SECRETS
ON THE CLOCK

By the Author

Hers to Protect

Secrets on the Clock

SECRETS ON THE CLOCK

by

Nicole Disney

2018

SECRETS ON THE CLOCK

ISBN 13: 978-1-63555-292-8

This Trade Paperback Original Is Published By
Bold Strokes Books, Inc.
P.O. Box 249
Valley Falls, NY 12185

First Edition: October 2018

Credits
Editor: Cindy Cresap
Production Design: Susan Ramundo
Cover Design By Tammy Seidick

Acknowledgments

First, I want to give a huge thank you to Bold Strokes Books for providing a home for so many wonderful stories over the years. I thank you as a reader, a writer, and simply a person for creating a place fantastic LGBTQ stories can be found. I am continually impressed with the beautiful quality of books that comes out of BSB and am so fortunate and happy to have been welcomed into the family.

Thank you always to my amazing family that has been so supportive my entire life, no matter how crazy my ideas and aspirations sounded. To my mom, for providing a home full of so much love and joy. Thank you for teaching me how to see the good in everything. You gave me the best gift a person can give in teaching me how to be happy. To my dad, who I lost before all this became reality, but who always knew it would. I miss you every day. To my wife, for being my fellow dreamer. For being by my side as we explore this beautiful and strange world together. The road never gets too dark with you walking it with me.

Dedication

To Cassandra, always and forever.

CHAPTER ONE

Jenna pulled on the suit jacket that was the last piece of her ensemble and cringed at the way it restricted her freedom of motion. She was proud of her promotion. At twenty-five years old, she was the youngest supervisor for Child Protective Services in the region, and it had taken dedication and long hours to achieve. But the pride came with a healthy dose of anxiety. Now she had to live up to the title, and her new boss was notoriously hard to please. Even with a host of new responsibilities to master and superiors to answer to, something much simpler had become a fixation: complete dread that the dream job she'd worked so hard to obtain was accompanied by a requirement to wear formal business attire.

It had taken hours of frowning at the discomfort of pantyhose, skirts, and heels before a salesperson had finally talked her into an expensive suit. At the time, she'd had to admit it was indeed the most comfortable option, and now, looking in the bathroom mirror, she also had to admit she looked good. She straightened her wavy hair and put mascara on her lashes. She knew many women who did this every day. In fact, they tended to be the type she preferred to date, so she'd witnessed the ritual a thousand times. Still, stumbling through the process, she felt like a kid who'd snuck into her mom's bedroom to play dress up.

"Wow, you look like a girl!"

Jenna jumped at the unexpected voice and turned to her sister, Callie. "I feel ridiculous."

"You shouldn't. You look amazing."

"It feels like too much."

"Isn't it required?"

"Business formal." Jenna blushed. "Whatever that means."

"It means what you're wearing is perfect."

"They're going to laugh."

Callie scanned her again, reassessing. She could always be trusted to be honest, even if it meant hurting feelings.

"They're not going to laugh," she finally said. "You look like a grownup now is all. Be confident. I know I would be if I was half as beautiful."

Jenna tilted her head, a rush of sadness flooding through her. She touched Callie's face, feeling the bumps and valleys of the scarring from her burns. "You *are* beautiful, Callie."

Callie shifted away. "Yeah, whatever. You better get out of here if you're going to be on time."

Jenna wanted to say more, something more powerful, more convincing, but they'd had this conversation a thousand times, and she never made any headway.

"All right," she said. "Have a good day then."

"You too," Callie said. "Knock 'em dead."

Jenna picked up the purse she'd purchased and draped it over her shoulder. She kissed Callie on her good cheek and headed for the door. "See you tonight."

"Bring me home a milkshake."

"Uh-huh." Jenna sighed and closed the door behind her. She passed by her old Volkswagen that sat unused in the driveway collecting sap under the scarlet oak trees and continued to her Acura. She loved her new car, but she wouldn't have bought it if she'd known Callie would never touch the VW. She pushed the irritation aside. Today was too important for her to be lingering on old problems. She sped through the quick drive to work and parked on the side of the building so she could enter through the door no one used. That was the only comfort she'd allow herself. She wouldn't slink through the halls like some kind of criminal. Callie had one thing right; confidence was key. She could do this.

She took one last look in the mirror and confirmed she didn't look like a clown, then opened her car door before she could chicken out. Her purse felt ridiculous bouncing against her side and trying to slide off her shoulder, but she grabbed the strap and kept moving at the swift pace she always did. Soon she was knocking on Paula Caliery's door without having come across another human. Perfect.

"Come in." Paula's voice rang out.

Jenna went in and closed the door behind her. "Good morning," she said.

Paula stood. She was a striking woman with pale eyes and hair so blond it was almost white. Her limbs were long, slender strips of muscle that made it hard to tell if she was fit or just so thin her skin betrayed every sinew. She'd been the manager for years, yet Jenna knew her more by her intimidating reputation than their limited face time. Paula shot her hand across the desk in a brisk jab.

"First of all, congratulations."

"Thank you," Jenna said. "I'm very excited about the opportunity."

Paula sat down and motioned for Jenna to do the same. "You already got the job. You can relax now."

Jenna laughed but knew she sounded stiff. Paula leaned back in her chair and crossed her legs, revealing a long, wiry thigh that seemed to never end. She scrutinized Jenna with a disarming scan down her body. Jenna imagined it was a motion that had made many men squirm before her, though she wouldn't call it flirtatious.

"You look great," Paula said.

"Oh, thanks."

Paula nodded and sat forward again. "So your training will be as streamlined as possible. A lot of it you already know. Supporting the caseworkers, answering questions, handling complaints. I have no concerns about your abilities with any of that."

Jenna nodded.

"One concern that was brought up when we were discussing your application, however, is that we know you're close friends with quite a few of the caseworkers."

Jenna knew something to this effect was coming, but she still felt her cheeks getting warm at the suggestion she couldn't be an unbiased supervisor. "Is that a problem?"

"I hope not," Paula said. "There isn't a rule that expressly prohibits it, but you can obviously see how a conflict could arise. It's common practice to distance yourself a bit to discourage anyone from putting any sort of inappropriate pressures on you."

"If you mean with evaluations, I plan to be completely fair and honest. I don't think any of my friends expect otherwise."

Paula nodded. "I don't doubt you. Nevertheless, we thought it would be a good idea to hand-select the caseworkers that will be assigned to you rather than just passing down Jordan's old crew. We'll start small at first. Let's say five caseworkers, and I'm doing my best to assign people to you that are not in your social circle. I think it will make it easier on everyone. However, if you start to receive any unethical requests, I'd like to know about it. I know that will put you in an uncomfortable position, but it will be in your best interest."

Jenna thought about her best friend, Sasha. They'd been hired as caseworkers together, along with another good friend, Adam, and they'd clicked instantly. Sasha knew how important this job was to her, and she couldn't imagine Sasha asking for anything compromising, but she had to admit she'd have a hard time turning her in if she did. The rest of them, Cole, Val, Suzie, they were more drinking buddies than close friends. She doubted they would dare to ask, but if they did she could handle it.

"I understand."

"Adam will be the one exception," Paula said. "He's in need of a new supervisor, and he has an excellent track record. We've all agreed he will be a good candidate to be matched with you while you transition to your new role." Paula uncrossed her legs and crossed them again the other direction. "Unless you believe otherwise."

"Of course not. I'm happy to have him," Jenna said.

"Great. I'll help you with the first few evaluations. After that you're free to fly. I'll be here if you have any questions, but I think you'll see my style is pretty hands-off."

"Sounds great." Jenna felt she was already in trouble before she'd even started.

"Last order of business." Paula sat forward again. "Your open cases. We'll need to pass them off to the others so you can focus on your new responsibilities. I'm dividing them up between everyone. Here's a list of who's getting what." Paula slid a paper across the desk. "You'll need to pass on any pertinent information to the correct people."

Jenna reached for the paper with numb fingers. She hadn't prepared for this. The thought of giving her cases away made her stomach turn to iron. She knew each of these families intimately and cared for the outcome of each. She scanned the list. The Stevensons and Craigs were going to Suzie. The Crenshaws and Saltoris to Adam. She looked up without reading further.

"Can I not finish out my open cases? I'd really like to see them through. They'll thin out soon enough as long as I don't take any more."

Paula threaded her fingers together and rested her hands on the desk. "You'll have a lot to do as it is. I don't think it's practical to expect you to learn your new responsibilities and continue with your previous workload."

Jenna knew she was wearing her feelings on her sleeve and tried to stifle them. She looked at the paper again, scanning for the name that mattered most. The Clarks. They were matched up with a name she'd never seen before.

"Who's Danielle Corey?"

Paula smiled. "Glad you asked. She's our new caseworker. She's filling your old position, and she'll be one of the members of your team."

"Oh." Jenna looked at the paper again. "That's great, her being on my team. I don't know if she should handle the Clarks, though. It's a complicated case, a lot for a new hire to take on. I've been working with them for two years."

"Sasha will be training her. She'll have support."

Jenna leaned back in her chair, weighing her words before she spoke.

"Problem?" Paula asked.

"They're difficult boys," Jenna said. "They don't warm up easily, and they'll be upset if I disappear on them. Sasha is fantastic, and I'm sure Danielle is too, but the kids know me."

"I understand it's difficult," Paula said. "Really. But you're going to have to get comfortable with delegation. Being a supervisor is a very different job. If it's not for you—"

"No!" Jenna interrupted. "It is for me. Promotion was always the plan. It's just…" Jenna sighed. She was losing ground. "It's a special case. I'll pass on the details of all the others, but it's really important to me to finish this one myself."

"It's been two years already. You know it could go on much longer. You want to keep it indefinitely?"

"What if I train Danielle on it? She'll get a chance to learn, and the boys will get to know her before I bow out. Once they're comfortable with her, if the case is open that long, I'll let her take over."

Paula tilted her head right and left as she thought it over. "It's unconventional, but a reasonable compromise. We'll go ahead with that, but if I see you struggling with your new duties because of it I'll have to pull you and give it to Sasha. Fair?"

"Fair."

CHAPTER TWO

Danielle hated the social pressure of a new job. It wasn't that she hated people; she didn't, but her first instinct in a new work environment was to quietly observe and study until she felt confident with the job. Then and only then did she feel comfortable goofing around with people. The problem was, by that time she'd already be labeled as a standoffish loner. It was a pattern she'd been battling since elementary school, and as much as she wanted it to be different this time, she was falling back into the familiar awkward and meaningless small talk that kept people at a distance. Her new trainer, Sasha, probably already thought she was dull.

"Let me show you where your locker is," Sasha said. She had sparkling blue eyes and hair that wasn't quite blond or brown. She led Danielle down a flight of stairs into a harsh yellow locker room that looked like it had been in need of fresh paint for at least a decade and smelled like citrus. Sasha pointed at number forty-six. It was probably only a foot wide and tall, not good for much except maybe a change of clothes, though she couldn't picture herself wanting out of the simple CPS polo bad enough to change at work. Danielle opened the locker anyway and was surprised to find a picture of a half-naked Victoria's Secret model taped to the door.

"Sorry." Sasha giggled and trotted over. "This locker used to belong to someone else. I guess she didn't quite finish cleaning it out."

Danielle laughed. "Did she quit?"

"No, got promoted, actually. Has a whole office for her pictures now." Sasha winked. "She'd probably die if she knew you saw that. I think it was a practical joke from one of the guys anyway."

Danielle shrugged. "Doesn't bother me."

"That's good. There are a lot of shenanigans around here. People with a sense of humor tend to do better. Anyway, if you want to leave anything in there, we'll hit the road in a few."

Danielle threw her jacket inside and followed Sasha back up the stairs and down the long hallway to the front doors. They still had about fifty feet to go when a woman in a gorgeous black designer suit rounded the corner and headed toward them. Danielle didn't make a habit of scrutinizing people's bodies, yet she was uncharacteristically aware of this woman's form beneath the loosely draped cloth.

"Damn, Thompson, that you?" Sasha called down the hall.

Danielle caught a glimpse of the woman's eyes and was almost startled by the brilliant shade of green that jumped across the room. The woman cut her curious gaze short as she shifted her attention to Sasha, who cleared her throat.

"I mean, Ms. Thompson. If I could introduce you to our new caseworker, this is Danielle."

Ms. Thompson's shoes clicked across the floor until she was standing in front of Danielle holding out her hand.

"Jenna."

Danielle accepted the handshake and was pleasantly surprised to find it effortless. She'd fumbled through more awkward handshakes than she could count.

"Danielle."

"Ms. Thompson will be your supervisor," Sasha said. "She'll be the one you want to go to with questions once you're out of training."

Danielle hoped the surprise didn't show on her face. Jenna was certainly dressed for the part, but she looked too young to be a supervisor. "Nice to meet you," Danielle said.

"I was just about to take her out on the road," Sasha said. "Unless you need her for paperwork?"

"Not quite, I do need her, though." Jenna spun toward Danielle. "I'm actually going to be taking you out on the road with me."

"Okay." Danielle could barely hear her own voice.

Jenna turned to Sasha again. "We're just going to check in with the Clarks. Then she's all yours."

"Oh, okay then."

Danielle caught both the look of confusion and the silent exchange between the women that said all would be explained later. The thought ran through her mind that the two might be lovers, but she blamed the idea on the locker incident and waved it away.

"This way," Jenna said. She turned and headed for the door at a pace that surprised Danielle and left her a few strides behind before she'd even started moving. She hurried to catch up and followed Jenna to a sleek Acura that looked brand new. Between the suit and the car Danielle couldn't help but wonder if her new boss was very well off, but there was something about her demeanor that seemed to indicate she'd seen rough times.

The moment they each closed their doors Jenna maneuvered out of her jacket so she was only in a silk cream-colored blouse.

"Hope you don't mind," she said. "Humidity kills me."

"Of course not." Danielle caught herself looking at Jenna's arms in some kind of aesthetic admiration that she wouldn't label attraction, but that she couldn't explain. The temperature gauge showed seventy-five degrees, enough to be uncomfortable, but nowhere near the heat a bad Memphis summer could bring. Jenna started the car and zipped out of the parking lot. Soon they were cruising at a smooth sixty miles per hour along a winding road surrounded by lush green woods on either side.

"So," Jenna said. "How'd you end up at CPS?"

"Oh, I've always wanted to work in this field, help kids. I finished my degree and was lucky enough to get hired on my first try. It almost felt too easy, come to think of it. I kind of thought I'd have to work a bunch of other jobs I didn't like first."

"Don't count your chickens." Jenna opened the sunroof.

"What do you mean?"

"This could turn out to be one of those jobs you don't like."

Danielle's nerves jolted. "You don't like it?"

"No, I do. A lot of people don't, though."

"Why is that?"

"You're going to get called a baby snatcher a lot. People think you get commissions for every child you remove. And the kids you're helping, they won't all want help, you know? Maybe you're taking them from an abuser and putting them with a loving family, but they won't understand that for another decade sometimes. All they know now is you're taking them from Mom." Jenna glanced over at her. "It's just not for everyone."

"Sounds hard."

"Sure, but the ones that really break your heart are the ones you have to leave behind. The ones you know are being hurt but you can't put together a strong enough case."

"Does that happen a lot?"

"Depends on the caseworker. We're going to do our best to train you well enough it never happens."

Danielle nodded and looked out the window. She'd been warned about most of this already, but it was somehow different to hear it from someone who actually did the job.

Jenna's gentle voice brought her back to the moment. "I'm not trying to scare you off," she said. "I'm sure it'll be a great fit. I just wanted to warn you it's harder for some people than others. If it's hard for you, don't panic. You can always talk to me or one of the other supervisors."

"Thanks."

"Probably not the best welcome aboard speech I could have made."

Danielle laughed and glanced across the car again. "No, it's good to know up front."

"So what about outside of work? Significant other? Kids?"

"Nope."

"Ah." Jenna adjusted the air conditioning. Danielle held back a chuckle, discreetly glancing at the open sunroof. "Well, that's simple."

"Yeah," Danielle said. She cringed as the conversation threatened to go stale. She forced herself to smile. "What about you?"

"No girlfriend. No kids. I live with my mom and my sister right now. It's not exactly a lady-killer kind of situation." Jenna flashed a dazzling smile and winked.

Danielle felt a rush of heat and knew she was blushing. She looked away and tried to stifle the surprising reaction. She very much doubted Jenna had a hard time with women with those eyes and her killer body.

"It's nice you're close with your family," she said.

Jenna shrugged. "I'm not sure how close we really are. It's more out of necessity."

"Really? Necessity? But you must make good money as a supervisor." Danielle said it before it occurred to her how inappropriate it was to bring up Jenna's income, but Jenna didn't miss a beat.

"I haven't been a supervisor long enough to even know what that paycheck looks like yet, but it's not a money issue. My mom is schizophrenic. She can't really live alone, and my sister is twenty, hasn't quite made it out of the nest yet."

"Oh God," Danielle said. "I'm so sorry. I shouldn't have assumed. That was..." Danielle trailed off and Jenna started laughing.

"Don't worry about it. No big deal."

Danielle hadn't expected such a personal revelation, and she felt strange now she hadn't offered more of an answer about her own family. She searched for a natural way to circle back around to a better answer, but Jenna was pulling over before she settled on anything. She stopped in front of a three-story apartment complex. The grass was littered with kids' toys, bicycles, lawn chairs, and beer bottles.

"Ready?" Jenna asked.

"Sure."

"We're just checking in on them, observing the conditions, making sure the kids are in good health."

Jenna spun toward an urgent tap on her window. She smiled and opened the car door.

"Hey, Raylon! How's it going, my friend?"

"Ms. Thompson! What'd you bring me?"

Danielle smiled at the genuine warmth in both their voices and hurried out of the car to get a look at their visitor. She circled the car and saw Jenna fanning out a collection of candy bars for a young black boy to choose from. His clothes were much too big for him, most likely hand-me-downs, but he looked otherwise clean, nourished, and happy. He grabbed a candy bar and started to pull, attempting to discreetly slip a second one out of Jenna's hand with it.

"No way, José."

"Aw, come on Ms. Thompson. Please?"

"You been doing well in school?"

"Yes."

"No, he hasn't," another voice sounded from behind them. Jenna and Danielle both spun. A second, older black boy was approaching.

"Hey, Deon."

"Hey, Ms. T." The boy walked over and casually pulled Jenna into a hug. Their obvious closeness surprised Danielle and made her feel out of place.

"That true, Raylon?" Jenna turned back to the younger boy who couldn't be more than eight.

"No. He's a liar."

"Nuh-uh. You never do your homework."

"Do too!"

"Copying your friends doesn't count."

"I don't!"

"All right, all right," Jenna interrupted. She fanned the candy bars in front of Deon for him to choose. He shook his head.

"Nah."

"Grownups like candy too, Deon."

He scanned the candy and reluctantly grabbed one. "Thanks."

Jenna nodded and waved Danielle closer. "Guys, this is Ms. Corey. She's going to be coming with me from now on."

Danielle felt blinded by the sudden spotlight, but she stepped closer to Jenna's side and waved at each of them. "Nice to meet you."

"Why?" Deon asked sharply.

"She's in training." Jenna smiled at Danielle. "Teaching her everything I know."

Danielle detected nervousness, maybe even fear in Deon's dark glare. His body said he was no older than fifteen, but his gaze felt years older. He broke the eye contact and looked back to Jenna.

"You dumping us on the new girl?"

"Of course not," Jenna said.

"You sure?"

"Yes." Jenna stared at him. "How are things?" The question was casual, but her quiet, deep tone communicated the more serious implication.

Deon waited a long second before answering. "They're okay."

Jenna nodded. "Come on. Let's go see your mom."

Raylon skipped toward the stairwell while Deon stood staring at Jenna another long moment. The contrast in their reaction was intriguing, and Danielle felt paralyzed by whatever was transpiring between Jenna and Deon. Jenna seemed to communicate with her eyes a lot, and Danielle wondered if she'd ever learn to speak the language. Jenna glanced back at Danielle and discreetly nodded at Raylon's disappearing silhouette, then led them after him. Danielle fell in stride next to Deon, a few paces behind Jenna.

"She walks fast," Deon said.

"I'm noticing that," Danielle said with a smile.

"This your first day or something?"

"It is, actually."

Deon smirked. "Thought so."

"Manners," Jenna said over her shoulder. They came to a thin wooden door that had fresh damage at the bottom. Whatever caused the impact hadn't gone all the way through, but splintered and cracked the wood.

"What's this?" Jenna asked.

Deon shrugged. "Don't know."

Jenna tilted her head in silent admonition.

"I don't. Came home and it was like that."

Jenna nodded at the door. Deon opened it and let them in. Danielle felt the poverty the moment they stepped inside. It wasn't the old television or the broken table or the stained surfaces, it was the anxiety in the air. It was the way the whole house seemed to hold its breath. Danielle felt the need to exercise discretion as she evaluated the home, but quickly noticed Jenna did not. She openly surveyed every corner.

A clatter and series of thumps sounded at the door. "God damn it, son of a bitch. Deon!" A husky female voice dripping with the syrup of a thick Southern accent filled the apartment.

Deon skimmed over Danielle for a reaction before he hurried toward the door.

"That'll be his mom," Jenna said.

A short, heavy woman waddled into the room. Her weight rocked back and forth as she battled the grocery bags in her arms. Deon trailed after her with the last of the groceries.

"What are you doing here?" she snapped at Jenna.

Jenna glanced at her watch. "We were scheduled for a nine o'clock visit."

"You shouldn't be in my house without me here."

"I apologize for startling you," Jenna said. "I didn't realize you weren't home. The boys just let us in a moment ago."

"You shouldn't be in here without me," the woman repeated.

"Neither should the boys, Ms. Clark."

Her brows dug into her face in anger. "You need to leave." She gave up on the grocery bags and dropped them on the floor. "I called down there and told them I wanted to reschedule."

"I tried to call you back and discuss the problem, but you never answered."

"So you just show up uninvited?"

"Again, I apologize for the inconvenience, but you know we can't just come over on an invitation basis. It's required you adhere to these visits."

Ms. Clark's eyes burned into Jenna with a fury. She finally shook her head. "I'll never understand why you all have to treat people this way. I just don't understand it." She started to gather the handles of the grocery bags. When no one answered, she let go of the bags again. The plastic slowly drooped with the weight of the contents and lazily slouched to settle on the floor.

"And who the hell are you lurking over there?" Ms. Clark turned her fiery gaze to Danielle.

Jenna was speaking for her before Danielle could even shake off the shock. "Ms. Clark, I'd like to introduce you to—"

"Yeah, yeah, nice to meet you. Can we get on with it?"

There was a slight tremor in Danielle's hands, a sudden layer of sweat on her palms. She hated that something so simple had triggered an adrenaline response. She couldn't be so easily shaken and had never thought she was that way before.

"How have Raylon's and Deon's school reports been?" Jenna asked evenly.

"Raylon has an F in math," Deon said from the corner.

"Do not!" Raylon yelled from upstairs.

"Do so!"

"And you're not doing any better, are you?" Ms. Clark snapped. Jenna turned to Deon and waited.

"Yeah, but my math teacher is a prick," he said.

Ms. Clark's gaze locked on to Deon with intimidating intensity. "Boy, you watch your mouth. Go put these groceries away."

Deon grabbed a single bag and silently left the room. Ms. Clark circled around to the couch and looked over her shoulder at the cushions a couple of times before she fell back and landed with a loud creak. Jenna was quiet until Deon was out of earshot, then directed her attention back to Ms. Clark.

"Have you considered a tutor?"

"They're not stupid; they're lazy," she said. "And I don't have money for that anyway."

"There are programs we could help them get started in."

"Won't help if they won't go. Deon wants to drop out when he turns sixteen."

"I see. He didn't mention that."

"Don't know why he would," Ms. Clark said. "You're not his mother."

"Of course not."

"Ms. Thompson, I've had a very long week, and I haven't been feeling well. If we could please make this a short visit. As you can see, the boys are in perfect health. They've got a roof over their heads and food in the fridge. Hell, they've even got a PlayStation. But they're young boys in the projects. Getting them to care about school is a lost cause, and it's hardly grounds for you to camp out in my front yard like I'm some kind of criminal."

"I'm not calling you a criminal, Ms. Clark. I'm here to put you in touch with resources that will help Raylon and Deon thrive. I don't doubt they're fed and clothed, but they'll need an education to be successful."

"Can't force them to learn."

"How's their attendance?"

"How should I know? They leave in the morning, and they come home in the afternoon. I guess they're going to school."

"Has the school notified you of any unexcused absences?"

"Phone was shut off."

"We can help you with that too."

"You going to cut me a check?"

"No, there are pro—"

Ms. Clark's shoulders were rounded heaps that started bouncing up and down as she laughed. "Another program. We don't want your programs. Then you'll be coming over here until the end of time. We just want to be left alone."

"There's also the matter of the damage to the front door," Jenna said.

"What about it?"

"It needs to be fixed."

"What makes you think I have money for that?"

"Ms. Clark, I understand money is tight; that's why I've offered to put you in touch with resources that can assist you. Whatever you choose to do, though, you are responsible for providing a safe and secure home for these boys. Not having money is not an acceptable answer."

Danielle was captivated by the display, watching Jenna shift back and forth between understanding and firm. Even having no experience watching anyone else work, she had a feeling she was watching someone with considerable skill.

"It is secure." Ms. Clark sat forward, resting her arms on her knees and glancing at the cigarettes on the table in front of her. "Still locks, just ugly is all."

"It's broken nearly through."

"It's as safe as any other door. Someone wants to break it they're going to break it, fixed or not."

"It needs to be fixed by our next visit. It's a requirement."

Ms. Clark shot to her feet with agility her gait moments before suggested she did not possess. "Or else what? Why are you doing this to me? You don't even have a reason to be coming over here anymore. Those boys are perfectly fine."

"After the seriousness of the accusations that brought us here, we're required to carry out recurrent visits."

Ms. Clark grabbed the edge of the coffee table and flung it across the room like it was made of paper. Liquid from a cup that was on it sprinkled Danielle's face, and she flinched at the unexpected crash.

"Those accusations were bullshit! My boys already told you so! Nobody laid a hand on 'em!"

"The conditions we found were unacceptable," Jenna said. "And this is not the way to get the visits to stop, Ladona."

Ms. Clark looked jarred by the use of her first name and closed the distance between herself and Jenna. She moved so she was inches away from Jenna's face like she was going to fight her. Danielle reached in her pocket and produced her phone. Jenna silently motioned for her to wait.

"The visits are never going to stop anyway," Ladona said. "You'll make sure of that, won't you? You'll always find something to bitch about! This time it's the door. Next time it will be something else. You're never going to leave us the fuck alone! You've already decided you're taking my boys from me one way or another, haven't you? Just because we're poor? You think telling me I have to come up with the money is going to make money fall from the sky? You don't know shit about not having money, little girl!"

Jenna held her ground, not moving an inch despite Ladona's lips nearly touching hers. She waited. Ladona's eyes were wide and bulging. She was still leaning forward, as if to make sure she'd have leverage if it did become physical, as if the extra hundred and fifty pounds she had on Jenna wasn't enough. Finally, her posture seemed to relax slightly even though she didn't back away.

"Mama, Ms. Thompson could have taken us away a long time ago if she wanted." Deon's voice came quietly from the door frame that connected the living room to the dining room. She spun toward him.

"Get your butt upstairs, Deon!"

"Ladona." Jenna drew her attention back. She waited until Ladona made eye contact again. "I don't want to take your boys from you. I know you love them very much, but this will not do. You can't throw things and try to start a fight."

"You'll know when I try to—"

"Ladona," Jenna cut her off. "This behavior is a fast track to those boys being taken away, and we need to get off it before we can't. Don't do something you're going to regret just because you're mad at me. It's not worth it."

Ladona's face wrestled with rage and tears. "You have no idea what it takes to raise them," she finally said. A tear spilled over. "You don't know what I do for them, and then you come in here telling me it's not enough. Telling me they were hurt when they weren't."

"I know it's a lot," Jenna said. "I understand you're angry we have to keep doing this, but I'm here to hear your side. I'm here to *be* on your side. I don't expect you to make money fall from the sky, but I do want you to take advantage of the opportunities I can put in front of you. *I* am money falling from the sky. I want to help you get your phone back on. I want to help you get the boys engaged in school again, at no expense to you so that you *can* afford things like the door. I know the boys want to be here. Help me make that possible for all of you."

"I just don't see why you have to act like I'm hurting them. I love those boys more than anything. They look hurt to you?"

Jenna quietly opened the folder she was carrying and fished out a business card.

"The boys don't appear to be in any immediate danger, no." Jenna held the card out to Ladona. "This is the number you'll need for that tutor. I hope you'll consider it. We'll check back on the twenty-third, nine a.m. again. The door does need to be fixed by then, but you can call me any time with questions if you need help. We'll find a way to get it done."

Danielle watched the standoff between them. Ladona was still a swirling array of emotions with tear streaks down her face and resentment building a barrier between her and the help Jenna offered. Jenna held out the card with steadfast patience. Danielle only realized she was holding her breath when Ladona finally snatched the card, and then she could breathe again. Jenna nodded.

"Hope you have a nice rest of your day, Ms. Clark." Jenna turned for the door.

"Bye, Ms. Thompson!" the boys called out in unison.

CHAPTER THREE

Jenna could feel Danielle watching her as they walked back to the car. She carefully avoided eye contact until they were inside, knowing the boys were probably watching from the window, listening. She started the car and headed back to work, then looked over her shoulder at Danielle. Danielle's dark, almond shaped eyes were pools of curiosity.

"What did you think?" Jenna asked.

"That was fantastic!"

Jenna laughed in surprise and relief. She'd been afraid she had exposed Danielle to too much too soon.

"Surprising," Danielle added.

"Which part?"

"I thought people were on their best behavior when we visit."

"You would think," Jenna said. "That's true most of the time, but Ladona isn't really like that. She pretty much says what she's thinking."

"I'll say. I thought she was going to hit you."

"Yeah, about that." Jenna took a breath. "I don't want you to think you have to put up with that. I chose to try to de-escalate her instead of leaving because I've been working with that family for a long time. I was confident I knew where she was with everything, but you're not required to take any form of abuse. If you ever feel like you're in any kind of danger you leave and call a supervisor, and the cops if it's warranted."

"I thought it was great you stayed," Danielle said. "You really turned it around."

"Thanks." Jenna felt a warm tingle travel through her skin despite the unease that still gripped her stomach. She'd hate for Danielle or anyone else under her supervision to get hurt trying to follow her example. She didn't consider her tactics reckless, but she handled the Clarks differently than any other family.

"You can always call a mental health counselor to help you too if you think they need that kind of intervention," Jenna said. "They're on the fourth floor of our building. I'll take you by sometime to meet them. We work with them a lot. Especially Tina."

"Tina." Danielle nodded. Jenna could see her mentally logging the information.

"Tina Richards. They all know what they're doing, of course, but I always get Tina if I can. I even asked her to work with my mom once. She's the only one I've ever seen really make a difference with her."

Danielle nodded again. Jenna could tell Danielle didn't know what to do when she brought up her family, and she couldn't help but be amused by it. Silence settled while Jenna waited for Danielle to find words.

"You think they're really best off with her?" she finally asked.

"Ladona?" Jenna sighed. "Sometimes she's a model parent; other times she's like this or worse. She's bipolar, so there are fluctuations. I care a lot about Raylon and Deon. There are a lot of things I wish I could change for them, but they want to live there. You have to be careful bringing what you think is best into the picture. I always start with whether or not they're safe and provided for, then move on to what they want. If those things are covered, I don't think I have much business pushing what *I* think is best on anyone."

"Sure," Danielle said. "That makes sense, but if she's that way to our faces I can only imagine what she's like when she's alone with them."

Jenna's stomach twisted at the suggestion. "Deon will tell me if she crosses the line."

"I hope so," Danielle said, doubt coloring her inflection. "They seem to really like you."

"They're great kids." Jenna felt her mind crawling back through the street toward the rundown apartment. Despite Ladona's accusation, she knew exactly what it was like to not have money, to open empty cupboards fifteen times a day.

She liked to think she knew Deon well enough to recognize the truth in him when he said they were fine, but she had been a skilled bluffer at his age, hidden horrible realities because she and her sister would rather suffer together than be placed in wealthier families apart. But she had to believe Deon was telling the truth. She had to trust that no matter how much he wanted to stay with his brother, he would know where to draw the line if the time came. And if he couldn't, at least he'd feel comfortable enough to open up to her so she could draw it for him.

"So," Danielle broke the silence and pulled Jenna back. "You said no *girlfriend*, right?"

Jenna felt a smile tugging at her face at the subject change, curious where Danielle could be going with such a question. "Uh-huh."

"Does that mean it's your locker I inherited, then?"

"Why would you say that?"

"Beautiful mostly naked girl on the door?"

Jenna burst out laughing. "Oh, God, did I really forget to take that down?"

Danielle beamed. "Apparently."

"Well, that's embarrassing. Hardly supervisory."

Danielle shrugged. "She's pretty, if that's what you're into."

Jenna grinned. "What the hell is that supposed to mean?" she asked. "What kind of girls do *you* like?" Jenna looked over and was surprised to see Danielle's cheeks flush. "Sorry, that was presumptuous."

"It's okay."

"Are you not out?"

The tension in Danielle's face evaporated, and she laughed. "Still presumptuous."

"Well?" Jenna looked over Danielle's slightly loose clothes, the way she was sitting, her simple hairstyle that said she never touched a hair dryer. It wasn't an exact science, but she was confident nonetheless. Danielle's deep brown eyes met hers and stuck there.

"Yes, I'm out."

"But you don't like talking about it?"

"I don't know," she said. "It's not a secret, but I don't advertise it either."

Jenna nodded. "Got it. Don't worry about me. I might seem like I have a big mouth, but I don't talk about people's business." Jenna pulled into the work lot, a little disappointed to cut the conversation short. She realized too late that bringing up Danielle's orientation was a far cry from the way she ought to behave as a supervisor, but they'd slipped into it so naturally she couldn't bring herself to worry about it.

"I'll help you track down Sasha," she said and turned off the car. Jenna reluctantly pulled her suit jacket back on and headed inside.

They tracked Sasha down in the break room. Her face lit up when Jenna rounded the corner.

"Hey, boss!"

"Ugh, don't do that," Jenna said. She chuckled when she glanced at the pile of empty creamer cups Sasha was accumulating. "No wonder you need ten cups a day, Sash; there's no coffee in there."

"Is it a frickin' crime to want my coffee to taste good?"

Jenna shook her head and took a seat, motioning at the empty chair to prompt Danielle to join them. Sasha finished stirring the twelfth creamer into her coffee and joined them at the table.

"So how was your first trip out?" Sasha asked Danielle.

"It was good," Danielle said. She raked her fingers through her long black hair.

"Anything noteworthy?"

Jenna glanced between them as silence stretched. Jenna knew Sasha was used to people warming up to her quickly. She was friendly and almost always happy, a natural conversationalist who rarely had to work to get people talking, yet Danielle seemed ill at ease around her.

"Ms. Clark was a bit feisty today," Jenna said when the silence became uncomfortable.

"Ah," Sasha said. "Thompson's throwing you right to the sharks, huh? Learn anything?"

"Yeah," Danielle said. "I think so."

Sasha looked at Danielle expectantly for a handful of seconds before she seemed to realize Danielle had no intention of elaborating. Jenna couldn't help but be amused by the way Danielle closed up. She wondered absently if she should be concerned, but something told her she didn't need to worry about Danielle.

"She got to see some de-escalation techniques," Jenna jumped in again.

"You? De-escalating?" Sasha teased her.

Jenna playfully scowled at her. "Yes, I am capable of a soft touch sometimes."

"You can tell me the truth when she leaves," Sasha said to Danielle.

Danielle cracked a smile and her shoulders relaxed. "We talked about the line between undesirable and unsafe circumstances, too."

Sasha threw up her hands. "Well, hell, that's pretty much the job. You're ready. What do you say we cut her loose, boss?"

"I'd say it sounds like you can spend the rest of the day showing her how to write reports in that case."

"Evil woman," Sasha said. "Been a supervisor for ten minutes, you're already one of them."

Jenna smiled and checked her watch. "Speaking of that job I got ten minutes ago, I'd better go do some work. You'll have to finish complaining about me behind my back like a normal employee."

"It's just not the same."

Jenna left the room, then lingered just outside the door until she heard the sound of conversation pick up again. Once she heard Danielle's low chuckle, she smiled and headed for her office.

CHAPTER FOUR

Danielle's feet felt weighted as she inched her way through the hall in her apartment complex. It seemed like years had passed since she left this morning. She slipped her key into the door and let herself in, more than a little disappointed to see that her roommate, Brianna, had already poured two drinks.

"Hello, dear," Brianna teased her and held out one of the cups. Danielle wasn't sure what it was, but she caught the distinct smell of liquor.

"What's this?"

"We're celebrating your first day of work, obviously."

"I don't know if I can, Bri," Danielle said. "I'm beat."

"Oh, come on," Brianna said. "Just have a drink and tell me all about it. I'll cancel the strippers."

Danielle accepted the drink, again getting a nose full of something strong and guessing it was only slightly diluted by whatever mixer Brianna opted for.

"So, tell me all about it." Brianna hopped on the brown leather couch and folded her legs under her. Danielle followed and slumped down, feeling she could sink into those cushions forever like they were clouds.

"Pretty much what I thought, I guess. I'll be in training until they decide I'm ready."

"That's a little open-ended, isn't it?"

"They said it usually takes about six weeks, but it's subject to change."

"So you'll be done in three?"

"For once I'm not sure I want to be ahead of schedule. It's kind of a lot. I don't mind the training," Danielle said.

Brianna studied her. Her wiry reddish hair was in its wildest state, probably just dry after a shower.

"A lot how?" she asked. "I've never seen you not want to overachieve. Did something happen?"

"No, not really."

"What gives, then? You got a hot trainer or something?"

"No," Danielle said. "Well, I mean, she's fine, but that's not why."

"She's fine, or she's *fine*?" Brianna wagged her eyebrows.

Danielle was used to Brianna commenting on the appearance of every woman she met, walked by, or heard existed. She'd done so even when they had been a couple, but since breaking up, it oddly made Danielle more uncomfortable than it ever had when they were together. When they were a couple, Danielle always knew it was just silliness. Since they'd decided to be friends, and especially since they'd moved in together, she was having a much harder time knowing the difference between Brianna joking, her having a genuine interest in someone, or outright snooping.

"Well, which is it?" Brianna pressed and grinned.

"She's pretty, I guess. I don't know." Danielle realized with a start that she was thinking of Jenna, and she was thinking Jenna was decidedly gorgeous. She was not, "pretty, I guess," nor was she Danielle's real trainer. She'd only spent a bit over an hour with Jenna and the rest of the day with Sasha. Sasha was beautiful too now that she thought about it, pretty enough she probably wasn't usually an afterthought. "They're both pretty, but I don't want to think of either of them that way."

"Whoa, hold on," Brianna said. "You have two trainers? And they're both hot? Score for you. No wonder you want to stay in training."

"It's not like that. Don't put it in my head. I have to work with them, and they're both my superiors. I don't want your filth popping into my mind while they're talking."

"Who said anything about filth?"

"Please, I know where this is going."

"Then you know me too well," Brianna said. She took a large gulp of her drink and pointed at Danielle's cup until she did the same. "So, if it's not that, what is it?"

"We went out on a case this morning, and the mom was kind of going off on Jenna."

"Jenna?"

"My supervisor, or…" Danielle paused. "Well, she was my trainer for the morning. They didn't really explain. But the mom on this case was getting crazy with her. She looked like she was going to hit her."

"Sounds intense. Did it freak you out?"

"No." Danielle remembered the way Jenna had motioned for her not to call for help. "Jenna obviously had it under control. It was cool to watch, but I don't know if I could have done that. It made me feel like I have a lot to learn."

"I say drag it out as long as you can." Brianna jumped up and rounded the bar into the kitchen, then poured a shot, threw it back, and poured again. "Training rules. You can't get in trouble." When Brianna returned she was carrying two shots.

"No way," Danielle said. "You know I can't do shots."

"Oh, come on. It's a special occasion."

"It's a Monday is what it is," Danielle said. "And I have to work tomorrow. I don't want to go in hungover on my second day."

"From one shot? No one's that much of a lightweight."

"I am so."

"You put too much emphasis on being perfect," Brianna said. "You know what works exactly as well as working hard and is a thousand times easier? Flirting."

"Please."

"I'm serious; it's a scientific fact."

"Uh-huh, and that study is published where?"

"The Journal of Successful Business Women with Social Lives."

"Please don't ever really become a teacher." Danielle laughed. "You'll destroy a whole generation of girls."

"Oh, lighten up. It's only degrading when it's men you're doing the flirting with. I promise."

Danielle's mind wandered to the picture of the model in Jenna's locker, her five foot eleven slender frame, oily and almost nude, her one in a billion bone structure and smoldering come-hither look reaching through the picture. If that was what Jenna was used to Danielle wouldn't be able to flirt her way out of two-minute tardy.

"Yeah, I think I'm just going to go ahead and work hard," Danielle said.

Brianna rolled her eyes. "Fine, you're no fun." Brianna took both of the shots and, as if it had an instant effect, she slouched deeper into the couch and let her head rest on Danielle's shoulder.

No fun. Danielle had heard the accusation her entire life. She was quiet in a crowd, early to rise, earlier to bed, careful with money, mindful about food, and unamused by drugs. The only people who had ever approved of it were her parents, and they weren't in her life anymore. Her studies had been a longstanding excuse to justify it all, but with nothing to stand in her way now, she had to admit it wasn't that she was afraid to have fun, it was that those things weren't her idea of fun.

"Danielle?" Brianna murmured.

"Yeah?"

"Will you mix me another drink?"

"I don't think you need another one," Danielle said.

"Do so."

"If I do it has to be your last one tonight."

Brianna shot up to a sitting position, suddenly energized. "No deal!" she said and bounded into the kitchen.

"I'm going to bed." Danielle stood up. Brianna protested from the kitchen, but Danielle ignored her and headed to her room anyway.

CHAPTER FIVE

A knock at Jenna's bedroom door sounded in unison with the chirp of her phone. She glanced at the screen and saw it was a message from Sasha.

"What is it?" she called to the door.

The doorknob twisted, and Callie walked inside. "Did you get more of my scar serum?"

"I haven't been to the store yet."

Callie shifted her weight and looked at Jenna expectantly. When Jenna didn't move she sighed. "Could you?"

"If I have time," Jenna said. "I had a long shift yesterday, might again today."

"Why?"

"It's a new job, Cal. There are probably going to be a lot of long days before I'm comfortable with it."

"Can't you go after?"

"I'm exhausted after, Callie. Why don't you just take the Volkswagen and go get it? That's why I gave it to you."

Callie stared at her like what she was saying was absurd, like it was a cruel joke. It used to break her down, but Jenna was learning how to wait Callie out.

"It hurts," Callie finally said.

Jenna's eyes pulled to Callie's scars like they did every time Callie mentioned them. She knew Callie's obsession with her scar serum had more to do with a desperate hope it would lessen their appearance than pain at this point, but Callie always brought up pain if she didn't immediately jump to retrieve more. It wasn't that she didn't believe her. Jenna knew the skin was sensitive, even after all these years, but that wasn't what was holding Callie back. What started as Callie avoiding her friend's birthday party at the age of eight because of her fresh scars had somehow turned into outright refusal to leave the house by twenty, but the steps along the way felt fuzzy and out of focus.

"Come on, Jenna, please?" Callie asked.

Jenna frowned. "I'll go after work," she said. "But I want you to take the trash to the curb."

"You're going to make me do chores to get my serum? That's a little messed up, don't you think? I need it, Jenna. It's not like I want to need it."

"It's not about the chores. You need to get out of the house. Get some sunlight and some fresh air. It's twenty feet, a lot easier than the store. Humor me."

"It's not humoring you if you force me."

"I don't want to force you. Please just do it."

Callie turned like she was about to leave the room, but it was only for dramatic effect. She quickly turned back to Jenna, this time with her hands resting on top of her head.

"Ten minutes in the backyard," she said.

"No."

"Come on, that's so much longer than it would take to take out the trash."

"Then take out the trash," Jenna said.

"I thought this was about getting sunlight, but obviously it's not."

"It's about making steps toward being part of the world, sun *and* people."

"You want to humiliate me."

"Of course not." Jenna stood up and started toward Callie. "You have nothing to be embarrassed about, Callie."

"Now you're just being stupid." Callie really left this time and slammed Jenna's door closed again.

Jenna sighed and rubbed her face with her palms. She flopped onto her bed and reached for her phone. She had half an hour to get ready and leave for work, which was fine under her old routine, but this getting dressed up stuff was time-consuming. She opened Sasha's text.

Enjoy the perks of your new job today and work from home! Going to be on the road with the new girl all day. Nothing to see here.

Jenna smiled at Sasha's thoughtfulness despite the fact that it was probably the worst day she could choose to work from home with her sister accumulating a demanding list of requests and an attitude to match.

How's she doing? Jenna texted back.

Seems fine. Little quiet. Will crush that today, don't worry. Wear sweatpants for me.

Jenna laughed and fished out her laptop. Working from home was a luxury she'd never experienced before. She imagined she needed a cup of coffee to do it properly, but she didn't want to go downstairs and deal with Callie again. She was only on her second email when her door burst open.

"Mom won't take her pills," Callie said, then slammed the door again.

Jenna sighed and shut her laptop. "Unbelievable."

Jenna dragged herself from the comfort of bed and headed downstairs. She started the coffeemaker and grabbed her mom's pills before heading to her room. When she opened the door, her mom was sitting on the floor in the corner. Jenna walked over to her slowly.

"Mom? What are you doing down there?"

"Feels nice down here," she said. "The walls make me feel safe."

Jenna walked over and sat with her back against the bed, across from her mom. She watched her mom's gaze dart around the room, waiting for it to fall on her face though it never would. She'd scan the room endlessly if Jenna didn't do something to ground her. She touched her hand.

"Mom," she said. "It's time for your medicine."

"I'm not taking it anymore," she said. Her eyes ricocheted around the corners of the room. Her auburn hair was streaked with gray and was tousled like she'd been pulling at it, covering her ears maybe.

"Why not?" Jenna asked.

"The government makes that stuff. It's not medicine; it's mind control. They're watching us, and they don't like anyone who knows what they're up to. They give us that to keep us foggy."

"But it helps you, Mom. It makes it so you don't hear the scary stuff."

"I haven't heard anything scary in ages."

"That's because you take the medicine, Mom."

"I'm not myself on it."

"Yes, you are. I know it makes you feel a little funny, but you're still you. You still know who we are. You still have fun and talk with us. Remember last week we all made dinner together and looked at old pictures? It was just like old times. When you stop taking your medicine is when you're not you. You start to think we're here to hurt you. You can't leave your bedroom. You hate it."

"No, I know things when my head is clear, and they don't like that so they have to dumb me down. They're poisoning me."

"Mom." Jenna squeezed her hand. "Look at me." Her mom's gaze did another lap around the room before she looked back at Jenna. "Mom, I would never let them poison you. It's medicine. I promise."

Her face quivered with fear and tears. "But you don't even know what those pills do."

"Sure, I do," Jenna said. "They just normalize your dopamine and serotonin levels so they're not out of whack. It makes your brain go all haywire when they're not right and you hear stuff that isn't real."

"Really?" Seeing her mom so afraid broke Jenna's heart. "You're sure?"

"I'm sure," Jenna said. "I wouldn't let them give you anything bad."

Her mom studied her face carefully. Jenna knew she was trying to decide whether or not to trust her, a scrutiny that had fundamentally shaken her the first time, but was just part of life now. Finally, her mom nodded and reached for a hug. Jenna pulled her in close and held her until she finally let go and held her palm out for the pills.

CHAPTER SIX

Danielle flipped through the folder Sasha had given her that detailed all the cases they were assigned to even though she'd practically memorized it over the course of her first week. The Clarks were the only case she was working with Jenna. She was shadowing Sasha on all the others, which she found disappointing despite Sasha's natural talent as a trainer. She figured she should be relieved, that working with her supervisor ought to be more of a pressure than anything, but she couldn't stop anticipating the next time she'd work with Jenna. When she confirmed what she already knew, that the address punched into the GPS was not among her papers, she redirected her attention to Sasha.

"Where are we headed?"

"We're swinging by for a visit with the Andersons."

Danielle pretended to read through her papers again. "I don't see them here."

Sasha glanced over and scanned her a few times before she sighed. "No, they're not ours. We're helping Adam out."

"Adam?"

"One of the other caseworkers. I'll introduce you to him sometime. He's a sweetheart. He's not in today, though."

"Oh," Danielle said. "So, when you call out you have to get someone to take your visits for you?"

"Not exactly." Sasha shifted. "You just call your supervisor and they have the scheduling department reschedule for you."

"So the scheduling department assigned it to us?"

"They probably would have," Sasha said. "If he had called out."

"And you lost me."

Sasha laughed. "I know. I'm sorry. It's kind of awkward. I don't want to ask you to keep secrets when you're so new, but this visit is kind of on the down low."

"Oh." Danielle was generally fine with keeping quiet. She'd never been much of a tattle, despite her own tendency to stay within the lines, but she still wasn't sure what to say.

"Adam is having problems with his boyfriend," Sasha said. "Bad problems. They might break up."

"And he doesn't think they'd give him the day off for that," Danielle surmised.

"Jenna is his supervisor." Sasha finally made eye contact, her hair catching in the light and falling around her face when she turned.

Danielle shrugged, confused again. "Jenna seems cool. She wouldn't be okay with that?"

"Jenna is extremely cool." Sasha laughed. "She'd probably give him a day off to catch up on laundry if he asked and he meant it."

"What's the problem then?"

"I don't know how much you've heard about everyone, but Jenna is a brand-new supervisor, and Adam is one of her best friends. He's the only friend of Jenna's they're letting her actually supervise, and she's taking it as a sort of test. If she starts letting Adam get away with stupid shit like calling out to fight with his man—"

"She'll look bad," Danielle said. "That makes sense, I guess."

"Adam told me this morning what was going on, and I just didn't even want it to make it to Jenna's plate, you know? She's already dealing with so much. So I just said I'd cover for him. I'm sorry if it puts you in a weird spot. I hope you're not—"

"It's fine," Danielle said. "Really, it doesn't bother me. I think it's nice. You guys are pretty close, huh? You and Jenna?"

"Yeah," Sasha said. "She's my best friend. We got hired together along with Adam. Cole, Val, and Suzie were hired together after us and joined the group. They're pretty close from training together, but we all hang out. Almost cost Jenna the promotion."

"How so?"

"I guess they thought it would be a problem, us all being tight."

"I feel like I'm missing out a little on the whole group training thing."

"You're right," Sasha said. "You're our first orphan in a while. They usually hire small groups. I think it's nice, gives people instant friends. Don't worry, though." Sasha smiled. "We'll adopt you."

Danielle felt a twinge of pain at the word adopt. It felt too on the nose. She'd come out to her parents two years ago and had promptly been disowned. She'd held out some flimsy hope they would come around, but once she hit the year mark without hearing from them, she accepted it would probably never happen.

"Really, though," Sasha said. "We should all have a get-together, welcome you aboard."

"You don't have to go to any trouble."

"Get out of here, having a party isn't trouble. You'll get to see what everyone is like when we're not in our polo shirts. We'll have a blast. Promise."

Sasha pulled into a cracked driveway. The windows on the old house were boarded up. The only thing that tipped them off anyone lived there at all was the hollow echo of dogs barking from the backyard. Sasha put the car in park and glanced at Danielle.

"Ready?"

Danielle nodded and got out of the car. She had an awful feeling about the place. There was a frightening quality to the neighborhood, to the way people walked down the street like it was a dare, to the sagging windowsills that seemed to gape at her and the boarded-up windows that looked like dead eyes. It was very much fact in Memphis that being the wrong race or wearing the wrong color in the wrong neighborhood was enough to get you hurt or killed. She got the feeling this was one of those places, and while being Asian usually put her on fairly neutral ground, she felt anything but safe now.

She passed through the chain-link gate and led the way to the door. She knocked, but nothing happened. Sasha knocked too. They let a full minute pass before they looked at one another. Danielle knew Sasha was feeling the same things she was. Danielle knocked again, harder, eager to get out of public view.

A swish blew the corner of the yellow drapes in the window to the left of the door. The movement seized Danielle's attention, but she saw nothing. She knocked again as loud as she could. Small fingers curled around the yellow drapes and timidly pulled back the edge, revealing two large, round brown eyes staring curiously into Danielle. Danielle and Sasha went to the window and leaned over to level with the small, tear-streaked face.

"Are you okay, honey?" Sasha asked through the glass.

The curly haired child stared at Sasha, but made no attempt to respond.

"Is your mommy home?" Danielle asked.

The child nodded.

"Can you get her for me?"

He shook his head.

"Why not?" Sasha asked.

The child looked over his shoulder and pointed at something neither of them could see. Danielle looked at Sasha.

"What now?"

Sasha didn't answer right away; she seemed to be searching for an answer. "Can you pull back the drapes?" Sasha asked the boy. He stared blankly. Danielle tried to motion it out, but he wouldn't move.

"I'm going to check the other windows," Sasha said. "See if I can see any more somewhere else. You keep talking to him. He likes you."

Sasha disappeared around the corner. Danielle looked back to the small brown face in the window. She put her hand against the glass. The boy cracked a smile and put his hand on the other side, matched up with hers.

"Very good." Danielle smiled. She put a finger on the glass and waited until he did the same. When he finally did, she had an idea. If she could get him to copy her, she could get him to pull the drapes back. She methodically alternated between something productive and something engaging, making faces at him, inching him to the left, doing a little dance, inching him over again. Finally, she made a sweeping motion with her arm, and he copied. The drapes swished away from the glass, and Danielle saw a woman on the floor twenty feet behind him in the kitchen. There was foam trailing from her mouth.

"Sasha!" she called, but she didn't wait for her. She removed the screen and motioned for the boy to back away. When he did, she broke the glass.

"What the hell?"

"There's a body," Danielle said.

"Wait!"

But she was already climbing through. The smell of death hit her so hard she thought she'd physically been stopped. She had to hold her breath to suppress a gag. The room was hot and the air thick. Sasha was behind her recounting what was going on into her phone, saying she needed an ambulance. Danielle had dropped onto a couch on the other side of the broken glass and felt stinging on her back. She must have cut herself though she hadn't felt the contact. Her focus shot around the room and landed on the curly haired boy. She reached out to him, and he stumbled into her arms. She realized his face was not only moist from tears, but also sweat from being trapped in the house as it had warmed up over who knew how long. She picked up the toddler, then unlocked and opened the front door. Sasha was standing in the doorway, her eyes wide.

"Yes, we'll be here," she said and hung up the phone.

She stared at Danielle with a look that said her disapproval was only one of a thousand thoughts she was having. Sasha assessed the room, glancing from Danielle to the toddler in her arms, from the body in the kitchen to every corner of the room.

"I'm—"

Sasha cut her off with a sharp motion of her hand. She stood like stone, listening. Danielle finally realized she was trying to figure out if anyone else was in the house. The thought was horrific to Danielle, that anyone would be ignoring a corpse in the kitchen. Danielle glanced over her shoulder to the body, careful to keep the child in her arms facing the other way. She thought she saw movement. Sasha seemed to see it too because she looked back to Danielle.

"Get him out of here," she said.

Danielle stepped onto the front porch and cradled the toddler's face against her shoulder, but she wouldn't leave. She watched Sasha carefully inch inside, checking over each shoulder incessantly. She leaned over the body for just a second before she bolted upright again and strode briskly back toward to the door.

"Bugs," she said. "Lots of bugs. Super dead."

Danielle could see Sasha's muscles tense and disgust take over her expression no matter how hard she tried to stay stoic. Danielle led them away from the house.

"My water," Danielle said.

Sasha was looking right at her but took several seconds to process it. Finally, she seemed to understand and riffled through the car until she emerged with a water bottle. She joined Danielle again and held the bottle up to the toddler's mouth. The boy caught on quickly and in short order had emptied what was left.

"How long do you think he was in there?" Danielle asked.

Sasha shook her head. "Long enough for there to be bugs."

"How long is that?"

"I don't know."

Sirens screamed, but they were nowhere to be seen yet. Danielle tightened her arms around the boy in her arms as if she could somehow squeeze the memories out of him.

CHAPTER SEVEN

Jenna went to her office thirty minutes before her scheduled meeting with Sasha and Adam just so she could sit in silent misery. Management had gone to great lengths to keep most of her friends out of her immediate responsibility, and yet Adam managed to get in trouble in a matter of days and Sasha had somehow found a way under her thumb.

The phone call from Paula had been terse and urgent. People weren't where they were supposed to be. A dead person was found. A trainee witnessed the whole debacle. Paula simply laid out the facts and told Jenna to handle it. She hadn't attempted to influence her decisions, which meant this was a test.

A timid knock on the door sounded ten minutes early. Jenna sighed. She knew it was professional to be a little early, but being on the other end of that appointment, she just found it imposing. She stood and smoothed out her pants and jacket, still not used to the fit and feel of fancy clothes. She opened the door. Sasha and Adam stood there with the exact same guilty face. She had an appointment with Danielle in an hour, but she'd decided to take her friends on together. She motioned them inside. Jenna circled her desk and sat, waiting for them to settle into their chairs before she spoke.

"Jenna, I—"

Jenna held up her hand and cut Adam off. He was always impeccably dressed, but he'd gone the extra mile today and was entirely striking in his tailored suit. His thick dark hair had been sculpted, yet looked somehow casual, and his expression was sharp and clear. He looked like he belonged on Wall Street, not in her office getting scolded for ditching work like a teenager.

"Two weeks," she said. "This is my *second* week."

"I know," Adam said. "I am so sorry, Jenna. I swear. Just write me up. Do whatever you need to do."

"Why wouldn't you just call me, Adam? I don't get it. You couldn't have possibly thought I wouldn't give you the day if you asked for it."

"I knew you would, but it's only your second week. I wanted to wait one more before I made your life hell."

Jenna felt her cheeks tugging into a smile, but she shook her head and forced herself to stay serious. "You don't have to treat me any differently than you would anyone else. If you need to call out, call out. Now it looks like you were trying to get away with something."

"It was my idea, Jenna," Sasha said. "I offered to take the visit for him."

"Why would you do that while you had a trainee?" Jenna asked. "Even if things hadn't gone the way they did, it could have gotten out that you covered for Adam and around to management. This was just a bad idea, guys."

"Because of Danielle? Come on, she wasn't going to narc."

Jenna stopped before she spoke too soon. She couldn't have an argument about the best ways to break policy. Her job was to enforce policy.

"I'm not talking about her deliberately trying to get you in trouble, Sash. I'm sure she wouldn't," Jenna said carefully. "But she's new. If she thinks that's common practice, if she casually mentions it to someone, or asks someone to do it for her because she saw you two do it, you see where I'm going."

Sasha nodded. "Sure, of course. We really are very sorry, Jenna. We were trying to help."

"I know that." Jenna sighed. "That's why I've been so miserable trying to figure out how to punish you."

"It's fine," Adam said. "Really. Don't sweat it. I know you have to write me up."

"I'm giving you a verbal warning," Jenna said.

"They'll give you hell if you go that soft," Adam said. "Really, do what you need to."

Jenna reached in her drawer and pulled out Adam's file, then slid it across the table. He opened it and looked inside.

"On the left you'll see that you haven't missed a day of work for two and a half years. Now, maybe that's because Sasha's been covering your shifts when you're not here, but I'm going to choose to believe it's because you're a model employee who has not had any behavioral issues in the entire time you've worked here," Jenna said.

Adam waited a long time before he finally nodded.

"On the right side of the folder is something you need to sign that states we discussed this, and that you understand you need to call in through regular channels when you can't be here."

"Of course." Adam scribbled his name without reading the paper and handed the folder back.

"All right, get out of here."

Adam looked at Sasha, then Jenna, then Sasha again, reluctant to leave.

"If you have to go hard on someone, it should be me," he said.

"I decided what was happening to everyone yesterday, Adam. This isn't a debate."

Adam's face changed six times in about a second and for the first time, Jenna saw him look at her like she was one of them. The boss. "Of course," he said.

"Adam," she said. He spun. "You and Sean okay?"

"Yeah," he said quietly. "I think so."

"Good." Jenna nodded. "Now go on, I promise I won't hurt her. And for God's sake, just pretend you're sick next time."

He smiled weakly and left the room. Jenna turned her attention to Sasha. They stared at each other for a long moment before they finally both smiled.

"What's my sentence?" Sasha asked.

"Same."

"Are you out of your mind?"

"Nope. Taking the visit for Adam makes you an accomplice in the same crime, and as far as I'm concerned that makes you deserving of the same punishment."

"Well, sure, as far as taking the visit goes, but what about the rest?"

"Ah, so good of you to bring up the dead body." Jenna reached into the drawer again and pulled out Sasha's folder. "I read your statement. Danielle broke the glass, is that right?"

"Yes."

"You asked her what she was doing. She said there was a body."

"Yeah."

"You told her to wait; she didn't."

Sasha shifted her weight. "Yeah, but—"

"Once she let you in the house, you told her to take the boy back *out* of the house."

"Well, yeah."

Jenna closed the folder with the statement inside and tossed it on the desk. "So you should be in trouble for what, exactly?"

"Danielle was my trainee. I was responsible for her. Even if I didn't do it, I let her."

"That's not what this says." Jenna pointed at the folder. "That says, and Danielle's is identical if you're curious, that you were around the corner when she decided to break the glass. That's not *letting* her. That's Danielle making a bold decision without consulting her trainer."

"She'd just seen a dead body. It was a normal reaction to want to barrel in there and help."

"I agree."

"It's my job to keep her from doing things she hasn't had the training to know not to do."

"Within reason."

"What do you mean, within reason?" Sasha's voice rose a little.

"If you'd been interviewing a client and Danielle had suddenly blurted out that they should go fuck themselves, would that be your fault?"

"Of course not."

"Well, neither is this then. You can't inform decisions she makes without you. You even managed to tell her to wait before going inside, and she ignored you. She says she ignored you right in her statement. Very honest of her to put that in there."

"You're just going to lay all this on her then?" Sasha stood up.

Jenna looked at her curiously. "Are you mad at me for *not* getting you in trouble?"

"I just don't think it's right to let me off scot-free because I'm your friend and blame it all on her. I didn't think you'd be like that."

"All right, first of all, it's got nothing to do with us being friends. I wouldn't throw the book at anyone over this. She saw something awful and she reacted. That's not your fault."

"Maybe not, but I still don't think it's right for her to take all the heat for this. Do you?"

"I do when I know I'm the heat and it won't be very hot."

The anger in Sasha's face was replaced with confusion. Finally, it seemed to register.

"What are you saying?"

"I'm saying I don't think anyone needs to get in a lot of trouble. People cover each other's shifts all the time. It's not cool, but it's not a huge deal either, and I'm not going to pretend it is just because a one in a million occurrence happened this time. I'm not going to get you in trouble for not psychically knowing what Danielle was going to do, and I'm not going to get Danielle in trouble for making a snap decision during her second week. I'm just not going to do it. Call it soft if you want, but I'm not going to go tough on you because you're my friend any more than I'm going to go *easy* on you because you're my friend. I'm comfortable explaining that to anyone who has a problem with it."

"Oh." Sasha's shoulders slumped back to normal.

"Now will you sit down and sign your verbal warning, you maniac?"

Sasha scanned Jenna's face, then she grabbed a pen to sign the warning. "So, I guess you're not bad at this."

Danielle was sitting in a chair in the hall when Sasha opened the door to leave. Jenna saw a brief exchange between them, but couldn't hear what they were saying. They looked much more comfortable than they had in the break room last week. She supposed rescuing a toddler from being stranded with his mother's dead body together could do that. Combined with the way Sasha got heated at the idea of Danielle getting in trouble, Jenna wondered if Sasha might have a little crush. Sasha identified as bisexual but only ever dated men, a habit she took plenty of flak over, but that typically seemed unlikely to change.

Jenna couldn't help fixating on the way the planes of Danielle's face moved as she talked. She had a face that was both soft and strong, and she had dimples Jenna had somehow not spotted before. Danielle caught Jenna off guard when she turned in time to catch her staring. Jenna grabbed her keys and met Danielle in the hall just as Sasha finally took off in the other direction.

"I thought we had a meeting?" Danielle said.

"More of a discussion. I figured we could have it while we're on the road if you're comfortable with that. I want to check in on Deon and Raylon."

"Sure," Danielle said. "That's great since it probably means I still have a job."

Jenna laughed. "You definitely still have a job."

Jenna waited until they were in her Acura before she spoke again to make sure no one overheard anything. After she closed the car door and started the engine, she looked over and met Danielle's eyes.

"So," she said. "You okay?"

Confusion passed through Danielle's face.

"You found a body," Jenna said. "In some stage of decay, and a boy trapped with it. We'll get to protocol, but first, I'm much more interested in how you're doing with that."

"I'm okay," Danielle said, but Jenna waited. "It was pretty awful," she added. "The smell was, I can't even start to describe it. You can't really breathe. It was so hot. I can't imagine being trapped in there. That boy…"

Jenna fought the instinct to reach out and touch Danielle. It's what she would have done for any of her friends or even perfect strangers when she was a caseworker, but as a supervisor it was basically a no-no.

"You can have a few days off if you need them," Jenna said. "It's important to process that kind of stuff."

"No," Danielle said. "No, I'm okay. You don't have to be careful with me. I know I screwed up. I know I wasn't supposed to barge in there."

"No, you weren't," Jenna said. "We don't have the authority to force entry. We have to call the police for that. And it's dangerous. If there was someone else inside still they could have hurt you. There could have been a suspect inside who killed that woman, or even just someone who lived there but didn't know what happened that could have thought you were breaking in."

"There's no way anyone could have not known she was in there. That smell—" Danielle broke off. "And it was a drug overdose, right? Isn't that what they said?"

"Yes," Jenna said. "It was an OD, and there was no one else in the house, but you couldn't have known that from outside."

"Of course," Danielle said. "I didn't mean to argue."

"It's okay," Jenna said. "It's not exactly in our orientation. You don't come across it often. Now you know."

"Really?" Danielle asked. "That's it?"

"That's it."

"Wow, the way everyone was talking around the office I thought I was in way more trouble."

"Well, if they ask, tell them I beat you."

Danielle smirked and her dimples came to life. Jenna could see how Sasha would fall for that. She wanted to pry about their relationship, but it wasn't appropriate. When she'd applied for supervisor she never realized the biggest thing she was giving up was the right to be inappropriate. Jenna put the car in drive and headed for the basketball courts.

When they pulled up, she was satisfied to see Raylon and Deon immediately. Raylon and his friends were building something out of rocks in the grass while Deon casually shot free throws. He tossed the ball to one of his friends when he saw her car pulling up. Jenna rolled down the window as he approached.

"Hey, Ms. Thompson," he said. "What's good?"

She hated the way he always talked differently around his friends, even when they were out of earshot. It was hard to watch a fourteen-year-old think he had to act tough. It was harder to know deep down that he *did* need to be tough. She spotted a purple shadow on his jaw.

"What's that?" she asked before he even made it all the way to the car.

"Nothing," he said.

She always gave him points for not playing dumb, but it wasn't enough. "Let me see."

He lifted his chin up so she could have a better look.

"What happened?"

"Just basketball," he said. "It gets rough sometimes."

Jenna stared at him, looking for some buried truth. She couldn't find it in the bruise or his eyes or his voice, but something inside still told her it was something much worse than basketball.

"Just tell me," Jenna said.

"I did, basketball."

"I don't believe you."

"What do you want to hear?" Deon asked. "You want me to tell you my mama did it? Or one of her boyfriends?"

"Did they?"

"No, but even if they did I wouldn't say."

"Why not?"

"You'll take us away if I say that."

"Haven't I always told you I'll talk to you about that before it ever happens?" Jenna said.

Deon looked at his feet. "Yeah."

"We've talked about stuff like this before, remember? Did I just take you and your brother away?"

"No, but now you have her with you." Deon nodded at Danielle. "So?"

"So it's not the same. I know you have to play by the rulebook now, Ms. T. I get it."

"Deon."

"Look, don't sweat it. It ain't even from that anyway. Just basketball." Deon turned and jogged back down to the courts before Jenna could stop him. She rolled up the window and merged with traffic.

"Damn it."

"You okay?" Danielle asked.

"Yeah," Jenna said. She could hear the frustration in her own voice.

"Am I messing this case up for you?"

Jenna looked over. "No," she said. "He's looking for any reason to distance himself. He wants to drop out and be a tough guy, and he knows I won't be okay with it so he has to start breaking ties. He's using you as an excuse. If you weren't here it would be something else."

"What do you think the bruise is from?"

"I don't know." Jenna sighed. "The original accusation that started their case was that Ladona was disciplining them by hitting them with objects, among other things."

"That's awful."

"All three of them say it isn't true, Mom and the boys. Ladona says the neighbor that accused her is just mad she's sleeping with her boyfriend."

"But Deon did tell you about something else that happened?" Danielle asked.

"The poverty is real, as you saw. When we first started working with them the place was unsanitary. The boys were malnourished. And Deon told me she slapped him once."

"Which probably means all the time," Danielle said.

Jenna looked over, surprised. She wanted to ask about Danielle's past, about what would make her assume such a thing. "Maybe," she said carefully. "Maybe not."

"Can't you just pull them out of there?"

Danielle exuded a confidence she hadn't just days before. Jenna wondered if the incident with the body could change so much so fast, or if Danielle was just starting to come out of her shell.

"Deon is exceptionally smart," Jenna said. "That bruise could be exactly what you think, but it could also just be basketball. You can't pull them out on something that debatable. If Deon doesn't want to be removed, he knows how the system works, what he can and can't say, and when he doesn't know, he shuts down completely. If it comes to the point he needs to be taken out of there, I'll have to get him on board with it. That will only happen if he trusts me."

"Why is he so set on staying there if she's hitting them?"

"Again, we don't know that she is. But their aunt is their next of kin, their only other kin, and she is only willing to take in Raylon. Deon would have to go to foster care."

"And Deon and Raylon don't want to be separated."

"You got it."

"In other words, he has a good reason to lie," Danielle said. "What makes you think he'd tell you?"

"He is exceptionally smart," Jenna said again. "And he loves his brother very much. I think he'll tell me if it gets bad, for Raylon."

A long, full silence stretched between them, and Jenna sensed it was filling up with unasked questions. She knew Danielle wanted to know if she really broke the rules for Deon like he implied, and she wasn't ready to answer. At the same time, her own questions were building about who Danielle was. And her mind kept wandering to Danielle and Sasha talking in the hall.

"How are you liking working with Sasha?" She hoped she sounded like a supervisor checking in on her newest team member, but she suspected she was rather transparent in her probing.

"It's fine," Danielle said and smiled. Jenna felt a tingle travel through her skin. The idea of Sasha checking Danielle out was making it impossible for Jenna not to do the same, and Danielle was gorgeous. Her teeth were exceptionally white, her hair was silky, and her eyes said she knew something she wasn't supposed to. Jenna couldn't guess the specifics of Danielle's Asian heritage, and she couldn't find a way to ask that felt natural, but in any case, she couldn't seem to keep her eyes off Danielle's amber skin.

"She's very nice," Danielle said. "And fun."

"She is," Jenna said. Those were only a couple on a long list of attributes Sasha possessed, along with wit and beauty. Despite always knowing her friend was a catch, Jenna had never felt threatened by her, and she wasn't exactly sure why she did now.

"She invited me out this weekend," Danielle said.

"Oh?" Jenna's stomach twisted. She hadn't been invited. Because it was a date? Or because she was no longer welcome at such gatherings? She wasn't sure which idea bothered her more.

"Yeah," Danielle said. "To Big J's. I guess it's tradition?"

Jenna laughed. "Oh, yeah. It is, I guess. It's always a good time. I'm sure you'll have fun."

"Are you going?"

"Not sure," Jenna said. "Haven't exactly been invited. They might not want a supervisor hanging out watching their mischief."

"That's crazy," Danielle said. "They love you."

"Do they?" Jenna looked over just in time to see Danielle's cheeks slightly flush, and she held back a chuckle as she realized Danielle blushed easily.

"Well, sure. They talk about you all the time."

"That's good to hear," Jenna said. "I've been trying to get this promotion for a while, but I'd hate to lose friends over it. Maybe it was a little naive of me, but I didn't really worry about that until it was too late."

"Well, I know I'm new," Danielle said. "But I'm pretty sure you don't have to worry. And you should consider yourself invited. I hope you'll come."

CHAPTER EIGHT

Danielle frowned at the pile of clothes on her bed. She couldn't remember the last time she'd struggled to pick an outfit, which might explain why the selection that made up her wardrobe was as sad as it was. Brianna poked her head into the room, observed the pile, then beamed and burst in the rest of the way.

"You need help."

Danielle sighed. "Yes, actually, I do."

"What are we going for? Maintaining the work image or shattering it?"

"Shattering."

Brianna went to the bed and sat down without looking through anything. "Something sexy?"

"Yes." She paused. "Well, no. Not like—"

"Sexy like you didn't mean to be?"

"Yeah."

"Who's the girl?"

"There's no girl."

Brianna scoffed. "Danielle, who's the girl?"

"There is no girl." Danielle ignored the face that jumped to mind. "I just don't want to be the little uptight Asian girl again. I haven't talked to anyone very much, and they haven't talked to me. I'm pretty sure they all think I just come home and practice violin every night or something."

Brianna smirked. "Oh, come on. It can't be that bad."

"You know what I mean."

"Well, no one will think you're shy next to me. I'm so loud we'll both get credit."

"Yeah, yeah. Can you just make me not look like a twelve-year-old boy?"

"Of course, I can," Brianna said. She started going through the clothes on the bed. "So, these two beautiful trainers of yours, will they be there?"

"Sasha will," Danielle said. "I'm not sure about Jenna." Danielle felt a stab of disappointment at the consideration Jenna might not show. She couldn't help but linger on the realization that if she found out right now Jenna wasn't going, she would no longer care what she wore. That was dangerous.

Brianna stood up and held a shirt on a hanger against Danielle's body, then pulled it away and tried another. "Did you call dibs on one of them yet?"

"Dibs? No."

"I could go after either one and you wouldn't mind?"

"Please don't," Danielle said.

"All right, we're getting somewhere. Please don't to which one?"

"Either."

"Well, you can't have them both, Danielle, that's not fair."

"I work with these people, Bri."

"So? I don't."

"This is a bad idea. Forget it," Danielle said. "I don't even want to go." Danielle slumped into her pile of clothes. Brianna slowly put the hangers down and came and sat by her.

"Isn't this a welcome party for *you*?"

Danielle raked her hand down her face. "Yeeees."

"Okay, so you have to go."

"Why? I didn't ask to be welcomed."

Brianna smiled and grabbed her arm. She pulled until Danielle was sitting again. "What happened to not wanting to be the quiet little Asian girl anymore?"

"You happened! With your sexy outfit choosing and girl hunting and shit faced being. It's just not me. I'm never going to be a party girl. I need to just buy a violin and get it over with."

"Oh stop. You don't have to be a party girl. Just go and talk and have fun. I'll do the drinking and girl hunting."

"Could you not? Just this time?"

"Don't drink or flirt? Why don't you just ask me to stop breathing, Danielle."

"Seriously," she said. "Please?"

Brianna sighed. "All right, fine. Just this once. Because it's a work thing."

"Thank you."

"And because I am *not* listening to you learn to play violin."

"Thanks."

Brianna started going through her clothes again and finally found something she liked. "Try this on." She tossed it into Danielle's hands. "And I'm doing your makeup."

"Thanks, Bri."

"Mhmm," she said. "That'll be twenty dollars for my services."

"Uh-huh."

Brianna cracked a smile, then took on a straight face again. "No seriously, I need twenty dollars. I—"

Ringing sounded from Danielle's laptop and cut Brianna off. Danielle looked over and saw her brother's picture on the screen. She launched from the bed to her desk and hit answer.

"Li!"

The screen filled with his face with his room at their parents' house in the background.

"Shh," he whispered. He hunching over the keyboard in an attempt to hide the screen. He glanced over his shoulder to verify the door was still closed. He looked older than the last time she'd seen him. His hair was longer and gelled, and his chest looked fuller, more muscled. A few lines had developed around his smile. At twenty-two years old, he seemed too young for that, but he had recently started med school. If that wasn't enough, she knew her situation with her parents stressed him out as much, if not more than her.

"Why didn't you call sooner?" she whispered. "It's been so long."

"They keep asking if I'm talking to you," he said. "I think they know."

"There's no way. We're too careful."

"I don't have long," he said. Danielle had never seen her brother so anxious. They'd been hiding the fact that they still spoke ever since her parents cut her out of their lives two years ago. He was always cautious, but not always scared.

"What's wrong, Li?"

"Dad is sick," he said. "He won't tell me what's wrong, but it's bad enough he hasn't been working for two weeks. He's home right now."

"Sick? How sick?"

"I don't know." Li checked over his shoulder again.

"You have to find out. You're the only one he'll tell."

"I tried," Li said. "He keeps saying it's nothing, that he just needs rest."

"Does he look sick? Come on, Dr. Corey, what's wrong with him?"

Li scoffed. "Please, I have no idea."

Something banged in the hall outside his door, and Li froze. Danielle found she couldn't breathe either. The idea of them being upset with Li for talking to her hurt just as much as their own refusal to talk to her.

"I better go," Li said.

Danielle felt tears building, but she wouldn't let them spill over, not for Li to see.

"Okay, call me soon."

He nodded, preoccupied with watching the door again. "Okay, love you." He closed the laptop before she could say it back.

CHAPTER NINE

Jenna's phone was exploding with text messages from her friends reminding her about Danielle's welcome party. The fear that she might not be wanted at these events anymore was extinguished, which was nice, but she was having doubts about attending.

She knew Paula was watching her carefully as she learned the nuances of her new job, and though nothing was explicitly said she could no longer socialize with the others, it was frowned upon.

She also had to admit she wasn't comfortable with how much she wanted to see Danielle. She'd always been good at being honest with herself, and even though a large part of her wanted to brush the notion away, she knew what she felt when Sasha lingered by Danielle was jealousy, however mild it might have been. She wasn't overpowered by Danielle's attractiveness or their comfortable conversations, but she didn't want to be. As a supervisor, she wasn't allowed to have any sort of romantic interaction with subordinates, and gentle as the fire might be between them, fires never needed alcohol. Her phone chimed again, and she read the message from Adam.

Bitch you better be on the way!

Jenna smiled and grabbed her jacket. Yeah, she was on the way. She couldn't deny she needed it. She missed her friends, and she didn't want to miss out on the fun. What she did tonight would set an expectation, both for her friends and her bosses, so if she wanted to keep hanging out with them, she needed to show up. Jenna hurried down the stairs and found Callie lying on the couch watching TV.

"I'm out of here," Jenna said. "Use my credit card if you want to order something for dinner; it's saved."

Callie rolled over onto her stomach so she could see. "Where are you going?"

"Out with friends. Work thing, sort of."

"Doesn't look like work." Callie scanned her outfit. "Bar?"

"Yeah."

"Must be nice."

"You'll be twenty-one before you know it. I'll take you to every bar in town if you want. I promise."

"Yeah, not what I meant."

"What do you mean, then?" Jenna asked.

"Must be nice to go out."

"You could go out too, Cal. You have a car and no curfew; the world is yours."

"Right, that helps." Callie's tone dripped with the sarcasm that had become her favorite weapon. "With what friends?"

"You'll make friends in no time. You just have to get out there."

"Yeah, because this just attracts people left and right." Callie gestured harshly at her face. "I said I want friends, not an audience." Callie had dark hair and bright green eyes just like Jenna, but the scarring on the left side of her face made her left eye a bit differently shaped than the other and her hairline higher. The skin looked a little too thin, too tight, with some bumps along the edges, and her lip curled up slightly on the side. It was noticeable. Jenna never claimed it wasn't, but Callie wasn't as horrifically disfigured as she clearly thought she was.

"Give people a chance, Cal. They aren't as awful as you think."

"Oh, they aren't? I just imagined people throwing rocks at me, did I?"

Jenna sighed. "That was terrible, Callie. I'm so sorry it happened. They were kids, though. Kids are awful. No adult is going to behave anything like that."

"Probably not, but they'll be thinking all the same things. No one sees me and thinks, let's be friends, or I'm going to ask her out."

"They would if you let them get to know you a little," Jenna said. "If you just—"

"You should go," Callie said. "You'll be late. Go have fun being beautiful."

Part of Jenna wanted to stay and keep comforting Callie, but she was starting to recognize their patterns as toxic. When she stayed she just felt like she was playing into Callie's agenda. She never changed the way Callie felt about her appearance. She would do anything to take back Callie's burns, but she couldn't, and she couldn't figure out how to help her see her life wasn't over.

Jenna grabbed her keys and headed for the door.

"Okay," Callie said. "Have fun. I'll just be here hanging out with *Mom*."

Jenna ignored the shiver of irritation and trudged for her car.

She could hear the hum of chatter and laughter from the bar the moment she pulled into the lot and was instantly grateful she did decide to come out. It was silly to think she couldn't handle a night around Danielle. She'd worked with many gorgeous coworkers in her life, and it hadn't been a problem yet. She wasn't a rabid teenager.

She made her way to their usual spot on the patio and saw Sasha and Adam shoot from their chairs to greet her.

"Hell yes!" Adam said. "You made it!"

Jenna felt a flood of relief seeing their smiling faces and barreled into a group hug. "You were right," she said. "I needed this."

She slipped into the chair that had become hers. Adam's boyfriend, Sean, was all smiles. His skin seemed to glow, and whatever had been pressing enough to jeopardize Adam's job seemed to be forgotten.

Val and the others streamed in from the bar in a roar of laughter as they balanced drinks and set shots on the table.

"Jenna!" Val chimed as she sat down. "Holy shit, I thought we'd never see you again. Have a shot, lady."

The chatter quickly turned to a constant buzz, and Jenna had a hard time hiding the fact that she couldn't stop checking over her shoulder for Danielle. Maybe she wouldn't show. That would certainly simplify things. She could use a nice carefree night with friends without having to worry about the impression she was making on a new employee, or the impression that employee seemed to be making on her.

Just as she started to think Danielle was probably a no-show, the signature roar of a greeting flowed around the table. She looked up, and Danielle was in the doorway with an understated smile that seemed genuine, if slightly uncomfortable. She was wearing skintight jeans with rips in them that made Jenna's mouth dry and a loose shirt with a beautiful artistic design that looked like it had been painted. It deceivingly hung freely from her shoulders, yet clung to her curves, and Jenna was much too aware of Danielle's perfectly proportioned form. Jenna realized with a tingle that Danielle was scrutinizing her just as closely. She looked away before it became downright inappropriate and was grateful for a new place to direct her attention when a woman came clomping through the doorway and squished onto the crowded patio.

"Who's your friend?" Jenna heard Sasha asking though she felt somehow far away. Jenna dared to look at Danielle again as she waited for the answer.

"I'm sorry," Danielle said. "This is Brianna."

"Hey, everyone," Brianna said. "Y'all ready to party?" Brianna did a quick shimmy and stirred up a round of laughs. She had voluminous, reddish brown hair, lots of makeup, and the type of clothes that took up a lot of space. A coat with a big, furry hood, a low-cut top with ample cleavage spilling from it, an oversized purse, knee high boots. And Jenna could tell her personality matched. She was surprised to see Danielle in such boisterous company, but how could she really know how Danielle behaved in her free time?

"Come on over, girls." Sasha pointed at the two empty seats between her and Jenna. Brianna bolted for the small opening between the wall and chairs, ensuring she would have the first pick.

Jenna laughed and braced herself as she realized Brianna was making an undisguised beeline for her. Brianna lunged into the chair and started shedding her bulky coat and purse, then turned her body toward Jenna as she crossed her legs and found a place for her elbow on the back of her chair.

"What was your name, hon?"

"Jenna. It's nice to meet you."

"Jenna, I just have to tell you real quick that you are absolutely gorgeous. Have you ever done any modeling?"

Jenna smiled and couldn't deny Brianna had a very warm presence that somehow amounted to something less cheesy than her parts.

"Can't say I have," Jenna said.

"Well, you definitely could if you ever got tired of your job."

"That's sweet of you to say."

"Tell me about this job of yours. It hasn't been long and already Danielle is telling me crazy stories. I bet you must have tons of them."

Jenna felt Brianna's leg brush hers under the table and knew it wasn't accidental. She was sure enough to presume Brianna preferred women, and she glanced at Danielle as she mused on the subject. Brianna certainly wasn't acting like anybody's girlfriend, and Danielle seemed unconcerned with it as she chatted with Sasha, but she still couldn't say she was confident of what the two were exactly.

She knew Brianna was still talking to her, still pointedly admiring her, but she couldn't seem to keep her attention on it despite Brianna's overtly sexual presence. Most of the women Jenna had been with in the past had been confident, sexual women. Women closer on the spectrum to Brianna than Danielle. That probably had a lot to do with her preference not to get involved too deeply. Relationships were just too complex. The second her love life started to bleed over into her home life, problems started, and she'd finally decided she simply couldn't do both properly. So why did her focus keep wandering away from Brianna, who fit the mold of a fun-only night, and who wasn't a coworker, and over to Danielle who was entirely off limits?

CHAPTER TEN

I'm so glad you came," Sasha said.

Danielle heard the words, but it somehow took her a long time to realize they were directed at her. When she turned and saw Sasha waiting, she put it together.

"Of course," Danielle said. "You're all so nice for doing this for me. Kind of a big show for one little person. I appreciate it."

"Don't worry, we like it," Adam said.

Danielle was still trying to recover from seeing Jenna outside of work for the first time. She was casually leaning back in her chair in a tank top and jeans. Her hair fell in loose curls instead of the straight locks Danielle was used to seeing, and the emerald color of her tank top played beautifully against her light skin. She was striking beyond belief, and even though Danielle had known she was beautiful, the full force of it had never hit her like a train the way it was now. No matter how she tried, she couldn't seem to stop the impact Jenna's gaze was making on her each time their eyes met.

It didn't help that Brianna had nearly tripped her to make sure to sit next to Jenna and had been drooling over her ever since. She couldn't say she was surprised, of course. Brianna loved the hunt, and Jenna was a prize anyone would brag over, but she couldn't continue to watch every word of the exchange.

She pulled away and noticed there were three people she'd never seen before at the table. Sasha seemed to read her mind.

"Danielle, this is Val, Suzie, and this is Cole." They each nodded at her.

"Well," Val said. "Now that the guest of honor is here I think it's time for shots."

"Oh, no thanks," Danielle said. "I don't drink much." A collective groan circled the table, Brianna leading the charge.

"Just one?" Val asked. "Something light?"

"Something light," Danielle conceded.

Val flagged down the server and ordered eight shots, but Danielle missed what they were. Val turned back to Danielle and Sasha.

"So, you two found a body? What the fuck?"

"Oh God," Sasha said. "Not again."

"Well, it's not every day you find a damn body, Sash, come on. That hasn't happened since…" She paused and looked up. "Shit, since Jenna did CPR on that one chick."

Danielle looked to Jenna. "You did?"

"Yeah," Jenna said. "Same thing, almost. Overdose. Except she was still alive when I found her."

"And you saved her?" Danielle said.

Jenna shook her head. "No. Tried, but she died."

"I'm sorry."

The darkness in Jenna's expression felt like it was physically pulling Danielle to her. Her hair was just past shoulder length, and Danielle found she couldn't stop sneaking glances along Jenna's collar and to the curve of her breasts. Her head swirled as she realized she was decidedly in forbidden territory. She tried to shake it off. What was wrong with her?

The server showed up with the tray of shots and set them all in the middle of the table. Danielle couldn't possibly guess what it was, but it looked like straight liquor, not something light. Everyone reached for a shot, and Danielle knew she had to go along. No one would understand or believe she was killing her entire tolerance in one gulp. She wouldn't be a mess, but she would be as drunk as she cared to get.

Sasha held up her shot. "To Danielle. The good ones always start with a bang."

Danielle watched Jenna and Brianna each take the shot effortlessly, then threw hers back, being sure not to make a face. Something spicy made its way down her throat. Danielle forced the cringe to disperse through her skin in a shudder. The burning almost seemed to intensify as time went by, and she wished she had water. She wanted to think she was imagining the way Brianna already seemed to be managing to touch Jenna quite a bit, but she knew she wasn't.

The group discussion quickly broke down into side conversations, and Sasha kept grabbing her attention. She should be glad. She usually was when she had someone trying to make conversation with her. It beat the hell out of sitting alone awkwardly trying to appear comfortable while also not look like she was intentionally isolating herself. But she found Sasha's voice kept failing to hold her attention. She kept losing track of the sentence before it finished, and damn it, she couldn't stop looking at Jenna's shoulders or the way Brianna was plotting to touch them. All Danielle could do was watch it happen out of the corner of her eye.

Brianna successfully lured Jenna into chitchat a couple times, but kept losing her again to the rest of the table. It seemed no matter the group, no matter the conversation, everyone always ended up calling for Jenna to join in. She had a story about everything, was friends with everyone, and was the energy in any group she joined. She was vibrant and comfortable in a way Danielle couldn't imagine being.

"Anyone need another?" Brianna asked, pointing around the table. Half of them raised their hands, and Brianna enthusiastically repeated everyone's choice of drink, then touched Jenna's shoulder. "Want to help me with a bar run?"

"Sure." Jenna graciously followed her inside to the bar. Danielle forced herself not to look after them or show her frustration. Jenna would never go for Brianna. And even if she did, that wasn't any of her business. Jenna was her boss. She repeated the words in her head a thousand times. Maybe it would even be better if Jenna did go for Brianna. It would take her mind off this impossible and inappropriate fixation she seemed to be developing.

Danielle turned back to Sasha and saw she was clearly waiting for Danielle to answer a question she hadn't heard. Danielle finally realized Sasha was wearing makeup and usually didn't. Her blondish brown hair had been trimmed and styled.

"I'm sorry, what?" Danielle felt her cheeks flush.

"I was asking how you and Brianna know each other."

"She was trying to figure out if you're gay," Adam mock whispered across the table. Sasha smacked his arm hard enough a loud thwack sounded, and everyone burst into laughter.

"You don't have to answer that," Sasha said. "Adam's an idiot."

"It's okay," Danielle said. "No. Well, yes, but no."

"Okaaay."

Danielle chuckled. "No, Brianna and I aren't a thing, if that's what you were getting at, but I am gay."

"Your loss," Brianna said from behind her. Danielle shook her head, but a round of laughter circled the table. Brianna started setting drinks down in front of people. Danielle suddenly felt warmth on her right side and the smell of campfire hugged her. When she looked over, Jenna was leaning down, placing a clear, bubbling drink in front of her.

"Oh, I really can—"

"It's soda water," Jenna said quietly. "Lime for effect." Jenna gently touched her shoulder before moving past and taking her seat again.

Danielle's fingers automatically moved to return Jenna's touch, but she was already gone, leaving the warmth of her hand branded on Danielle's skin.

CHAPTER ELEVEN

I bet they snuck off for a quickie," Adam said.
"She said they weren't involved," Sasha said.
"So?"

Jenna watched the two bicker about where Brianna and Danielle had gone. She'd been curious for ten minutes before either of them had noticed. When Val, Suzie, and Cole split off for the bar a few minutes later, they finally saw the group had gotten much smaller. It caught Jenna's attention immediately because it had been Brianna who'd gotten up first, and it was a relief to have her personal space back. Danielle had gone after her a few minutes later, but she didn't look happy, not the way Jenna guessed she might if she'd been going after a quickie.

"I'll be back," Jenna said and got up.

"Not you too," Sasha said.

"I'm just going to get some air."

"We're outside," Adam sneered playfully.

"You know what I mean."

"I really don't, but okay, beautiful."

Jenna laughed and hugged him on her way past. She pushed through the crowd in the bar. It was filling up inside, and she knew she stood little chance of spotting them. Instead, she just went to the parking lot to confirm Danielle's car was still there. It was. A ripple of relief made its way through her body. She really should get some air before she saw Danielle again.

When she made her way over to the benches that were probably meant to be a smoking area, a muffled voice cut through the quiet. She followed the sound until she could tell it was two voices, female voices. The sounds were indistinct, maybe not even words. Jenna's stomach jolted as she wondered if Adam was right after all. She took another step and had to suppress a laugh. It wasn't the sound of sex; it was puking.

Jenna circled the Jeep that hid them and saw Brianna curled over, puking in the grass while Danielle held her hair and scolded her.

"Doing okay over here?" Jenna asked and smiled.

Danielle looked up miserably, and Jenna couldn't contain a chuckle. She knelt by the two of them and put her hand on Brianna's back.

"Let it go, girl," she said.

Brianna flashed the rock 'n' roll horns without lifting her head.

"I better get her home," Danielle said.

"Oh," Jenna said. "Okay."

"No way," Brianna said. "Give me five minutes and I'm good for another drink. No big deal."

"You don't need to drink more," Danielle said.

"'Kay, Mom." Brianna sat up and flipped her hair over her head. "Voila! Let's get back in there."

Brianna grabbed each of them, swaying both directions before she was confident enough to let go.

"Good as new," she said. "Really." Brianna headed back inside without waiting for them. Jenna was surprised to see her go after the way she'd clung to her all night, but she was relieved. When she looked back to Danielle she saw anger in her face.

"You okay?"

"Yeah," she said. "She just does this every time. I'm sorry you had to see that."

"It's okay." Jenna laughed. "I've seen way worse, trust me. You should have seen my twenty-third birthday."

"Thanks," Danielle said. "Well, I should start trying to talk her into leaving."

"Why?" Jenna asked. Danielle looked surprised by the question. "She's drunk, but she's fine. None of us are going to let her get into any trouble. Don't bother yourself with it."

Danielle seemed to think it over before she finally nodded. "Yeah, I guess I could just let her do whatever, couldn't I?"

"Sure." Jenna shrugged. "Want another drink?"

Danielle met Jenna's eyes like she'd just asked something very serious. Jenna let Danielle stare into her, not sure what she was looking for. Was she taking it as an advance? Was it? She had to get her mind under control.

"Could we bring it back out here?" she finally said. "I'm just not sure I'm ready for the crowd again yet."

"Sure," Jenna said. "I'll get the drinks." Jenna's heart started pounding as she saw Danielle sit on the bench outside, though she wasn't sure why. She turned and headed for the bar, ordered their drinks, and looked at Danielle through the glass door while she waited. Danielle was absentmindedly combing her fingers through her hair, and Jenna craved the tangles around her own fingers. This was exactly why she'd been afraid to come out tonight. She couldn't be swept up in this. She couldn't start her career this way. Or end it this way, more to the point. She should bump into the others and bring them outside with her. She should come up with a reason to leave.

But she didn't. She accepted the two drinks from the bartender and headed back outside. Danielle was standing now, staring up at the sky.

❖

"Good stars tonight?" Jenna's voice reached up from behind her and encircled her. Danielle felt the ocean sway of her buzz from the shot of mystery liquor and slowly turned as she tried to pull together enough composure to answer.

"Good moon," she said.

Jenna handed her a glass, and they each downed a couple of sips. The warmth of the alcohol traveled down her center and pulsed through her. Jenna took a seat on the bench that was just far enough away from the entrance of the bar that it was quiet. Danielle looked down from the sky and came to sit by her.

"I think it's great you take care of your mom and sister," Danielle said.

She could see Jenna was caught off guard by the remark, and a second passed before she answered.

"Thanks," she said. "There are plenty of people who disagree. Sasha thinks I need to kick Callie to the curb and make her grow up."

Danielle raised her eyebrow. "I can't imagine kicking my brother out. If he lived with me, that is."

"I didn't know you have a brother."

Danielle looked down into her drink self-consciously, then glanced up again. "I guess I didn't tell you much that first day when you asked about my family. It's kind of a bad situation. But I do have a little brother I love to death. He's going to be a doctor."

"That's awesome," Jenna said. "Doesn't sound like a bad situation. I would kill for Callie to have that kind of ambition."

"Li is great. My parents are the bad part. My dad, really. He disowned me when I came out."

"Oh, Danielle, I'm sorry."

"It's okay," Danielle said. It wasn't okay at all, and she knew she wasn't doing much to hide that. The pain still felt raw and fresh, despite the two years that had passed.

"What about your mom?" Jenna asked.

"She does what he says. She comes from a traditional Chinese family. She feels the need to honor his wishes, so she doesn't talk to me either. Li still does, but we have to hide it."

"That's awful."

The words were simple, but Danielle could somehow feel so much more in them than was on the surface. She met Jenna's eyes and wished Jenna would touch her, but she knew that wouldn't happen. Just because they were outside of work didn't mean there weren't still professional boundaries. They were starting to feel rather thin even without them touching.

"You and Brianna seem close," Jenna said. "Like you've been friends for a long time. Surrogate family?"

Danielle stared at Jenna a long time trying to dissect the question, trying to figure out if there was more to it or not. Was she interested in knowing if she was attached? Or if Brianna was? Or was it just what she said? Trying to explain her relationship with Brianna was somehow proving to be fruitless. She couldn't make the words come out. She was embarrassed to admit the inappropriate, busty, barfy flirt who'd been attached to Jenna's hip all night was her ex. She barely wanted to claim her as a friend, and she couldn't bear imagining what Jenna would think when she told her they used to go out, what she would think of their living arrangement now. She would have to have her doubts about them being strictly platonic, and even though that shouldn't bother her, it did. But she was way ahead of herself. She didn't owe an explanation of the people in her life to her boss, and thinking she did meant she was crossing a line.

"Yeah," Danielle finally said. "Surrogate family, you could say that. We've been friends a long time. Since before my parents disowned me, and we moved in together after. It did feel a little like family, I guess, just being around someone who had known me so long."

Jenna nodded. "I'm glad you have her, then."

Danielle felt the pressure of Jenna's gaze crushing into her and felt the need to lighten the mood, but as soon as she spoke she just kept bringing it crashing down. "She has a crush on you, you know?" Danielle said. "Brianna."

Jenna laughed. "I don't know about that. She seems like the flirty type that doesn't mean much by it."

"She is the flirty type," Danielle said. "But trust me, she wants you."

"How can you be so sure?"

Danielle laughed softly. "I mean look at you, for one. You're gorgeous." She wanted to reach out and gather the words back up, but it was too late.

She felt like she could actually see the adrenaline race through Jenna's skin, and even though she knew it was wrong, she couldn't help the thrill it gave her to rattle Jenna just a little.

"Well, thanks."

"And like you said, we've known each other a long time. I know how she acts when she's interested."

"And that's bothering you?" Jenna asked.

A jolt traveled through her own skin at the remark, and her heart thundered in her chest. Was Jenna actually inviting her to cross the line? Or had she just had too much to drink?

"Yes," she said. "It bothers me."

"Why is that?"

She tumbled into Jenna's intense gaze. "You know why."

Danielle's stomach flipped, and a shiver ran down her spine as she stepped closer and touched Jenna's cheek. Her heart pounded as she waited for something to happen, for Jenna to pull away from her touch, to wake her up from this dream, but it didn't happen. Jenna felt stiff, like maybe she wasn't breathing, but she was still boldly staring into her.

Danielle gave in and closed the remaining distance between them. Their lips met softly at first, but when Jenna wrapped her arms around Danielle and pulled her closer, their bodies touched and a surge of energy awakened. The trembling of nerves fell away, and Danielle deepened the kiss, opening her mouth to Jenna and teasing her with her tongue. Jenna grabbed a handful of Danielle's shirt and pulled her closer. Danielle's head was swirling in disbelief this was happening. She could barely think.

"Danielle." Jenna barely parted their kiss to whisper it. The sound of her name on Jenna's breathless lips sent another rush through her entire body. "They're right ins—"

Danielle curled her fists around Jenna's shirt and gently pushed her until she backed up between the cars, out of view of the bar. She backed Jenna into the side of a large black SUV, then crashed into her with an urgency she'd never felt. Jenna responded to her energy with the same eagerness, and Danielle felt Jenna's fingers weaving through her hair, her body crushing against her as the heat of her kiss made Danielle dizzy. Danielle let her hands wander Jenna's body as she pressed her into the SUV, holding her against it at her waist, feeling up her lean abdomen and over her breasts. She felt the rumble of vibrations as she tore a low moan from Jenna's throat. She was pulsing with need as they lost themselves in each other's warmth in the cool night.

A drunken yell ripped through the parking lot. "Jenna? Where the fuck did you go?"

Danielle pulled away. She felt disoriented and hazy from the desire, like she'd been ripped from a dream too soon. She saw Jenna gradually come back to the present too. "You better go back," Danielle said. "They're looking for you."

"I—"

"Jenna!" Sasha was too close to escape. Jenna and Danielle jumped away from each other and tried to look natural. Jenna's eyes stayed on hers another second. They were intense and full of desire and different in the dark in a way that made her breath catch.

"Sash," Jenna said after a second. "Over here."

Sasha squinted into the darkness, then clumsily started toward them. "What the hell are you doing creeping around over there?"

"Just chatting," Jenna said.

"Oh, hey, Danielle," Sasha said. "Didn't see you at first." Sasha looked at each of them a couple of times before suspicion finally took over her face and she stared at Jenna.

"Brianna wasn't feeling well," Jenna said. "She didn't want to make a scene, so she slipped out here."

"Brianna's in there taking a belly shot off some chick at the bar," Sasha said without breaking eye contact.

"Yeah, second wind puke, I guess."

Danielle studied Jenna curiously, watching her try to smooth it over as if it was a lie even though it had really happened. She was still swimming in Jenna's touch. She realized she'd never seen Jenna look disarmed before, and she found it inescapably endearing.

"Right," Sasha said.

"Brianna and I had a little disagreement," Danielle said. "I wanted some air before going back in. Jenna was nice enough to keep me company."

"Oh." Sasha bought into Danielle's explanation much more readily and turned to face her. "Are you okay?"

"Yeah, sure," Danielle said. "Just stupid roommate stuff."

"Okay, well, you guys want to head back in?"

"I should actually take off," Jenna said.

Danielle shot a look at Jenna, struggling to keep her obvious surprise that was verging on alarm at least a little hidden.

"It's getting late," Jenna added.

"Seriously?" Sasha asked, checking her watch. "It's like, midnight. You're usually an all-nighter."

"Yeah, I know, but I should get home and check on Callie. She wasn't thrilled with me for coming out tonight."

"Come on, Jenna," Sasha whined. "You haven't been out in forever. Have some fun. Callie's a grown-up."

"Another time," Jenna said. "I promise."

Danielle thought she saw some kind of remorse or apology hidden in Jenna's fleeting eye contact, but she couldn't possibly work out what it meant, what she was feeling. Jenna turned and started through the parking lot.

Jenna had woken something inside her, made her do things she'd never even thought about doing, and she couldn't stop wanting more. She knew if Jenna stayed they'd end up in bed together. They shouldn't let that happen. It would jeopardize Jenna's entire career. Her need was relentless, but if Jenna had the strength to run, she had to let her.

"You better be taking a cab," Sasha called after her.

"Yep!"

CHAPTER TWELVE

Danielle drove to work in silence. Her mind was too busy to handle music, no matter how relaxing. The party felt like it happened years ago, not just days before. From the moment Jenna's lips left hers she'd thought of nothing else. She couldn't stop replaying the way Jenna had walked through the parking lot that night, leaving her and Sasha behind.

Danielle knew she hadn't mistaken Jenna's desire. She'd felt it in the way Jenna had melted into her arms, pulled her closer, the vibration of her quiet moan. But she'd taken off just minutes later. She ran. Maybe her kiss wasn't welcome, enjoyable or not. Come to think of it, of course her kiss wasn't welcome. It could get Jenna fired, and all she'd heard about Jenna from their coworkers was how hard she'd worked to get where she was. It was completely out of line to come on to her. Danielle couldn't remember a time she'd wanted to kiss someone so badly she'd thrown common sense to the wind.

She would just apologize, say that she shouldn't have gotten so carried away. It was the only way she could salvage any sort of comfortable working relationship.

Danielle made her way to the locker room, hoping to sneak in and out, but Sasha was sitting on the bench with her head leaned back against the locker. She shot upright when Danielle walked in.

"Good morning," she said.

"Morning. You okay?"

"Yeah, just tired. Did you have fun at the party?"

"Yes, it was so nice of you to organize it," Danielle said. "It was fun seeing everyone outside of work. You're right; everyone's really different."

"Especially Jenna, huh?"

Danielle searched her for an underlying meaning, some damning implication, but she looked innocent enough.

"Yeah, I guess."

"That's the Jenna we all know and love," Sasha said. "We're all still adjusting to supervisor Jenna."

Danielle wasn't sure what to say. Jenna seemed friendly, open, and social at work, too. The major difference Danielle saw was the way she looked, which she did have to admit turned her world upside down. "Seems like you pretty much get the best of both worlds," Danielle said.

"Sort of." Sasha crinkled her face as she thought it over. "She's usually a bit more, I don't know, wild? Just seems like she's on her best behavior. Can't remember the last time she left so early. Or so, alone."

"Oh." Danielle recoiled from the idea of Jenna hooking up with someone else. She hoped her reaction wasn't as dramatic on the surface as it felt inside.

"Sorry," Sasha said. "I shouldn't even be talking about her like that. You two just seem to be getting close. I figured she wouldn't mind."

"I wouldn't know," Danielle said. "I do need to see her, though. Training meeting."

"Right," Sasha said. "Head on up to her office, I'll wait for you in the break room. I need a lot more coffee anyway."

Danielle started toward Jenna's office, her stomach in knots. She was making too much of the kiss. Jenna hooked up with people all the time and probably hadn't given it a second thought. She was glad to know before she made even more of a fool out of herself making a big deal out of something trivial.

Jenna's door was open when Danielle approached. She gently knocked on the doorframe anyway and stuck her head inside. A dazzling smile sprang to Jenna's face. She was wearing another suit today, looking better than anyone had a right to in an office. Danielle couldn't believe Jenna's sexiness had somehow blindsided her at the party. It seemed so obvious now, and Danielle couldn't un-see Jenna's bare shoulders in that tank top or the lines of her hips.

"Come on in," Jenna said. Danielle stepped inside and paused at the door, undecided about whether or not to close it. She glanced at Jenna and saw her waiting with curiosity to see what she would do. Finally, she pulled the door closed and sat in the chair across the desk. She thought she saw Jenna smile ever so slightly, but maybe she imagined it.

"How have you been?" Jenna asked.

"Great."

Jenna let an unsettled silence pass as she seemed to ponder the short response. Eventually, she grabbed Danielle's file and opened it.

"I think you're progressing very well. I don't have much to go over."

"Okay."

"Sasha says you're picking everything up quickly, that she hasn't had to tell you anything more than once. How are you feeling with the report software?"

"Fine," Danielle said. "Maybe another time or two and I think I'll have it."

"Great," Jenna said. "Do you have any questions? Concerns?"

"No." She didn't mean to be short. Jenna hadn't done anything wrong, but it was the only way she knew to convey that she understood what happened between them was an unnecessary risk for Jenna, and that she didn't expect anything from her.

"Okay, then," Jenna said slowly.

Danielle headed for the door.

"Danielle," Jenna said. She turned around. "About the other night."

"Forget it," Danielle said. "I'm sorry I kissed you. I won't tell anyone."

"Oh," Jenna said. "Sure, if that's what you want."

"I don't drink often," Danielle said. "I know I kind of threw myself at you. It was inappropriate of me."

"I don't recall complaining."

Danielle managed a detached smile, but it wouldn't touch the stone in her chest. "I know how much this job means to you," Danielle said. "I would never say anything that would jeopardize that for you. I promise I won't do it again." Danielle could get in trouble too, but it wasn't even worth mentioning compared to what Jenna could face as her superior.

Jenna studied her for a long time. Danielle felt her skin tingling under Jenna's gaze, and she hoped Jenna would refute her logic. As the warmth in her eyes turned to fire she was sure she would, but then Jenna took a breath.

"That's probably for the best," she said. "For both of us."

"Right." Danielle nodded. "Well, I'll see you around." Danielle bolted out the door before Jenna could say anything else.

CHAPTER THIRTEEN

Something about Sasha's invitation to lunch felt more forceful than usual. Jenna could sense there was something on her mind even though she hadn't said so. Ever since her promotion, Jenna wanted to spend most of her spare time alone, but she knew she should fight the urge. She didn't want to lose touch with her friends, and Sasha was already starting to feel further away somehow. They'd agreed to meet at their old favorite lunch spot, Bubba's BBQ. When Jenna walked in, Sasha lit up and stood to hug her.

"I'm so glad you came!" Sasha said.

"You think it's too early for a drink?"

"Hell no," Sasha said. "Let's get our day drink on."

Jenna smiled and slipped into the cracked leather booth, then ordered a Long Island.

"That bad, huh?"

"No." Jenna laughed. "Everything's fine. I've just been a little busy. Stressed."

"Tell me about it," Sasha said. "Fuck that job. Come back to caseworking."

"Trust me, I've thought about it. Just growing pains, though, don't you think? I'll get used to it."

"Of course," Sasha said. "I was kidding. I'll kick your ass if you come back. It'll get easier."

"I know. I just miss you guys."

"We're still here," Sasha said. "Nothing has to change."

"Thanks."

Their drinks came and Sasha stared off into hers while she stirred it. Eventually, she looked up again, a serious expression on her face.

"Friday night was fun," she said.

"Yeah."

"Extra fun for you?"

"What do you mean?"

"Well, I'm no expert, but it looked like I stumbled on something between you and Danielle."

Jenna concentrated on keeping her face neutral. She'd never had a reason to hide anything from Sasha before. She'd always trusted her completely, but something inside her was whispering to lie now.

"I could tell you thought that," Jenna said. "You were kind of glaring at us. You have a thing for Danielle or something?"

"What?" Sasha shot back in her chair in surprise. "What the hell gave you that idea?"

"I don't know, you were really upset about her possibly getting in trouble over the body thing. Then you seemed sort of upset when you thought you saw something happen between us."

"When I *thought* I saw something happen between you?"

"At the bar."

"In between the cars." Sasha raised an eyebrow. "Where no one could see you."

"Brianna really was sick. She was out there puking when I came outside. I'm sure being out of sight was the idea when they walked over there."

"Wow, something totally happened," Sasha said.

"Where did you get that out of what I just said?"

"From the part where you won't deny it."

"Nothing happened," Jenna snapped, annoyed Sasha was forcing her into the outright lie she didn't want to tell.

Sasha stared at her for a long moment before she finally took a breath. "It's just because I care about you," she finally said. "You're Danielle's supervisor. They'll crucify you if they find out."

"There's nothing to find out."

"They'd demote you for sure, maybe even fire you."

"I know."

"It's exactly the kind of shit they were afraid of when you applied, remember? You would have had the job the first time if it wasn't for your relationship with everyone. If that bothered them, just imagine sex."

"Sash, I said I know."

"It's just not worth it. Danielle is great, but—"

"You done?"

"Yeah." Sasha sighed. "Don't be mad at me. I'm just trying to look out for you."

Jenna slowly shook her head. "You never answered my question, either. Do you have a thing for her? Is that what this is about?"

"Please." Sasha snorted. "I mean she's gorgeous and everything, and very sweet, but we have zero chemistry. There's no ulterior motive, Jenna. I wouldn't do that. I'm just worried about you. I don't want you to do something you'll regret."

Jenna took a long sip of her drink. She knew Sasha wasn't buying it, and she was right, of course. It was a bad idea. She hadn't expected the kiss, but she hadn't been able to stop, either. That didn't matter now. Danielle understood. She'd been quick to blame the alcohol and sweep it under the rug, so quick it stung a little. But that was insane; she should be thrilled with Danielle's reaction. It was going to save her ass.

CHAPTER FOURTEEN

Danielle couldn't understand why she was so exhausted at the end of every day. The hours were reasonable, the work enjoyable, her coworkers friendly, yet by the time she made it to her apartment every day, she had nothing left. Her view upon opening the door was, as usual, Brianna sprawled on the couch with a drink hanging loosely from intoxicated fingers. Brianna twisted her head awkwardly to see Danielle come inside, then sprang to life.

"Hey!" She walked over and pulled Danielle into a hug. Danielle endured the sloppy embrace. She recognized the signs that Brianna was too drunk to avoid. "How was work?"

"It was fine," Danielle said. Work was awful. She knew Jenna would want to forget about the kiss, but hearing her say so out loud left the echo of it swirling through her. It was torture trying to hide the visceral reaction she had every time Jenna passed her in the hall, and being trained by Jenna's best friend just seemed like a cosmic joke to top it all off.

"What's wrong?"

"Nothing," Danielle said.

"Bullshit," Brianna said. She stood and ping-ponged off the walls into the kitchen and poured a drink. She downed it, then poured another before she moved back to the couch. "Brianna loves drama," she said. "Let's hear it. You're embarrassed you got drunk the other night, huh? And you had to face everyone today and you feel all cruddy about it?"

"A little," Danielle said, though her embarrassment was more specific than that.

"Trust me, you behaved normally," Brianna said. "You have nothing to be embarrassed about."

Kissing Jenna in the parking lot had definitely not been normal behavior, not for her, but she couldn't tell Brianna that. She'd never tested the way Brianna might react to her interest in another woman, but if she was going to do so, now certainly wasn't the time, when Brianna was already several drinks in. Instead, she just said, "Thanks."

"Sure." Brianna shrugged. "So why didn't you tell me your coworkers look like models?"

"I told you they're pretty."

"Yeah, but pretty doesn't really do it, does it? They are delicious!"

"It's just better for me not to think of them that way," Danielle said. "They're off limits."

"Says who?"

"The rules."

"That only applies to your boss, right? The mega-hot one?"

"Not really. Relationships are off limits altogether. Jenna is just even more off limits."

"Perfect, 'cause I want that one. You can have Sasha."

Danielle felt her jaw tighten. "She's not a piece of meat, you know? And I'm not going to *have* either one."

"Suit yourself. You need to bring Jenna over sometime, though. I think she was interested up until I puked."

Danielle rolled her eyes. "I'm sure."

Brianna jumped to her feet again and headed back into the kitchen, returning with the entire bottle of vodka this time. She slumped back onto the couch, took off the lid, and glanced at Danielle for a second while she seemed to decide whether or not to drink straight from the bottle. With another sideways glance at Danielle, she poured a modest amount into her cup and threw it back.

"You seem off," she said. "Does it bother you to hear me talk about other girls or something?"

"Of course not." Danielle slumped onto the couch next to her.

"'Cause we've been broken up for like, a long time now."

"I know."

"I mean you broke up with me," Brianna snapped. A spark of anger flared up, and Danielle braced herself for the storm.

"It was mutual," Danielle reminded her.

"What the hell are you up my ass for, then?"

"I'm not."

"I can fuck whoever I want to fuck," Brianna said. She took a sip from the bottle. She rocked slightly from side to side when she looked back at Danielle. "I can drink what I want to drink and fuck who I want to fuck."

"No one's arguing with you, Brianna. Fuck who you want to fuck."

"Just not your boss?"

"Preferably."

"If you're jealous, just say so."

"I'm not jealous," Danielle said.

"You sure? Because we can have a little thing on the side if you want." Brianna wagged her eyebrows playfully. "If you need a reminder that I love you."

Brianna slid her arm around Danielle's shoulder and pulled her closer, the teasing light leaving her eyes, replaced by the dark swirls of desire Danielle hadn't seen directed at her in years. Brianna leaned toward her. Danielle realized with horror she was trying for a kiss and abruptly pulled away.

"Are you crazy?" she asked. "No way."

Brianna laughed and pulled away. "Oh yes, I forgot, casual sex isn't your thing."

"No, it's not," Danielle said. "And this isn't a jealousy thing. I'd just rather you didn't hook up with my boss. I don't want those worlds to cross. Is that so much to ask?"

Brianna's face turned hard just as quickly as she'd melted into Danielle's side. Keeping up with Brianna's emotions required intense focus she was exhausted with giving.

"You don't get to ask me shit," Brianna said. "You treat me like you're my damned mother."

"Fine," Danielle said. "Go for it then." Danielle was vibrating with the anger she was restraining.

"Why do you always treat me like this?" Brianna's voice quivered.

"What are you talking about? You're the one freaking out."

"Oh sure, just play innocent."

"What do you want me to say, Brianna?"

Tears spilled down Brianna's face. She looked a decade older, and Danielle could see how far away she was, how unnecessary it was for her to give so much credence to her irrational switches, but she couldn't seem to stop. She wanted to ask how much she'd had to drink, but that would only set her off.

"You treat me like I'm a fucking joke," Brianna said. "Just because I like to have a few drinks? That's not weird, Danielle, you are! Loosen the fuck up!"

Danielle sighed. Brianna was at least a little right. She did treat her like she was a nuisance at the least, and a joke at worse times. She was just so tired of taking care of Brianna. Jenna's advice ran through her mind. *Don't bother yourself with it.* Why couldn't she seem to just leave Brianna be? Brianna didn't want her help any more than Danielle wanted to give it, but she found it impossible to ignore her tears.

"You're right," Danielle said. "I'm sorry."

"Huh?" Brianna was slumping into the couch, fighting sleep.

"I said I'm sorry."

"What are you talking about?" Brianna reached for the bottle and took another swig.

"Never mind." Danielle sighed and started to get up.

"Wait!" Brianna said. "What are you talking about?" Anger surfaced again, and a wave of exhaustion slammed into Danielle.

"You said I treat you like a joke," Danielle said. "I said I'm sorry."

"You don't treat me like a joke," Brianna said. "You're the only one who gives a shit about me at all." Brianna wrapped her arms around Danielle's neck, pulling her back onto the couch. "Sit with me for a while."

"I really need to get to bed," Danielle said.

"Fine." Brianna pushed her away. "Go! You don't care about me anymore."

"Of course, I do."

"No, you don't." Brianna was on the verge of tears again.

Danielle sighed and accepted she was in for a night of complete madness.

CHAPTER FIFTEEN

Jenna walked over to where Callie was sitting on the couch and set several bottles of her serum on the coffee table.

"Peace offering?" she said.

Callie surveyed the bottles, then looked up at Jenna. "It's a good start," she said and smiled. "Mom was a handful the other night when you went out, though. I think you owe me a milkshake, too."

Jenna circled the table and sat down next to Callie. "What do you mean, a handful?"

"Kept looking out the blinds like crazy. About bit my head off when I asked what was wrong."

"What'd she say?"

"Asked if I saw them."

"Saw who?"

Callie shrugged. "Who the hell knows? *Them.*"

"What'd you do?"

"Nothing."

"Nothing?"

"What could I do?" Callie said. "I would have only made it worse."

"You should have called me."

"I was mad at you, remember?"

"Still."

"Like you would have answered. I knew you were out dancing or hooking up or whatever the hell you do."

"Callie."

"What? It's true."

Jenna sighed. "I'm worried about her. That's twice this week she's had paranoia episodes."

Callie shrugged. "Probably skipping her meds again."

"How could she?" Jenna asked. "We watch her take them every day." But even as she said it she knew Callie was probably right. Her mom's illness was consistent and under control when she was properly medicated, but the medications themselves were always the first thing she became suspicious of, which sent her into a downward spiral that was difficult to pull her out of. Jenna put her hand on Callie's shoulder, then headed for her mom's room.

As she walked up the stairs she heard the shower running. Perfect. Jenna slipped into her mom's room and glanced around for obvious hiding places. She checked the drawers and inside small boxes and knick-knacks. When she checked the pillowcase she found it, a small plastic bag with at least thirty pills inside. They were all partially dissolved, like they'd been in her mouth for a minute, then taken out. Jenna sighed just as the shower turned off. Her mom emerged from the bathroom wrapped in a towel, bringing the humidity of her boiling hot shower with her.

"What are you doing in here?"

Jenna held up the bag of pills. "What's this?"

"None of your business is what it is. What are you doing sneaking around my room?"

"Looking for this. You can't skip your meds, Mom. We talked about this."

"I can do whatever the hell I want," she said. "I'm a grown woman. No one can make me take pills I don't want to take."

"You're right, Mom. I can't make you take them, but you need them. You get scared when you're not on them, and pretty soon I can't take care of you anymore. You'll end up back in a facility."

"Are you threatening me?"

"No, I'm just telling you what will happen. That's what happens every time. You always think coming off the meds is going to make you better, but it never does."

"I think better off them."

"No, you don't."

"Yes, I do! I won't be one of the sheep! I won't be like you! They're coming for us, and I'm going to know about it. Oh, you'll be sorry one day. That's for sure. You'll see I was right all along."

"That stuff's not real, Mom. It's just your illness."

"It's not an illness. I'm special. I see things they don't want us to know."

Jenna paused to keep her voice from climbing. "Mom, I need you to trust me. I know it seems real, but it isn't. The longer you're off your meds the worse it's going to get."

Her mom's eyes narrowed. "Trust you?"

"Yes."

"Are you working for them?"

A jolt ran through Jenna's limbs. She was rarely the subject of a direct accusation. It was a nearly impossible thing to talk her way back from.

"Of course not," Jenna said. "Mom, it's me. You know I would never do anything to hurt you."

"They got to you, didn't they? They brainwashed you too."

"No," Jenna said. "No one got to me."

Her mom's stare glistened with tears. "They turned you against me, didn't they? Not you too, Jenna."

Jenna searched her for recognition, for any semblance of the bond they shared, but all she could see was suspicion and fear.

"Why don't you put some clothes on, and we'll talk about it downstairs?"

"I don't want to talk about it. I want you to leave. I'm not taking those damned pills anymore. They're poison."

"They're not poison."

"They make my brain stop working." Her mom stepped closer. She stared at Jenna like she was daring her to do something. "What else would you call it?"

"They make your brain work better, Mom. They just stop the scary thoughts and the voices."

"The voices protect me," she said. "They tell me about the bad ones. I need them."

"There are no bad ones."

Her mom laughed. "Of course there are, Jenna. Don't be stupid. You just don't see them. You're one of the sheep, but the voices tell me the truth."

"It's not the truth."

"It is so!" her mom screamed. "They chose me!"

Jenna felt anger rattling up her bones. Why couldn't she break through? Why couldn't she make a difference with someone?

"I'm special!"

"No, you're not!" Jenna yelled.

Jenna felt herself sprawling away before the pain in her face registered. When she regained her orientation in the room, she looked to her mother. She'd dropped her towel and was standing naked in front of her with her hand raised.

"Get out of my room!" she yelled. "Get out of my house! You're one of them! You're not my daughter!" She walked toward Jenna as if to hit her again, but Jenna backed out of the room and slammed the door shut. She turned and jogged down the stairs. Her face was on fire. She powered into the kitchen. Callie spun on the couch.

"Jenna?"

"Stay away from Mom today," Jenna said. "Don't go in there."

"What happened? Are you okay?"

"Just don't go in there. I'll deal with it later. If she comes out, go to your room. Lock it if you have to."

"Jenna, what the hell happened?" Callie jumped to her feet and shot across the room, but Jenna snatched her keys off the counter and headed for the door.

"Jenna!"

CHAPTER SIXTEEN

The sun was hitting harder than usual today. The humidity was smothering, and Danielle felt like she'd never completely dried off from her shower. She sat in the parking lot waiting for Jenna. It was their day to check on Deon and Raylon, but Jenna hadn't been in her office or the break room. Once Sasha said she didn't know where else she could be, Danielle stopped asking, realizing Jenna was obviously running late and trying not to draw any more attention to it. Danielle couldn't pretend she hadn't been anxiously awaiting their next day together, but it wasn't just time moving at a crawl anymore. Jenna was very late.

Just as she was about to give up and go back inside, Jenna's Acura pulled into the lot. Danielle stood up as Jenna pulled up next to her and got into the car.

"Well, good morning," Danielle said as she closed the door. "Have a late night?"

"I'm really sorry," Jenna said in a flat tone.

Danielle quit smiling and dropped her plan to tease Jenna. "Are you okay?"

"Yeah."

"No, you're not," Danielle said. She could tell Jenna had been crying. "What happened?"

"Nothing." Jenna put the car in drive and checked for traffic over her shoulder. When she turned her head, Danielle made out a faint red mark on her face. Danielle grabbed the shifter and put the car back into park before Jenna could hit the gas. Jenna looked over, surprised. Before she could say another word, Danielle touched her cheek.

"Who did that?" She surprised herself with the intensity of the fury in her chest.

"Danielle, it's fine. I'm fine."

"Then tell me what happened."

Danielle's heart broke as she watched tears spring back to Jenna's eyes as if they'd never left. Before they could spill over, Jenna physically shook them away and turned her attention back to the road.

"Not here," she said.

Danielle wanted to insist, but Jenna was too preoccupied with being seen to really talk. She sighed and nodded, and Jenna pulled away from the curb. Danielle didn't even have a right to know. She certainly didn't have a right to hold Jenna hostage until she gave up the information, but she couldn't let it go.

She let Jenna drive in silence, hoping she'd break it, but in just a few minutes they pulled up outside the Clark apartment and parked. Again, Danielle hoped Jenna would say something, but she turned off the ignition and reached for the car door.

"Jenna."

"After."

"I'm not going to forget," Danielle said.

"I know."

Danielle gave in and opened the car door, following Jenna up to the apartment. Jenna snapped a picture of the new door before she knocked. Ladona opened immediately.

"Hey, Ms. Thompson. You see the new door?"

"I sure did," Jenna said with enthusiasm Danielle hadn't expected her to be able to muster. The pain she'd read so easily in Jenna in the car vanished.

"Come in, come in," Ladona said. "I don't think I caught your name last time, sweetie. What was it?" It took Danielle a second to realize Ladona was talking to her. She was beaming at her, and pleasant though she was, Danielle felt a little unnerved by the change in her personality.

"Danielle Corey."

"Very nice to meet you, Ms. Corey. I'm so sorry for the last time we spoke. I was having a bad week."

"I understand."

"Can I get you two anything to drink? I was just fixin' to make some lemonade."

"No, thanks," Jenna said. Ladona motioned for them to sit down, and Jenna promptly did so, motioning for Danielle to join her. She remembered Jenna saying Ladona fluctuated, but the idea of a genuine one-eighty was a little suspect to Danielle. Jenna put her folder on her lap and took out a pen. "Let's jump right in," Jenna said. "How have things been?"

"Much better," Ladona said. "We got that door fixed, got groceries in the fridge."

"How about that tutor?" Jenna asked.

"Yes, ma'am, I called them. They were very nice. Raylon's been in twice now."

"And Deon?"

"Ms. Thompson, Lord's honest truth, I can't get the boy to go. I tried everything."

Jenna nodded gravely and wrote something down, then looked up. "You mind if I try to talk to him?"

"Course not. Talk sense into him if you think you can. I know he's smart enough, but he just won't go."

"Is he in his room?"

"Yep. Go on up."

Jenna nodded and stood. Danielle followed her up the stairs, curious what condition they'd find the bedrooms in. Jenna had obviously been upstairs before since she went directly to the room in back and knocked. Deon appeared in the frame without a shirt on. He was more muscular than Danielle expected, well on his way to being a man and in her opinion, probably beyond much influence he didn't want. He already looked older than he did when she'd met him just a couple of weeks ago. Whatever activities were replacing school were aging him. He nodded at each of them and let them inside. When he turned, Danielle spotted a long, purple bruise across his back.

"What the hell is that?" Jenna asked.

Deon sat in the desk chair and put his feet up on his bed. He casually lit a cigarette and took a drag. Something about the colors of the white and brown cigarette brought the entire stark room into focus. The cheap white blinds were kinked and bent and turned every which way. The hard brown carpet was meant to last, but had obviously been pushed beyond its limits. Jenna grabbed the cigarette right out of his mouth and put it out.

"What the hell do you think you're doing?" she said. "You're fourteen."

"It's just a cigarette," he said.

"It's not just anything. Those things kill you."

Deon rolled his eyes and leaned back in his chair again. "My mom send you up here to tell me to go to school?"

"Everyone wants you in school, Deon." Jenna sat on the edge of his bed. "Let's talk about that bruise on your back first, though."

"You see how my mom is acting all sweet now?"

Jenna paused at the subject change. "Yeah."

"'Cause she feels bad. That's why."

"Did she do that?"

Deon looked out the window. "Nah."

"Someone she invited over here?"

"Nah."

"What do you mean then, Deon?"

"Nothing. She's just always nice after I get hurt."

"How'd you get hurt?"

"Basketball."

"That's it." Jenna stood up. "I'm pulling you two."

"What?" Deon's focus snapped over to Jenna, his tough-guy demeanor shattered. Danielle studied Jenna's face, trying to figure out if it was a bluff. She certainly had enough evidence to pull them. Danielle would be relieved to see her do it, but she knew Jenna didn't truly want to. And at the same time, if it was a bluff it was a damn good one.

"You want to play games with me, Deon, I'm pulling you," Jenna said. "This is not our agreement. I said I'd let you call the shots as long as you were honest with me and as long as you understood certain things are unacceptable."

"I can't be honest with you anymore with her here!" Deon gestured at Danielle.

Danielle looked at Jenna, silently asking if she should leave, but Jenna didn't even look at her.

"What makes you think anything has changed just because she's here?" Jenna asked.

"I know you can't be breaking any rules in front of little miss new girl."

"I don't make decisions I can't live with, Deon. Our arrangement isn't a secret. If the day comes that I have to explain it, I can, but I can't explain leaving you here with bruises that came from God knows where. I can't do that to you. I can't do it to Raylon. I agreed to let you decide if you should live here or not because I could trust you, but if that's gone the deal's gone. So, it's your turn to make a decision, Deon, what's it going to be?"

"Fine," he said.

"You going to tell me the truth?"

"Yeah."

"Okay, start with the bruise on your face last week at the basketball court."

Deon's head bowed as he looked at the floor. Danielle leaned forward, staring at Deon's face in suspense. He looked so strong next to the paper-thin desk that supported his muscled arm, but she knew it was an illusion. He wasn't old and wise; he was sad. His muscles weren't bulging; he was cut because he was too thin. "Mama's boyfriend slapped me," he finally said.

Danielle knew her reaction was visible and tried to wrangle it in, but Deon's focus was on Jenna, and she was made of stone.

"What happened?" she asked.

"Him and Mama got in an argument. She told him to leave and he wouldn't, so I told him to go, and he slapped me."

"Did she call the police?"

"No."

"What did she do?"

"He left after he hit me," Deon said. "That's when she got the new door."

"And what about your back?" Jenna asked.

"It was just Raylon."

"Excuse me?"

"Raylon got pissed and threw the PlayStation. He didn't even mean to hit me. It was an accident."

"He didn't mean to hit you?"

Deon looked at the floor again and scratched the back of his neck. "He was trying to throw it at Mama."

"Why?"

"Because she made him go to a tutor."

Jenna raked her hand down her face and sighed. "And why do you think he doesn't want to go to school, Deon?"

"Come on, that's not fair."

"He thinks the world of you, Deon. Wants to be just like you. You think it doesn't affect him when you refuse to go?"

Deon stared at his feet. "If I go back to school will you let us stay?"

Jenna looked disarmed by the question and glanced at Danielle for the first time. Danielle was surprised by the conflict she saw in Jenna. Everything Jenna said she said with complete confidence and conviction. Danielle had never seen uncertainty in her face. Jenna looked back to Deon.

"It doesn't sound like you're safe here, Deon. I can't let people hit you."

"They're not," he said. "Raylon doesn't count, and that guy is gone."

"And what if he comes back?"

"Mama won't let him. She hates him now. Honest."

"You swear?"

"I swear! Ms. Thompson, please don't take us away. Raylon needs me. He'll go berserk without me."

"Deon, look at me," Jenna said. "I know you love Raylon, and I know you want him with you, but I know you don't want some man hitting him. If he hit you, he'll hit Raylon. Did this guy really stop coming around?"

"Yes, Ms. Thompson. I swear."

Jenna stared at Deon for several long seconds before she finally took a breath again.

"You get your butt back in school," she said.

"Okay." He nodded. "I will."

Jenna snatched the pack of cigarettes off his desk. "And no more of this shit," she said. "Crazy."

Deon cracked a smile. "Thanks, Jenna."

When they exited the room, Raylon was crouched in the frame of his bedroom door down the hall. The frame's white paint was chipped, and the brown wood exposed beneath was tearing in strips. Jenna crouched by him. He looked as small as a cat and like he was on the verge of tears.

"Are you going to take me away for throwing the PlayStation?" he asked.

"No, honey," Jenna said. "Let's not do that again though, okay?" He nodded.

"Are you scared to be here?" Jenna asked.

Raylon shook his head. "Deon doesn't let anything bad happen."

Jenna nodded and touched his head before walking down the stairs. Ladona was waiting at the bottom. She looked paralyzed.

"Well?" she asked.

"Deon says he'll go back to school," Jenna said.

Her eyebrows arched in surprise. "Just like that?"

"Yes," Jenna said. "But you call me if he stops going again."

"I sure will. Thank you, Ms. Thompson."

"He can't have bruises again, Ms. Clark. I need you to understand that. Whoever needs to go for that to happen, they need to go."

Ladona looked Jenna in the eye in silence for what felt like an eternity. She seemed afraid to answer, afraid to argue, afraid to acknowledge it, afraid even to breathe. Finally, she nodded, her round, soft face taking a tone of sincerity and cooperation Danielle hadn't seen before.

"I wouldn't let that son of a bitch back in here to save my own life," she said. "You have my word."

"You have to call the police if he tries. You have to protect them, Ladona, or I'll have to."

CHAPTER SEVENTEEN

Y ou're not really leaving them there, are you?" Danielle asked.

Jenna felt the air squeezing out of her chest. Her mind was scrambling in a million directions, and she couldn't even start to chase one thought before another darted through her mind. She took a breath and started the car.

"Yes."

Danielle's hand sprang into her vision and turned the car back off. When Jenna looked to the passenger seat Danielle was staring at her.

"You do that a lot, don't you?" she asked. "Put the car in park, turn it off?"

"No," Danielle said. "I don't. But you said after, it's after."

Jenna sighed. "Coffee."

"What?"

"Let's go get coffee, and I swear we'll talk."

Danielle eyed her, but finally nodded. Jenna knew stalling wouldn't work forever, but she needed more time. She wasn't sure how much to say, and it was a conflict she wasn't used to. She usually knew the exact distance she wanted people at, but Danielle was confusing. If Danielle disagreed with her decisions strongly enough she could really affect Deon and Raylon, and the promise Jenna made to them. It was safer to tell her as little as possible, but some strange, untrustworthy part of her was bizarrely possessed to tell Danielle everything.

They ordered their drinks in silence and found a place to sit on the couches in the back corner of the cozy coffee shop, across from one another. Danielle took a sip of her drink and waited quietly. Jenna felt her heart start to race again as she prepared to speak.

"I'm not sure where to start," she said.

"Why does Deon keep saying you break the rules for him?" Danielle asked. "Do you?"

"I use my discretion."

"I don't know what that means, Jenna."

Jenna felt a tingle go down her spine hearing Danielle say her name. She found it difficult to hold Danielle's strong and steady gaze. She felt Danielle's hand on her knee, and her head snapped up.

"You can trust me," Danielle said. "Just tell me what's going on. If you're ever going to turn this case over to me I need to know."

Jenna pictured Danielle checking in with the boys alone. She couldn't shake the feeling that the case would be over quickly if that ever happened. Danielle would pull the boys out of the house, separated or not. Paula could tell Jenna it was time to put Danielle in charge of the Clarks any day, and if she didn't do something to change Danielle's mind, that would be their fate. It didn't need to be about trust or attraction or closeness. It was her job to explain things to Danielle.

"I don't always record everything I see over there," Jenna said. "That's what he means."

"Like what?"

Jenna sighed and searched for an example. "Deon got in a fight with another kid once. I didn't report it. Things like that. Things that could tip the scales when they shouldn't."

Danielle seemed to think it over. "The bruise last week?"

Jenna felt her insides clench up, wanting to hold back, but she had to be honest. She shook her head.

"You didn't put it in the report?" Danielle's face plainly fought a battle with her expression, and Jenna couldn't stop the chuckle that came out of her.

"You need to work on that," she said. "You can't look shocked when the kids tell you something awful. Scares them quiet."

"I don't understand," Danielle said. "I know you care about them. Why would you cover that up? Don't you want to stop it?"

"Of course!" Jenna felt her first surge of anger. "I care about those boys like family."

Danielle's expression was soft. "So explain it to me."

Jenna sighed and touched her face, awakening the tenderness where her mom slapped her. She fought the emotion that came with the pain. "I just understand them," Jenna said. "And they want to stay there."

Danielle waited a beat, then sat back in her chair again. "That's it? They want to be there? They're kids, Jenna, they don't know any better. They don't know any alternatives. They don't know what life can be like. Aren't you the one who said sometimes they don't know it's for the best until they're older?"

"Yes, I did." Jenna sighed. "But it's more complicated than that. Kids know way more than they're given credit for. They know what foster care is. They know they may be separated. Deon knows he may or may not like his foster family. He knows what Raylon's life will be like with his aunt. They know their mom is sick. He's old enough to see the big picture. I wouldn't let Raylon make the calls, but Deon…"

"But you can't possibly put that big of a decision on his shoulders. It's too much."

"It's not all on him. I'm not expecting him to make the decision. I'm just making their opinions worth something. I'm over there all the time monitoring them very closely. If I need to take them out of there, I will."

"But Deon has been hurt twice already," Danielle said. "Where's the line?"

"I believe what Deon told me today. Do you?"

Danielle blinked in surprise. "Yeah," she finally said. "I believe him. But you didn't know the story yet when you decided not to report it last week. I know you didn't buy that basketball crap."

"No," Jenna said. "I didn't, but I trust Deon."

"How can you possibly say that when he was obviously lying?"

"He just needed a little time. I knew he'd tell me. I knew he'd make the right call."

"But he's just a kid! Anything could have happened."

Jenna watched Danielle fight her rising anger and made sure her voice didn't change as she answered. "I know he's just a kid, but I also knew he'd make the right choice. I know what a kid his age is capable of understanding, especially one as bright as he is."

"How could you know that?"

"Because I grew up that way," Jenna said. Adrenaline jolted through her and her palms started sweating. She forced herself to look at Danielle even though everything in her screamed to shut up. "I was Deon," she said. "And no one would listen to me. No one cared what a kid had to say."

Danielle was visibly shaken as she tracked the subject change. She looked from Jenna to the floor, then to her face again.

"Remember I told you my mom is schizophrenic?" Jenna said. Danielle nodded. "Her symptoms began when I was going into my teens. She lost her job. Soon we were poor. CPS got involved. They clearly wanted to take us away, but that would have most likely meant my sister and I would be separated. I wanted to talk to them about it, but it was just a checklist for them. It was yes and no answers, and if there were a certain number of yeses, that was that. I never felt like I could tell the truth without that being the end. The lengths my sister and I went to in order to keep that from happening..." Jenna had to look away thinking about Callie, about her scarred face and the way she lived to hide it from the world.

"I'm sorry, Jenna."

Jenna couldn't look at Danielle. She didn't want to see pity in her face. "All I had to go on was what my mom told me, and that was skewed by paranoia. If someone had explained things to me, not just written off my opinion because I was young, I might have told the truth. There has to be a safe space for conversation, or you'll never get anywhere. I could have told them what they needed to know, but they couldn't see past their little survey. I might have made different decisions if they had. Better ones. Everything could have been different."

"You think the surveys are too rigid?"

"I think the surveys are a tool and should be treated that way. They don't do the job for you. They don't tell the whole story. A kid that knows you're going by the survey knows to just lie until you leave. *That's* how kids in bad situations get left there, not from what I'm doing."

Danielle sighed. "I want to agree with you, Jenna, I do. I'm just not sure. You did what you set out to do with Deon. He trusts you and he told you the truth. But now what? Now your hands are tied honoring that trust, and he's still there."

"They're not there because my hands are tied. I never promised Deon I'd do whatever he wants no matter what. I just promised his voice would mean something, that I would listen to the whole story instead of freaking out the second he tells me something scary," Jenna said. "He knows if I take them away one day it will be because it's what's truly best for them. He knows I won't do it lightly. I'm not ignoring what's going on in that house just because I didn't report it. I made him tell me the truth, and now that he has I think they're better where they are. That asshole who slapped him is gone. They both said so and I believe they meant it. I hate that it happened, Danielle. Trust me, I do, but getting slapped isn't the worst thing that can happen to him. Losing Raylon is."

When Jenna finally dared to look up again, Danielle was staring into her.

"And you know that firsthand." Danielle touched Jenna's cheek where she knew she must be developing a bruise. Danielle touched so softly she barely felt it, and Jenna turned into Danielle's hand, her warmth and softness. Her stomach twisted, and she pulled back. She couldn't let Danielle touch her and expect to keep her head about her. Danielle was patient but curious. "Your mom did that?" she finally asked.

"Yes," Jenna said. "She's sick; she can't help it."

Danielle's brow somehow became even softer. "That doesn't mean you should have to take it."

"I can't put her away," Jenna said. "It wouldn't be right."

"How often does this happen?"

"Not often." Jenna could see Danielle didn't believe her. "In clusters," she amended. "She's fine until she comes off the meds, then it's a bit of a free-for-all until we can get her back on them. She's going to need a shot. They last much longer, long enough for the medicine to do its job. Getting her back on pills is a losing battle.

They have to accumulate in her system again to work, and getting her to take pills long enough for that to happen while she's in this state is pretty much impossible. But getting her to a doctor isn't much easier. It's just going to be rough for a while, but she'll stabilize."

Danielle nodded solemnly. "Jenna, if you ever need help, or a break, anything, you can call me."

Jenna felt sucked inside Danielle's stare. She couldn't pull away. They were both leaning toward one another. They'd inched to the edge of their chairs so much now they were only a foot apart. Jenna wanted to touch her. Her entire body screamed for it. She gently cupped Danielle's cheek. When Danielle's eyes fluttered shut at her touch, Jenna let her fingers slowly slide into Danielle's impossibly soft hair. She was drawn to Danielle, and she felt powerless against it. There were inches between them now, screaming at her to end the distance. She knew she wouldn't be able to fight it another second, and a rush of panic streamed through her. She pulled back. What the hell was she doing? She was going to lose everything if she didn't stop.

"We should get back," she said.

Danielle seemed to snap back to reality just as quickly. "Right," she said. "Work."

CHAPTER EIGHTEEN

Danielle knew it was before sunrise without looking at the time. A dream of Jenna had woken her, and the real situation with Jenna was now keeping her up. She couldn't stop thinking about the bruise on Jenna's face, picturing her mom hitting her, picturing it when Jenna was just a kid, imagining her hiding the abuse to stay close to her sister. And that stormy look in Jenna's green eyes when the pain of those thoughts had blended with need, with want. She knew Jenna had been a breath away from kissing her. Just the memory of it had her stirring in bed. Dreams of Jenna's breath over her skin were becoming a nightly problem.

Danielle thought she imagined the first knock on the front door. Her bedroom was in the back of the apartment where she rarely heard the door at all, but the house was silent in the early hours of the morning. It came again, a gentle tapping. Danielle got out of bed, some insane part of her expecting it to be Jenna. Maybe her mom was out of control again and she was taking Danielle up on that break from her crazy life.

Danielle passed Brianna's room. The door was cracked open, and Brianna was splayed across the bed in her underwear, passed out after another night of drinking. Danielle pulled the door closed and went to the front. She checked the peephole, then yanked the door open.

"Li!"

A smile exploded across Li's face. He stepped into a hug and squeezed her tight. Danielle pulled him inside. "God, it's so good to see you," she said. "Sit down. Tell me everything."

Li stiffly removed his shoes and moved to the couch. "I can't stay long," he said. "I have class in an hour."

"Okay." Danielle sat next to him. "What brings you, then? Is Dad okay?"

"He's okay," Li said. "Unfortunately."

"Oh, Li," Danielle said. His face was full of stress again. She missed his youthful joy, the way he lit up so easily. "You don't mean that."

"I really do, Danielle. I thought I wanted him to be okay, but when he finally told me he was fine…" Li paused and took a breath. "I was disappointed. I didn't even realize I had all these thoughts about me, you, and Mom together again until he said that, and then I realized I was hoping he really was sick."

Danielle hugged him. "It's okay," she said. "You miss the way things used to be. That doesn't mean you want him to be sick. It's not the same."

Li's eyes watered, something she hadn't seen since before he was a teenager. "You don't understand," he said. "He found out we've been talking."

Danielle's insides froze. "How?"

"He thought he had cancer. That's why he was staying home. Turns out he doesn't even have it. The tumor was benign, big baby. But he was getting his affairs in order. I don't know what they told him, but they had him really spooked. He was snooping through everything in the house, looking at old stuff, going through pictures on the computer, and he found one of our email chains. I thought I was being so careful, but I guess I forgot to delete one."

"What did he do?"

"He wouldn't talk to me for a while. Eventually, he came in and told me I have to stop talking to you. He won't pay for medical school if I don't. Says he'll disown me too. He says you'll never go back to normal if I keep making you think it's okay to be gay."

"Go back to normal?" The familiar fury at the way her father talked about her flooded her body. "What the hell does he—"

"Forget it, Danielle," Li said. "He's a jackass. I'm going to tell him to disown me if he really wants to. I'm his only son. He won't do it."

Danielle's muscles tensed, and she shook with anger. Her father had broken her heart when he cut her out of his life. He'd broken it tenfold when he'd taken her mother from her too. Li was the only one willing to disobey him, and now he wanted to take that from her too? Danielle examined Li's face again. He'd been crying well before he'd made it to her apartment. A protectiveness of her little brother replaced her rage, and she grabbed his hand.

"Dad doesn't make empty threats."

"We'll hide it again," Li said. "Better." But the words fell flat. Danielle knew he didn't believe it any more than she did. He knew what she'd say, and she had to be the big sister and say it.

"If he finds out again he won't forgive you." The words were coming out of her mouth, though where she found the strength she wasn't sure. "You can't jeopardize medical school. It's all you've ever wanted. Do what he says."

"I can't," Li said. "It isn't worth it. I'll find another way."

"You'll never get financial aid. They have too much money."

"I'll..." He choked up before he could finish.

Danielle shook her head. "It's okay, Li. I understand."

Li put his head in his hands and pulled his hair. "I'm so ashamed."

Danielle put her arms around him and pulled him into a hug, knowing it would be the last for a long time. He turned and hugged her back.

"The second I'm done with school we'll go back to normal. There won't be anything he can do to either of us then."

"He could take your inheritance."

"He can have it."

"You better study hard," Danielle said. "If you even think about being set back a year to party I'll kill you."

"I'll study so much, Danielle. You'll be proud."

"I already am, Li." Danielle didn't realize she was crying too until she saw that her cheek left a wet mark on his shirt. She released him and stood up.

"I guess you better start now," she said. "You'll be late for class."

Li pulled her into one more tight embrace before he finally headed for the door. He looked broken, but Danielle knew his future would be so much brighter this way. She couldn't take his dream from him, no matter how much it would hurt both of them not to see each other.

"Danielle." Li spun just outside the door. "Take this." He pulled a ring from his pocket. "It's Mom's. She gave it to me, but it's for you."

"She said that?"

Li shook his head. "No, but you know how she is. She can't. It was her mother's, though, then hers. It's meant to be yours. She gave it to me last night after Dad said I had to stop talking to you. I think she knew I would come to you. She knew I'd give it to you. I think it's what she wanted."

Danielle struggled not to let her emotions overcome her as she accepted the ring.

"I hope it makes you think of both of us if you're ever feeling alone," Li said. "A reminder we're thinking of you too, and we love you."

When Danielle closed and locked the door, she turned to find Brianna standing in the hallway, looking at her.

"You okay?"

"I think so," she said. "I can do it for him."

CHAPTER NINETEEN

Danielle's weekly training review was scheduled in ten minutes, and Jenna still wasn't sure how she was going to reclaim the professionalism they'd agreed to stick to. Somehow the policy seemed a million miles away and more than a little irrelevant, though she knew that was just her mind playing tricks on her. She had to get a grip. Danielle said they shouldn't cross the line. There was no reason for her to be struggling with a decision that was already made.

She fished for Danielle's papers, along with Sasha's training notes. Sasha still had nothing but good things to say, and Jenna knew at some point Paula would start asking questions about why she wasn't putting Danielle in charge of the Clark case. The only way she could think to avoid the problem was to continue working very long hours and turning in immaculate work so Paula wouldn't have a reason to want to lessen her workload.

Danielle tapped on the door as she was already entering. "Afternoon," she said. She was in tighter jeans than usual that showed off the shape of her legs. Jenna realized she was staring and forced herself to look at Danielle's smile instead.

"Afternoon," Jenna said. "How was your day?"

"Sasha and I just did the rounds. Nothing crazy." Danielle slipped into the chair across the desk. "I think I like these reviews at the end of the day. It's nicer than doing them in the morning."

"Coast out the end of the shift?" Jenna asked.

"Exactly. Plus, if you yell at me I can just go straight home and cry."

Jenna laughed. "Please. Do I really seem like the yelling type?"

"No, but I'm sensitive," Danielle teased her.

Jenna slid the training notes across the desk. "No secrets here," she said. "All good."

Danielle eyed Jenna suspiciously, then grabbed the notes and read through them. "Wow," she said. "I didn't realize Sasha thought I was doing such a good job. She never really says so."

"She thinks you're ready to be released on your own," Jenna said. "What do you think?"

"I think I learn a lot more from you than Sasha."

A tingle ran up Jenna's spine. "That's nice of you to say, but I'm not sure how many of my habits you really want to pick up."

"I don't think they would have promoted you if they didn't like the way you work."

"Thanks." Jenna couldn't seem to stop lingering on Danielle's body, and wherever she shifted her attention it quickly felt inappropriate. Danielle's black hair, her warm complexion, the way she held most people at a distance all made for a mysterious presence she wanted to be closer to. She wanted to be the one allowed under Danielle's layers. "So, what do you think?" she asked. "You ready to do the job on your own?"

Danielle seemed to consider it for an eternity before she answered. "I think so."

"And the Clarks, how are you feeling about them?" Jenna tried her best to hide the anxiety she felt even mentioning them. Danielle knew the job, and Jenna was expected to release the case to her, but she didn't want to hand the boys off to anyone. She didn't know if she even could, no matter what Danielle said.

"I think I'm ready," Danielle said. "But I'm not sure they are. They're attached to you. And I know it's a special case to you."

Jenna returned Danielle's steady gaze. Danielle knew *she* wasn't ready. That's what she was really saying, and she was right. "It is." Jenna's voice came out in a whisper. She couldn't hold a fully capable employee back for her own benefit, but she couldn't deny she'd tried to think of reasons to. "What about your other cases? Are you comfortable with them?"

"Absolutely."

"All right," Jenna said. "What if we release you from Sasha? I'll continue working with you on the Clarks, and if you have any questions on your other cases you can ask me?"

"That sounds perfect."

"I guess that makes this our last training check-in," Jenna said.

"I guess so."

Jenna stood up. "Well, congratulations." She held out her hand. Danielle's hand slipped into hers as she accepted the handshake. Why did it feel so out of place? Had they strayed that far outside the lines? Jenna circled the desk and led the way to the door to see Danielle out. Danielle stopped just inside the frame.

"Listen, Jenna, everything you told me about Deon and Raylon, and your mom, all of it, I understand. If it ever becomes my case I'll do my best to do what you would do."

"Thanks," Jenna said. "That means a lot."

"It meant a lot that you told me what you did."

Danielle's eyes had a shine to them, the unmistakable reflectiveness of tears. Just as she was sure she saw it, it was gone.

"Are you okay?"

"Yeah," Danielle said, but the tremor in her voice said otherwise.

"Danielle, what is it?"

"Nothing," she said. "Nothing, I'm so sorry. Just thinking about you and your mom made me think of my brother."

"Li?"

Danielle nodded.

"What about him?"

Danielle shook her head. "No, I shouldn't. I shouldn't bother you with it. I'm so sorry. You're trying to work."

"Danielle."

"He just came to see me early this morning. It's not a big deal."

"Is he okay?"

"Sure, yeah, he's great. He just can't talk to me anymore. My dad found out we were talking and threatened to stop paying for college. But he's going to stop talking to me. He'll be a doctor, and everything will be fine." A tear spilled down Danielle's cheek. She wiped it away like lightning. "I'm fine," she said. "I'm fine. I'm really fine. I wouldn't want him to do anything different. I'm so sorry, I can't believe I did that."

"It's okay, Danielle. You can cry."

"No," she whispered. "No, I shouldn't. Not here. I shouldn't dump this on you. You're my boss."

Jenna felt paralyzed by how wrong that word felt. Boss. It wasn't close to describing her relationship with Danielle. It didn't remotely capture it. It wasn't even in the same universe. Danielle's tears were gone; she was composed again, and she even smiled.

"I really am fine," she said. "It's what I want for him."

Jenna felt trapped in Danielle's eyes. They were burning into her, and the passion was stirring into desire. She felt almost panicked that this was their last meeting, and she knew she shouldn't. The space between them felt wrong. The mask of work felt strange. She'd wanted to hold Danielle while she cried, not something a boss would do, not even the way a friend would do it.

She longed for Danielle's touch, wanted her to move closer and take the kiss she wanted the way she had at the party. But Danielle would never do it. She wouldn't be the one to break their agreement, and Jenna understood why. The risk was hers to take. The consequences would be hers to bear. Danielle wouldn't be the one to put her in that position, and she shouldn't be.

Danielle turned for the door again, and Jenna impulsively pushed it closed before it was too late. When Danielle turned to her in surprise, she stole the kiss she knew they both wanted.

Danielle's sharp inhale sent arousal plunging down her, and she wrapped her arms around Danielle and pulled her closer. Danielle locked the door. The quiet click of it twisting sent a thrill through her, and Jenna fell into the heat of Danielle's kiss. She backed her into the door and pressed against her, wanting Danielle's hands everywhere. When Danielle's tongue brushed over her lip, she thought her knees might buckle on the spot. Jenna traced her hand down Danielle's soft neck, moving down to her breasts. Danielle pulled away from their kiss just enough that their lips parted.

"Jenna, are you sure?"

"Yes," Jenna said. "I can't stand it. I need you."

"Then take me."

Their lips crashed together again. Danielle's hands were on her chest, moving under her suit jacket and pulling it off. Jenna grabbed

Danielle's hips and pushed her back into the room, stepping until Danielle backed into the edge of the desk and sat on the surface, then grabbed her knees and pulled them apart, moving between them. Jenna wove her fingers through Danielle's hair and pressed her body between her legs. Danielle moaned into their kiss, and her fists tightened around Jenna's blouse as she leaned back onto the desk.

Jenna kissed down Danielle's neck, gently pulling with her teeth at the sensitive skin until Danielle was writhing under her. She moved her hands under Danielle's shirt, feeling her way up the smooth, hot skin of Danielle's stomach until she reached the swell of her breasts and gently took Danielle's nipple between her fingers. Danielle muffled her moan against Jenna's neck and wrapped her legs around Jenna's waist. Jenna pushed against her center again, and Danielle collapsed onto the desk under her while she tugged at Jenna's blouse buttons until she could rip it off.

Jenna undid Danielle's belt, then the button, until she was able to slip her hand inside Danielle's pants. Danielle pulled Jenna into another kiss as she shifted her hips toward Jenna's hand. Jenna brushed Danielle's clit with the softest of touches and Danielle reeled in her arms.

"Fuck me, Jenna, please. I can't wait anymore."

Jenna cupped her hand under Danielle's neck and slowly plunged inside. Danielle's back arched off the desk, and Jenna covered her moan with a kiss. The sound of papers fluttering through the air and hitting the ground did nothing to distract from Danielle's nails dragged down her back as she plunged again, deeper. Danielle's reactions to her every movement made her head swim. All she could think about was tasting every inch of her. She pressed her body into Danielle's clit while she fucked her slow and deep. Danielle's fingers made their way into her hair again and held her fast against her body. Her hips started moving faster, and she pulled Jenna against her even harder.

"I'm going to come," Danielle whispered in her ear. Arousal shot through Jenna, and she fucked Danielle faster and harder until the first wave of Danielle's orgasm took over and her back arched off the desk. Her arms tightened around Jenna's body, and her nails dug into her back. Jenna moaned and pressed into her harder. Danielle's moan ripped through Jenna, and she felt undone by her need for Danielle's touch. Danielle buried her face in Jenna's shoulder and tried to stifle the sounds of her own ecstasy, then finally collapsed onto the desk. Jenna waited, relishing the pulses of Danielle's orgasm before she removed her fingers. Danielle gently touched Jenna's face, then leaned up and kissed her.

A knock sounded at the door. Jenna and Danielle both leapt in surprise. Danielle started to button her pants. Jenna motioned for her to be quiet.

"Jenna? You in there?" Sasha called as the door handle twisted, catching on the lock.

Jenna grabbed her blouse and yanked it on. "Yeah," she said. "Just finishing a few things up."

"You seen Danielle?"

Jenna and Danielle stopped to look at one another, and they both had to stifle laughter. Danielle's fingers started working on the buttons of Jenna's blouse while Jenna grabbed her jacket.

"Maybe half an hour ago," Jenna said. "Told her she could leave after our meeting."

"Her car is still here."

Jenna pulled her jacket closed. When she turned to look at Danielle, she'd already dived under the desk. Jenna cracked her office door open enough to not look strange, but kept it closed enough to remain uninviting. Sasha was eyeing her curiously.

"You lock your door?"

"I still can't get used to these stupid suits," Jenna said. "I may or may not take most of it off the second I know Paula has gone home for the day."

Sasha laughed. "I won't tell."

"Thanks," she said. "Maybe check the locker room for Danielle. Or the break room. She was talking about heading out."

"Okay." Sasha frowned. "I guess I'll look around one more time. I was hoping to catch her, congratulate her on finishing training and all. I assume you did release her, right?"

"Yeah," Jenna said. "Of course. No reason not to. You gave her glowing reviews."

"She earned them."

"I'm sure."

Sasha finally seemed to stop and examine her, and Jenna became very self-conscious, sure her hair was pure craziness. She was also certain her blouse was askew and she did everything she could to keep her jacket safely closed over it.

"You doing okay?" Sasha asked.

"Yeah, absolutely."

"You sure? The work getting to you? Seems like you've been locked away in here a lot."

Jenna shrugged. "It calls for long hours, but nothing I can't handle. I'm kind of glad to be out of the house, honestly."

Sasha's scrutiny landed on the bruise on her cheek. "You used to come knock back a few beers and talk with us when that happened. Seems like more effective therapy than work."

"It definitely is," Jenna said. "Maybe this weekend?"

Sasha lit up. "Yeah? Great!"

"Well, you better hurry up if you want to catch Danielle. She didn't sound like she was going to hang out long."

"Right, see you this weekend then."

Jenna closed and locked the door again and breathed out in relief. Danielle emerged from under the desk with a sexy smirk on her face and her hair tousled. "Do you really work naked in here when no one's looking?"

Jenna laughed. "Would you like that?"

"Of course, I would." Danielle kissed her jaw. "Wouldn't mind getting you naked right now."

"I think we might be pushing it on office nakedness for one day."

Danielle wrapped her arms around Jenna's waist. "Well, I simply must see you naked somewhere."

"Take me home with you." Jenna kissed Danielle's forehead, but Danielle stiffened in her arms. "Something wrong?"

"No," Danielle said quickly. "Home is just not very homey for me."

"What do you mean?"

"I don't really want us to be around Brianna."

Jenna felt herself pulling away though she didn't physically move. She'd heard things like that before, and it was usually code for, "I'm not as single as I let on." She hadn't seen any indication Danielle and Brianna were an item at the party. In fact, Danielle had outright said they weren't, and she couldn't imagine Danielle doing something like that, didn't want to, but she'd been shocked before.

"Oh," Jenna said. "I see."

"Hey," Danielle said, drawing Jenna's gaze back. "It's not like that. I promise."

"You don't have to explain anything to me," Jenna said. "This was kind of, unexpected." Jenna let her hands fall. Danielle grabbed them, pulling Jenna back to her.

"No, it wasn't," she said. "I mean the timing, maybe, but I'm not shocked. Are you shocked?"

"No."

"I haven't been able to get you out of my head since we met. This wasn't some mistake I made, and there's nothing shady going on, I promise. Brianna is just," Danielle sighed. "She's just a real pain in the ass. I'll explain it all later if we can go somewhere else tonight. I swear."

Jenna searched Danielle's face and realized she would go anywhere with her, Brianna or no. Danielle had gotten deep under her skin, and if there were some hard truths in between them, she'd deal with it later. "My home isn't exactly warm and fuzzy, either," Jenna said. "You'd have to deal with my sister, and my mom."

"That's okay," Danielle said. "I'd like to meet them. I know they're important to you."

Jenna raised her eyebrow. "Sure, they're important to me, but they're no walk in the park."

Danielle squeezed her hand. "That's okay," she said. "Really."

Jenna shook her head and laughed. "Okay, you asked for it."

CHAPTER TWENTY

Danielle's heart jumped when Jenna pulled into the driveway in front of a sweet two-story house with black shutters. There were tall, lush trees hanging over the driveway and yard. She imagined it had been someone's dream home at one point, but from what she knew of Jenna's past, the dream had fallen apart. Jenna's hand landed on her knee.

"I feel like I should prepare you," she said.

"You already told me about your mom," Danielle said. "I'm not going to get scared off." Danielle wanted to soothe Jenna's trepidation, but she could see she wasn't.

"Brianna can't possibly be worse than—"

"She is," Danielle said. "She'll ruin the whole night." Danielle felt a twist of guilt as Jenna's eyes swam with confusion and suspicion. She had to explain Brianna. She had to tell Jenna the reason she dreaded them being in the same place wasn't because Danielle was seeing them both, but because Brianna would be out of control drunk and would bother them all night falling on the floor, banging on the doors, talking too loud, flirting with Jenna, crying, puking, asking for a ride to the liquor store. It would be nonstop. And after explaining what a mess Brianna was, Danielle would somehow have to find a way to also tell Jenna that she'd dated that mess. And that despite all of that, that she also wasn't crazy for not being able to kick Brianna out like any normal person would.

She sighed. It was impossible to hope Jenna could understand all that. As much as she wanted to believe she could tell Jenna anything, everything in her life told her otherwise. Every time she'd dug down and exposed the rawest, scariest truths, she'd been cut off. Kicked out of her family, forbidden from speaking with her mother, tracked down and severed from her brother. People never seemed to understand the way she wanted them to, no matter how hard she tried to explain. Part of her still wished she'd never even come out to her family. Had it really been so bad in the closet? She had her family then, and it wasn't like it stopped her from dating. Maybe honesty was overrated. Jenna squeezed her hand and pulled her back to the moment.

"I told you about my mother, but I haven't told you about my sister," Jenna said. "She's…"

Danielle squeezed her hand. "Whatever it is, it will be just fine."

"She's never seen me bring someone home, for one."

"That's got to be a line." Danielle laughed.

"Nope."

Danielle wrapped her hand behind Jenna's neck and pulled her into a soft kiss. She licked Jenna's lower lip and delighted in the soft groan it pulled from her.

"I'm going to lose my mind if you don't touch me soon," Jenna whispered.

"We should probably get inside, then."

Jenna pulled back and nodded. Danielle couldn't imagine what she was so concerned about, and she was so fixated on Jenna's breath-taking face she couldn't concentrate long enough to venture a guess.

"She has scars," Jenna said. "Bad ones."

"Oh," Danielle said. "Is that all?"

"She's sensitive about it. She doesn't really let people see her."

"Okay," Danielle said. She looked Jenna in the eye to show she was taking it seriously, though she wasn't the slightest bit concerned. "I'll be respectful."

"Of course you will," Jenna said. "I'm more worried about her."

Danielle laughed. "Okay, well, I have thick skin. Can we go inside now so I can rip your clothes off?"

Jenna smiled and opened the car door. She guided Danielle through the front. The doorway led to a small foyer that connected to the living room. Danielle spotted Jenna's sister stretched out on the couch and couldn't help but draw a parallel to Brianna in the lazy way she was lying that seemed to suggest she rarely moved. She had dark wavy hair like Jenna's, but Danielle could tell her hairline was higher than usual. She couldn't see much more than that from a distance. The girl labored to a sitting position.

"About time," she said. "Did you bring—" She spotted Danielle and her back straightened. Her face clouded with darkness.

"Callie, I'd like you to meet Danielle," Jenna said.

Danielle raised her hand in a half-wave. "It's good to meet you," Danielle said. Jenna took her hand and guided her into the living room. Callie scooted backward as if she could disappear through the back of the couch. She locked onto their entwined hands, then trailed up in obvious scrutiny. As they joined Callie on the couch, Danielle saw the full extent of her scars. They were severe, but Jenna's warning had braced her for worse. They weren't so bad she'd expect Callie to hide from people. Danielle was careful to neither avoid nor stare at Callie's face.

Callie glanced between her and Jenna half a dozen times. She looked like a trapped animal searching for exits, and Danielle was hit with a wave of guilt for insisting on invading Jenna's space. Callie's space.

"How's Mom?" Jenna asked.

Callie's gaze darted around the room again before it finally landed on Jenna. She shrugged. "In her room."

"Have you had dinner? I could make you some food."

"Is she staying?" Callie eyed Danielle but spoke to Jenna.

"Yes," Jenna said.

"Until when?"

"Callie, don't be rude," Jenna said.

"It was just a question."

"As long as she wants."

Callie turned to Danielle. "How long is that?"

Danielle's first reaction was to laugh, but she held it back when she saw Callie wasn't joking at all. Danielle knew if she really was the first woman Jenna had brought home, a certain level of protectiveness was to be expected, but as she thought about it, she didn't detect protectiveness from Callie so much as outright anger and possessiveness.

"Until morning, I guess," Danielle said. Her stomach twisted as she glanced over for Jenna's reaction. She had pictured them spending the night together, but they hadn't talked about it explicitly. Jenna could expect her to leave after they finished satisfying their carnal cravings, but Jenna's warm smile calmed her fears.

"Gross," Callie said. "So this is your sex pad now?"

"Callie," Jenna scolded her.

"What? I can't say sex? We're all adults, aren't we?"

"One of us sure isn't acting like it," Jenna said. Danielle watched the exchange in fascination. Some part of her had expected Callie to be perfectly polite despite Jenna's concerns.

"What are you looking at?" Callie's attention spun on Danielle in an instant.

"Nothi—"

"You know, I know my face is fucking melted, okay? I do own a mirror."

Jenna grabbed Danielle's hand and pulled her to her feet. "Don't even answer her."

Callie scoffed. "Don't cross paths with the schizo. Don't talk to the burn victim. You should make a warning sign for the door before you let people into your freak show, Jenna."

"Stop it, Callie," Jenna said as she started for the hallway. She paused and looked over her shoulder. "I expected better out of you."

"Please, it's not my fault you brought your Asian fetish into the den of horrors."

Danielle felt Jenna's arm flex and shake, and she pulled to start back toward Callie. Danielle tightened her grip on Jenna's hand and drew her toward the hall. She had no idea where Jenna's room was, but she knew it was the other way. Jenna resisted for a second, but when Danielle gently pulled again, she consented and went up the stairs.

Danielle followed her into the second room on the left. Jenna closed the door and locked it, then ran her hands through her hair and tugged in frustration.

"I'm so sorry, Danielle. That was so—"

Danielle grabbed Jenna's hips, stopping her from pacing. "Hey," she said. "I was warned."

"No," Jenna said. "A warning doesn't cover that. That was inexcusable."

Danielle chuckled. "That is nowhere near the first time I've heard something like that. She's upset, and that's an easy direction to go with it. You told me we shouldn't come here, and I pushed. That's what happens."

Jenna's eyes were colored with both pain and concern. Danielle felt guilt washing over again that she hadn't just taken Jenna home to her place instead, but when she pictured Brianna drunkenly hanging all over Jenna and pounding the door at four a.m., she just wanted to be anywhere else.

On top of that, she wanted to find a way to tell Jenna who Brianna was to her. She kicked herself for not just telling her at the bar when she'd asked. She felt stupid for talking herself out of it, for relying on the delusion their relationship would remain professional and that it wouldn't bite her in the ass. At the time, it was easy to think Jenna didn't need to know, but it was different now. She had to find a way back around to the subject, but she couldn't figure out how to do it without making Jenna suspicious. She hated the idea of Jenna being uncomfortable with her living situation when she knew she wasn't ready to change it.

She stepped closer and kissed Jenna's neck. Jenna was stiff, upset and resistant. Danielle kissed her way up to Jenna's ear. "Besides," she said. "I know you don't have an Asian fetish. I saw your locker, remember?"

Jenna finally laughed and wrapped her arms around Danielle. "Still, I'm so disgusted that came out of her mouth."

"Be disgusted with her later," Danielle said. "I'd rather you were turned on by me for now." Danielle trailed her hands down Jenna's flat stomach and hooked her fingers in the waist of her pants, feeling Jenna's warm skin tremble at her touch. Danielle kissed her way along Jenna's jaw. Jenna's warm smell took over her senses, and she gave in to her need for Jenna's lips, taking the kiss softly at first, then getting lost in it when Jenna parted her lips with her tongue.

Danielle pushed Jenna backward until the back of her knees hit the bed, then lowered her onto it, crawling on top of her as they went. Jenna pulled at her shirt, but Danielle couldn't bear to let any space between them. She gently pushed Jenna's legs apart with her knee, never breaking their kiss. Jenna clawed at her shirt, and she felt it sliding over her skin. Jenna's warm hands on her burning skin sent a rush of arousal through her, and she was so intoxicated by Jenna's touch, her tongue, that her kiss was becoming wild with abandon.

Danielle grabbed the bottom of Jenna's blouse and pulled it over her head, moving immediately to Jenna's bra. Jenna arched off the bed to allow Danielle's hand to the clasp while Jenna caressed down her back. Danielle tossed the bra aside. The contact of her skin with Jenna's made her weak and energized her all at once. Jenna's breasts perfectly filled her hand, and her light pink nipples were hard. When Danielle took one into her mouth Jenna's hand tightened in her hair as she sucked in air sharply.

"God, that feels so good," she said. "I need more of you."

Danielle continued to work Jenna's nipples with her fingers while she nibbled on her neck.

"I want you to fuck me," Jenna whispered.

The words traveled to her core and made her pulse with desire. "Oh, I'm going to fuck you," Danielle said. Jenna moaned and squirmed in her arms. "Do you have any idea how much I've wanted to fuck you?"

Jenna found her lips again and moaned into the kiss, raising her hips in a plea for contact. Danielle undid the button to Jenna's pants and ripped them down her legs. Jenna's slim figure was toned and soft in all the right places. Her cheeks were flushed with desire, and her hair was wild and tangled. Danielle removed the rest of her own clothes while Jenna watched with dark, hungry eyes. She sat up and pulled Danielle back onto the bed, turning her onto her back and climbing on top.

The view of Jenna straddling her left her helpless with need, and she pushed her hips up as Jenna ground against her. Danielle was quickly getting close to the edge, but she wasn't going to get caught up in coming again before Jenna. She slipped her hand between their bodies. Jenna was so wet Danielle knew she could enter her right then, but she teased anyway, determined to be Jenna's undoing. Jenna leaned down as if she couldn't manage to stay upright and kissed her.

"Please," she said, never letting their lips separate.

Danielle spun her fingers through Jenna's hair and slowly plunged inside. Jenna's moan made her feel like her skin was on fire with lust. She fucked deeper, letting Jenna control the speed as she rode her. Danielle used her other hand to tease Jenna's nipples until a moan tore through her. Jenna's head went back, and her rhythm slowed. Danielle sat up and held Jenna against her as she came in her arms. Finally, Jenna went weak in her embrace, and she collapsed to the mattress.

Danielle wrapped her arm around Jenna's shoulder and pulled her close. Jenna only snuggled up long enough to kiss her neck, and then she was trailing kisses down Danielle's stomach. She lingered on Danielle's hips, her breath tickling the sensitive skin until Danielle was squirming. The warmth tormented her until Jenna finally covered her clit with the soft fire of her mouth. She arched off the bed in ecstasy. Each caress of Jenna's tongue took more of her strength away, and she was completely helpless to resist a single whim Jenna might have. When Jenna slipped her fingers inside without breaking the contact of her mouth, Danielle fell into a fuzzy blur of sensation. Her orgasm took her and she felt the vibration of Jenna moaning in pleasure as she came in her mouth.

When the aftershocks of her orgasm subsided, she pulled Jenna up next to her. They faced each other, their arms gently draped across one another. Danielle touched Jenna's face. Jenna lit up with a warm smile.

Danielle knew they had to come back to reality sometime, but she couldn't even vaguely entertain reality right now when Jenna was fulfilling all her recent dreams.

CHAPTER TWENTY-ONE

Danielle woke to the soft clink of dishes downstairs. She slowly sat up, smiling at the dull ache in her muscles as the night rushed back to her and she remembered she was in Jenna's bedroom. The doorknob twisted, and Jenna emerged with two coffee cups. A warm smile spread across Jenna's face. She walked the rest of the way into the room at a much more relaxed pace, like she'd been trying not to make noise before. Danielle soaked the image of Jenna in and let it fill her. She was still swimming in Jenna's smell, her touch.

"Good morning." Jenna handed Danielle the cup of coffee. "Figured you might not want to risk running into my family after yesterday."

Danielle smiled and took the cup, pulling up the covers and inviting Jenna back into bed. Jenna slipped in next to her and settled into the nook under Danielle's arm. Jenna fit against her perfectly, and she breathed in the comfort and ease of her.

"What are you up to today?" Danielle asked.

"I have to get some work done," Jenna said.

"On the weekend?"

"Yeah, I didn't finish my reports yesterday."

"Someone interrupt you?" Danielle teased her as she kissed Jenna's ear, gently grabbing her earlobe in her teeth. She felt a shiver run over Jenna's skin, and Jenna turned into a kiss.

"I guess that's why they think workplace relationships are bad," Jenna said.

Danielle felt the weight of the words crushing her and pulling her down even though they were meant to be a joke. "Yeah," she said. "I guess we should probably talk about that. I don't want to get you in trouble, Jenna."

"We had our chance to stop," Jenna said. "We failed miserably. I failed miserably."

Danielle couldn't help but smile, but the stone remained heavy and solid in her chest. Jenna was risking so much for her. She couldn't help but dread and fear the day Jenna would resent her for it. "I never should have kissed you," Danielle said. "I got this whole mess started."

"Are you saying you want to stop?"

Danielle's stomach dropped. She looked up sharply, relieved to see the same dread in Jenna's expression. "No," she said. "I don't want to stop. I'm just not sure what to do now."

"Me either." Jenna took a deep breath. "All I know is you're all I can think about. I don't know if I can keep my hands off you."

"I don't want you to."

"We could hide it," Jenna said. "Until we can think of something better?"

Jenna spoke the suggestion sheepishly, like she was afraid of Danielle's reaction, but she'd thought of nothing else for days. She'd gone around and around in circles trying to figure out what to do with her feelings, and she kept winding up at an image of them hiding their relationship away. She'd just been too afraid to suggest it. It felt wrong, asking Jenna to sneak around, hiding their feelings when really she wanted to shout them to the world.

"Yes," Danielle said. "It's the only way I can think of too. We can't possibly be the first to run into this problem."

Jenna laughed, and Danielle finally breathed with relief. Suddenly, the whole issue seemed smaller. Plenty of people hid workplace relationships. They had to. It couldn't possibly be that rare, but they couldn't take it lightly. She could get in trouble, the kind of trouble she could live with, but Jenna could lose her job entirely, and Danielle refused to be the cause of that.

Danielle leaned forward and kissed Jenna gently, letting it settle in her mind not just that they were agreeing to hide the relationship, but first of all, to have one. She loved the idea, but it brought both of their homes raging through her thoughts. Brianna. Callie.

"Jenna, about last night," she said. "I feel really bad for making you bring me here. I didn't mean to start problems between you and your sister. I don't want you to feel like you have to start a war with her over me, over what happened."

A knot bunched in Jenna's jaw. She looked just as angry as she had last night when it happened. "It's not your fault," she said.

"It kind of is, though," Danielle said. "You told me it was a bad idea, and I pushed because I didn't want to be around Brianna. I told you I'd explain later. I think I should now. I know what it sounded like to you, and I can't stand you thinking that."

Jenna turned toward her on the bed and seemed to stiffen. Danielle took a breath, trying to figure out where to start.

"When I got upset that night at the party because Brianna was wasted, I told you she does it all the time. I didn't mean she just likes to party a lot. She's an alcoholic."

"Oh." Jenna smiled. "Is that all? You had me scared."

"It's a real problem," Danielle said. "It might not sound like a big deal, but—"

"You're right," Jenna said. "I'm sorry. I didn't mean it like that. How bad is it?"

Danielle's chest tightened as she pictured the last couple years of her life, Brianna's decline from a lively and fun but stable and dependable friend into the disaster she was now. She'd liked to drink more than average even when they were dating, but it had taken another year for it to become clear it was an issue she couldn't control. It had been devastating to watch, and Danielle somehow wound up becoming the one Brianna turned to again and again. She witnessed Brianna's herd of friends thin, fill, and thin again as the many people she met at the bar inevitably tapped out.

"She drinks all day every day," Danielle said. "She goes to bed when she's finally so drunk she passes out. Doesn't remember much the next day. She acts crazy a lot of the time. I just knew if I took you over there she wouldn't leave us alone. We'd be taking care of her all night in between her hitting on you. I just wanted some real time with you."

Jenna squeezed Danielle's hand. "Sounds like a hard way to live," she said. "You deal with that every night?"

"Most nights."

"Has she ever tried to get help?"

Danielle shook her head. She knew the pattern of thoughts Jenna would go through. Many people had done the same. Danielle had done the same, but she never found a solution.

"She doesn't think she needs it," Danielle said. "Of course."

"She doesn't do anything..." Jenna paused. "Abusive, does she?"

Danielle felt a knot form in her throat while she considered how much to say. The more she told people, the more she was pressured to kick Brianna out, and she simply couldn't do that. She couldn't abandon someone she cared about. She knew too well how it felt.

"She doesn't hit me, if that's what you mean."

"I mean it in the broadest sense," Jenna said.

"She goes into rages sometimes," Danielle said. She took a forced breath. She had to trust Jenna. Her family was just as complex. She'd understand. "She breaks stuff. She can get mean, call me names. She lies a lot. Then she cries, falls on the floor like a little kid until you take care of her. It used to upset me, but she has no idea it even happened the next day. Usually it doesn't seem worth it trying to stay mad at her. It just upsets her when I'm mad, and it starts her on a whole new rampage. I try to ignore it."

"Danielle, you know that's not healthy, right?"

"I know." She felt like she could read everything Jenna was thinking straight out of her brain. "But I don't know what to do about it. She doesn't want help, and I can't throw her out on the street. She can't take care of herself. God knows what will happen to her."

"Does she have family?"

"They cut her off."

"Maybe for good reason," Jenna said. "You don't have to let her treat you that way."

Danielle's stomach twisted, and the urge to shut down slammed into her full force. She knew Jenna's reaction was normal, that she was just trying to look out for her well-being, but she'd had too many people try to tell her how to handle Brianna, too many people who thought the answer was to throw her out and let her drown, who tried to impose their opinions like the law, like her father. They all seemed to think Brianna would get her life together if she was forced to, but Danielle knew better. She knew with a certainty that ran all the way into her bones that Brianna could not handle a sink or swim ultimatum. She'd sink. And no matter how crazy Brianna got sometimes, Danielle couldn't just let that happen. There had to be a better way.

She grabbed Jenna's hand and squeezed. "I know it's not okay," she said. "I know something has to change, but I can't just throw her on the street, and I can't get her to go to rehab yet. I'm dealing with it the best I can until I can think of something better."

"But—"

Danielle cut her off with a kiss. "You don't have to solve this," she said. "I just wanted you to know. I couldn't stand you thinking I didn't want you there because I was seeing her or something."

"It crossed my mind," Jenna said.

"I'm not," Danielle said. "I promise." She wanted to keep going. She wanted to tell Jenna Brianna was her ex. It was information she should be aware of, but Jenna was already having trouble understanding. She already thought Danielle should refuse to deal with Brianna. If she added that they used to date to the mix, who knew how she'd react? She would probably think that was some hidden key that explained her willingness to put up with Bri. If Jenna demanded she get rid of Bri, she wouldn't be able to do it, and she couldn't lose Jenna over that. If she just gave her more time she'd understand.

"I believe you," Jenna said.

"Thank you."

Danielle jumped to her feet, eager to put space between them and the topic of Brianna. "I guess I better let you get to work," she said. "Do you mind if I use your shower?"

"Of course not," Jenna said. "Right through there."

Danielle kissed Jenna, letting the heat of her mouth ripple through her skin. When she pulled away, the sparkle in Jenna's eyes wrapped her in longing. She made her way into the bathroom and turned the shower up as hot as she could stand.

❖

Jenna watched Danielle disappear into the bathroom. She wanted to stop her. She wanted to talk about Brianna more, but she knew Danielle wasn't ready to hear it. She was keenly aware Danielle hadn't asked for her opinion, yet she'd still had a hard time not giving it. She'd seen Danielle clam up and shut down, and that had been enough to silence her. She would have to go at Danielle's pace.

They already had enough to think about as it was. They had to find a way to cover their uncontrollable lust at work, and she needed to figure out how to keep Callie in check before she went too far and did some real damage. And between all that, she just wanted to enjoy Danielle and get to know her more at whatever pace felt right.

Jenna started downstairs to search for breakfast. When she got there, Callie was sitting silently at the dining room table. Jenna paused, then walked past her and opened the fridge.

"Have a fun night?" Callie asked.

Jenna's shoulders tensed with anger at the sound of Callie's voice. She wasn't ready to talk to her, but she couldn't avoid it. She grabbed the orange juice, poured a glass, and sat at the table across from her.

"It's not just fun, Callie," Jenna said. "I really like her. I thought you would know that when I brought her home. When have I ever done that?"

"Never."

"When have I ever treated this house like a 'sex pad'?"

"Last night."

"Damn it, Callie, even if that were true it doesn't give you the right to act the way you did."

"And what gives you the right to bring random people over here? You know I don't like to be around people."

"I live here too, Callie. I pay the bills. I have every right to bring people over."

"But you can leave, Jenna. You can do this somewhere else. I can't. I'm trapped here. You took my one safe place and you brought someone into it without so much as telling me."

Jenna grit her teeth, then slumped back into the chair, all her energy drained. "I guess I could have warned you," Jenna said. "I will next time."

Callie shot forward in her chair and slammed her palm on the table. "Next time? You have got to be fucking kidding me."

"No, Callie, I'm not kidding." Jenna kept her voice calm and steady. "I told you I really like this woman. Doesn't that matter to you? Doesn't my happiness matter?"

Callie crossed her arms and stared at the table. Jenna was struck by how childlike she looked with her ridiculous, protruding, pouting mouth.

"Callie, you have to know I would never bring anyone here who would be cruel to you. Give Danielle a chance. For me."

Callie looked at Jenna for a long time before the corner of her mouth finally twitched into a smile. "Ah, fine. Jeez. You're like, in love, aren't you?"

The words sent a jolt through her. "I—"

Jenna's gaze tore from Callie when Danielle filled the door frame at the bottom of the stairs. Her hair was still wet, and her clothes clung to the curves of her body. Danielle smiled when they both looked over at her.

"Sorry," Danielle said. "I didn't mean to interrupt."

"It's okay," Jenna said. "We were done, and I'd better get to work."

Danielle nodded. "All right. Well, I hope you have a good day, Callie."

Callie looked at Jenna, then finally nodded at Danielle. "You too. Good to meet you."

CHAPTER TWENTY-TWO

Danielle watched Jenna make her way into work before she started her car. Even from behind, even from two hundred feet away, Jenna was so gorgeous Danielle could barely breathe. She couldn't believe they'd somehow wound up in bed together. She couldn't believe Jenna hadn't pled temporary insanity in the morning, that she would risk her career to be with her, but she couldn't seem to tell Jenna it wasn't worth it. The feeling she had when they were together, the way the air filled with their energy felt worth it. It felt special.

It only took a few minutes for her to drive home in the light Saturday morning traffic. She tried to open the door to her apartment quietly, hoping Brianna would still be passed out from a night of drinking. When she slowly cracked the door open, Brianna was sitting on the couch staring at her. She raised an eyebrow as Danielle finally slipped inside.

"Well, look at you sneaking around," she said. "I thought there was a slight chance you would have some innocent explanation for not coming home, but alas, the sweet Danielle has finally indulged in a one-night stand."

Danielle breathed with relief as she recognized Brianna was sober. She smiled and went to sit on the couch.

"So?" Brianna asked.

"So what?"

"Who was she?"

Danielle groaned. "I don't want to talk about it."

"Oh, hell no," Brianna said. "Danielle, I can and will die from information deprivation. Why does everything have to be a big secret? Just tell me."

"Do you really want to know?" Danielle asked. "Think about it."

"What do you mean?" Brianna pulled away in surprise. "God, don't tell me you think I still have a thing for you."

"I don't know," Danielle said. "I didn't. But then you wanted to hook up that one night."

"What?" Brianna's face filled with what looked like genuine shock. "What in the hell are you talking about?"

"You…" Danielle paused as she realized Brianna had no memory of the event and wished she hadn't even mentioned it. As often as it happened, it still surprised her every time Brianna failed to recall major events. "You tried—"

"If I did that I was just wasted and horny. Purely physical needs clashing with a lack of inhibition. Don't be full of yourself. I'm so over you. We covered this when we moved in together, remember?"

"Yeah."

"Okay, so who is she?"

Danielle sighed and rubbed her face. "Jenna."

"Your boss?" Brianna nearly yelled the words and sprang in the air while she turned to Danielle, crossing her legs on the couch so she could face her squarely.

"Yes."

"After all that talk about how inappropriate it was?"

Danielle groaned. "Yes."

"Well done," Brianna said with a mischievous smile. "My little Danielle is all grown up and sleeping with her boss."

"Knock it off," Danielle said. "I'm a horrible person. She could get fired."

"She must really like you then."

Danielle nodded. "I think so."

"Not a one-night stand after all," Brianna said. "You could do a lot worse. She's sexy as hell. And I was only around her for a night, but she seemed cool."

"She is."

"So, when are you seeing her again?"

"At work, I guess." Danielle laughed.

"You should bring her over sometime."

"Really?"

"Yes, Danielle." Brianna rolled her eyes. "That's what you do when you like someone. You do like her, don't you?"

"Of course, I do."

"Okay, then."

"You won't hit on her?"

Brianna scoffed. "Oh, come on. I wouldn't do that."

Danielle raised her eyebrow.

"Okay, well, my natural flirtatious aura doesn't count. You know I can't help that. But I would never go after someone you're sleeping with, Danielle. What kind of person do you think I am?"

"You promise?"

Brianna huffed. "You're honestly going to hurt my feelings if you don't knock it off."

"Okay, okay," Danielle said, but the problem with Brianna was that no matter how great her promises were when she was sober, all bets were off once she had a few.

CHAPTER TWENTY-THREE

Jenna stacked her reports into a pile and tapped them on the desk to straighten them. She went up the hall to Paula's office and slipped them into her mailbox. She had the hang of her new responsibilities, and they weren't taking quite so long anymore. Things were finally feeling easier, and she knew it was more than a little because of Danielle. The work hadn't changed; her mood had. Everything just felt better. Whoever decided workplace romances were a bad idea was out of their mind. The weeks that passed since she started sneaking around with Danielle had been some of the smoothest she could remember. She'd never been so happy at work, or anywhere for that matter, in her life.

She checked her watch. Only an hour left in the day, which probably meant people had already stopped working. She took the stairs down to the break room and smiled as the familiar hum of end-of-day chatter came from the small room. She turned the corner and saw Sasha, Adam, Val, and Danielle laughing over coffee. Danielle glanced at her from the back corner, and the warmth there brought a smile to Jenna's face.

"Oh, shit. We're busted," Adam said and laughed.

"Damn right," Jenna said.

"Take it easy on us, boss," Val said. "We've only been here for..." She checked her watch, then playfully cringed. Jenna pretended to crack a whip, but pulled up a chair and straddled it.

"Any war stories today?" she asked.

"Oh no," Sasha said. "No war stories for you. We're saving them until you actually come out with us this weekend. It's the only way to get you to come along."

"Aw, come on. That's not necessary."

"What we really need to talk about is what you're doing to get management to put a vending machine in here," Adam said.

"Yeah, that's what I spend my time on, all right," Jenna said. Danielle made her way from the corner to the table and sat in the free chair. Jenna couldn't believe how powerful their stolen seconds of eye contact could be. It never took more than a glance to completely undo her.

"You're coming out with us this weekend, right, Danielle?" Val asked.

Danielle glanced at Jenna with a question dancing in her eyes, but Jenna just raised an eyebrow and waited.

"Sure," she said.

Jenna's mind flooded with the images of the charade they'd have to put on all night. It sounded impossible in a casual environment. She could barely keep her hands off Danielle even with the clear-cut boundaries of work. Just as she thought it, Danielle's foot touched her ankle under the table and moved up her leg. When Jenna looked over, Danielle was seemingly paying no attention.

"Well," Danielle said abruptly. "I'm going to take care of a few last things before the end of the day. I think I left a file in my locker."

Jenna couldn't get up too soon, but the moment Danielle left, Jenna lost her ability to process a thing anyone was saying. She heard herself laughing, but she was already swimming in Danielle's smell. When ten minutes passed, she stood.

"All right, guys, I'd better get some work done. Especially if I'm going to spend my weekend with you scoundrels."

"Hear, hear," Adam said. "No more weekend work."

Jenna pushed her chair in. Sasha was leaning against the wall by the door. When Jenna tried to pass she discreetly hooked Jenna's arm and looked her in the eye.

"Be careful," she said under her breath.

Jenna met her intense gaze. She refused to acknowledge Sasha's rattling accusation, in admission or denial. She passed by and headed for the locker room after Danielle, checking behind her as she went.

The locker room was empty when she got there. She checked each row for stragglers, but it was quiet. When she got to the last row,

Danielle leaned against her locker with her arms crossed, her shirt unbuttoned far enough to dance with the line of decency.

"I was starting to think you wouldn't come," Danielle said.

"How could I not?"

Jenna walked over until their thighs were touching. She could feel Danielle's breath on her cheek. She met Danielle's lips with her own, instantly lost in the softness of them. Danielle grabbed Jenna's suit jacket and pulled her around the corner, opening the supply closet door and pulling Jenna inside. Jenna laughed as she let Danielle drag her away.

"What are we doing in here?"

"Can't find the staples." Danielle kissed the hollow at the base of Jenna's neck. "I'm new around here. Can you help me?"

Jenna smiled and grabbed Danielle's hips, then turned her around.

"Did you check this shelf?" She pressed into to the shape of Danielle's back, letting her breath brush over Danielle's skin. Danielle groaned and reached behind her, running her fingers through Jenna's hair with one hand, grabbing her leg with the other.

"I don't see them," Danielle said.

"Oh." Jenna put her hand on the back of Danielle's neck and gently guided her head down until she was bent over. "How about the next shelf down?"

Danielle pushed her ass into Jenna as she pretended to search. Jenna raked her nails down Danielle's back and returned the pressure Danielle was supplying until her clit was screaming for release. Finally, Danielle stood again and lunged at Jenna, meeting her mouth in a passionate, urgent kiss. Danielle pushed her until she was against the opposite wall, then reached between her legs and stroked her clit.

"You better stop that," Jenna said breathlessly. "You'll make me come."

"Surely you can come up with a better threat than that," Danielle said.

The sound of a door closing made them both freeze even though a second of reflection told them it had come from the floor above. Jenna looked back into Danielle's waiting gaze.

"We really need to stop doing this at work," she said.

"I know," Danielle said. "Come home with me."

"Really?" Jenna knew the big cheesy grin on her face gave away any hope she had of acting smooth, but she didn't care.

"Really. I can't promise Brianna won't ruin it, but we can try."

"She can't possibly act worse than my sister did."

"Don't tell her that; she'll think it's a bet," Danielle said. She fished Jenna's phone out of her pocket and punched in her address. "Meet you there." Danielle kissed her cheek and disappeared back into the locker room.

Jenna waited awhile for Danielle to clear the area, then emerged from the closet. She took the stairs to her office two at a time, eager to gather her things for the weekend and get to Danielle's house. Danielle's house, she loved the idea of being there with her, even if it came with Brianna, even if it came with chaos. She didn't doubt Danielle's assessment of Brianna's drinking. She'd only seen Brianna for a night, and though she hadn't taken the fact that Brianna drank to the point of vomiting all that seriously, Danielle knew her much better. Even so, she'd never been the type to scare easily, and she couldn't picture a drunken antic severe enough to make a night with Danielle not worth it. Just as she reached her office door Paula called her name from two doors down.

"Jenna, that you?"

Jenna fleetingly wondered if she could get away with pretending she hadn't heard, but that was childish. She begrudgingly made her way to Paula's doorway.

"I was just stopping—"

"Come on in," Paula said. Jenna slowly digested Paula's serious expression and came down from the euphoria of Danielle. "Close the door."

Jenna obliged and took the seat opposite Paula. "Everything okay?"

"I'm afraid not."

"Is it my evaluations? I can take another look at them if they're not up to par."

"Your evaluations are wonderful."

Jenna wore her puzzled expression freely, hoping it would end the suspense Paula seemed to want to build. Paula leaned back in her chair in the same way she always did that made her legs seem like they went on and on.

"I'm afraid we need to discuss an accusation that's been made against you."

"An accusation?" Jenna felt her pulse pick up as her mind scrambled through every important decision she'd made during the week. She couldn't come up with anything questionable. "What accusation?"

"It's been brought to my attention that you're having a romantic relationship with Danielle Corey."

Jenna felt her blood drain, and she knew she was pale. The way Paula phrased it didn't sound like a question, but if there was any doubt, Jenna was quite sure she was transparent.

"I thought we made it clear that being too close to your subordinates could be problematic. A relationship is beyond that concern; it is in direct violation of policy. I'm sure you're aware of that." Paula set her pen on top of a file on her desk. Jenna couldn't help looking at it, wondering if it was her file, if this was Paula's way of telling her she was about to end her career with what she would write inside of it.

"I'm aware," Jenna said. She hated the way her voice came out so quiet and decided she wouldn't let it happen again. She would take what was coming to her with whatever dignity she could muster.

"Is there anything you'd like to say?"

"Where is this accusation coming from?" Jenna asked.

"I can't release that information to you."

"Someone who wants my job, I imagine."

"The only thing we need to discuss is whether or not it's true."

Jenna leaned back in her chair, a bizarre calmness coming over her. She could lie. She could say it was made up, and Paula likely couldn't prove anything. But when she pictured Danielle she knew it wasn't a passing fling. Hiding it would only get harder, and one of these days the accusation would come with evidence and a termination notice if she lied.

"It's true." Jenna hardly recognized herself. Even when she'd given in and kissed Danielle in her office she didn't really believe she was setting a match to her career, certainly not so soon, and she had to admit a big part of her didn't expect to get caught at all. She figured it would end when she or Danielle found hiding it intolerable.

"It hasn't been long. I was going to ask about her being transferred to another supervisor soon. It hasn't affected her training or evaluations in any way, I assure you."

Paula nodded grimly. "I'm sorry to hear that," she said. "I had very high hopes for you."

Jenna's stomach twisted. "What are you saying?"

"This issue is more than frowned upon," Paula said. "It's inexcusable."

"Are you firing me?"

Paula studied her for a long time. "No. I'm not firing you, but you cannot continue to work as Danielle's supervisor, obviously." Paula opened the file on her desk and slid a stack of papers to Jenna.

"There are a few options here for you to consider. The first is a request to transfer to the Nashville branch. If you want to both remain a supervisor and continue your relationship with Danielle, you can turn that in to me. I can't guarantee they'll grant the transfer, as your file will include this incident, but you may apply. If they don't hire you, you'll have to choose from the other options. The next is a resignation form. If you decide to resign, I will personally provide you with a good reference and leave this information out in the hopes you find a new career quickly and painlessly. The last is a form that states you will no longer carry on a relationship with Danielle. Jenna, this one allows you to keep the job you have now, at this location, and Danielle will be assigned to a different team with a different supervisor, but this will come with some steep discipline, and it will be a final warning. If you sign this and it comes to light that you are still seeing Danielle, you will be terminated. I want you to consider each of your options very carefully before you get back to me. I'll give you the weekend."

Jenna took the papers with numb fingers. "Thank you." She stood and headed for the door. She couldn't feel her legs.

"Jenna," Paula said. She turned. "You are very good at what you do. Most would have simply been fired. I hope you understand that."

Jenna nodded. "I understand. Thank you."

"I won't be lenient twice. Choose carefully."

CHAPTER TWENTY-FOUR

Danielle rushed home, hoping to get there ahead of Jenna early enough to clean a little and see how well Brianna was likely to hold up. When she went inside, Brianna was in her usual place on the couch with a drink in her hand.

"Hey," Danielle said as she burst through the door.

"Well, hello," Brianna said.

"Jenna's coming over. You're still cool with that, right?"

Brianna sat up straighter. "Sure. Any reason you're having a panic attack about it?"

"I'm not. I'm just going to clean up real quick."

Brianna looked at her blankly for a few seconds before she registered what Danielle wanted. Finally, she sprang to her feet.

"Ah, you want me to help you clean."

"If you don't mind."

"Wow, I've never seen you like this before." Brianna gathered the dishes from the coffee table. "Did you run around like a psycho before I came over? Back in the day?"

"Huh? Oh, no. The place was already clean."

Brianna laughed. "You calling me a slob?"

"No."

"Kind of, though."

"Come on, Brianna, please?"

"I'm cleaning. I'm cleaning."

Jenna knocked on the door just fifteen minutes later, but the place looked remarkably better. Danielle couldn't pretend that had been her major concern, though. Brianna was at least a few drinks in already and wasn't likely to stop. And even that was secondary to the fact that she still hadn't managed to tell Jenna that Brianna was her ex. She should have never invited Jenna over, not before that was handled, but the words just came out, and now she would be forced to handle it once and for all.

When Danielle opened the door and saw Jenna standing there, all her problems seemed to melt away. She smiled and invited Jenna in.

"Hello again," Brianna said.

"Hey," Jenna said. "Good to see you."

"Good to see anyone Danielle will break some rules for." Brianna nudged Danielle playfully. "Secret affairs are so sexy."

Danielle scowled at Brianna. She held her hands up innocently. "Don't worry. I'm going out."

"You are?"

"Yep, house is all yours. I'll be home at some point, so don't get too carried away." Brianna slipped her arms around Danielle and pulled her into a hug. "Actually, get carried away if you want. Who am I to complain about walking in on some naked ladies?"

"Bri," Danielle said.

"All right, all right, I'm leaving." Brianna dashed out and closed the door.

Jenna hooked her thumbs in her jeans, and a crooked smile stretched across her face. "That wasn't so bad."

"No, it wasn't," Danielle said. She was so relieved she only now realized she'd barely been able to breathe before. She was free to tell Jenna everything. Brianna wouldn't blurt it out, wouldn't be able to sabotage her. "Come sit. I want to tell you something."

"That's funny," Jenna said as she went to the couch and sat down. "Me too." She put the files she was carrying on the table and rubbed her face.

"Don't tell me you think you're working tonight," Danielle said.

"No, just didn't want to leave them in the car. Sensitive stuff in there."

"Aw, you're secretly a sucker for the rules too."

"I don't know about that."

Danielle saw names on each folder tab. Some she recognized, others she didn't. When she saw the Clark file, her curiosity was piqued. What did Jenna have access to that she didn't?

"Can I look?"

"In the files?" Jenna glanced at the stack. "Sure," she said. "If you want. Just don't tell anyone."

"Of course not." Danielle picked up the first file. She flipped through the pictures, shaking her head as she examined them. Many were of disgusting living situations, homes with holes in the walls, with dead insects piled in corners, dog feces and urine puddles. She closed the file and went to another. The first picture was a little girl with a black eye. Danielle shook her head again as the girl's sorrow seized her chest.

"You inherit all the worst cases?" Danielle asked. Jenna smiled weakly, but Danielle held her gaze. "Seriously."

"Yeah, pretty much." She shrugged. "I go through all my team's cases. I choose the ones I think could use extra attention. Those tend to be the worst ones."

"Wow," Danielle said. "I guess that makes sense. I just never thought of it that way. That must be really hard. It's like your work is a compilation of all of our worse moments."

Jenna shrugged. "I'm just a supporting role, though. I'm not as close to it as you guys."

Danielle closed the file. "I know it still affects you, Jenna. Do you ever feel like it's too much? With your history?"

"Sure, sometimes." Jenna's serious tone told Danielle she'd found the nerve she suspected was beneath the surface. She wanted to know everything about Jenna, every secret corner.

"What was it like?" Danielle asked. "Growing up with your mom?"

"It was a lot like what you see with Deon and Raylon. One day it's great, the next..." Jenna paused. "The next you're scared out of your mind."

"What were you afraid of? That she'd hit you?"

"No," Jenna said. "She did occasionally, but that was over before I had time to be afraid of it. It was scarier when she was scared."

Danielle was lost in Jenna's green eyes. They seemed a shade deeper in the dim light and they were swirling with the past.

"What was she afraid of?"

"She thinks people are after her. She used to think someone was trying to shoot her pretty often. Lots of ducking. When you're a kid you don't really know any better. You end up in the delusion too."

"That's awful."

"We didn't really know what we were looking for or running from. We just knew whoever *they* were, they wanted to kill us. I actually liked it better when we were on the lookout, checking the peephole or the blinds. It felt like we were all together doing something. When it really got bad she couldn't even do that. She'd just cower in the corner, talking to herself. She stopped making sense. Word salad, they call it. Words out of order. Impossible to follow. She wouldn't eat, wouldn't bathe, wouldn't leave the house for weeks. We'd run out of food. That was the worst of it, watching this woman who was your world, your protector, completely fall apart. That's when I really felt unsafe."

Danielle melted watching Jenna wrap her arms around her own shoulders, like she was hugging the scared child she used to be.

"I don't understand how CPS didn't take you away."

Jenna scoffed. "Our caseworker was a joke. She didn't care. Just there to collect a paycheck. She's the reason I wanted to be a social worker."

"You knew you could do it better?"

"Exactly. She wanted to remove us, but she thought that was the end of her job. She didn't want to talk through it with me, so I just lied. I knew how to bullshit. Callie and I would clean the house. We'd shoplift some food, set up the table with our homework like we were all doing just great."

"But…" Danielle paused, trying to figure out how to phrase it. "But if your mom was so ill, why didn't you want to be removed? Wouldn't it have been better for all of you?"

Jenna sighed. "Yes," she said. "It would have been, but at the time all I knew was I didn't want to be separated from my sister. I didn't even want to be separated from my mom. Maybe if the caseworker had actually taken the time to explain that they could try to keep us together, that my mom would be able to try to get us back once she was stable again, maybe I would have felt differently, but we'll never know. At the time it was just us against her. She never gave me a chance to get to know or trust her, so all I had to go on was what my mom said about them."

"And she hated them."

"Of course."

Danielle grabbed the next file, the Clark file. She flipped it open, and the first picture was of Deon with his shirt off. He was emaciated to the point he barely looked like himself. Danielle felt her breath catch, and she quickly closed the file.

"That was the day I met him," Jenna said.

Danielle was shaken. She hadn't expected the difference in impact that knowing Deon made. "I…" she paused, feeling tears coming on. "How did they not get taken away that day?"

"They did," Jenna said. "Temporarily. They stayed with their aunt while Ladona got treatment. They went back when she stabilized. Deon and his aunt had a lot of issues while they were over there. It's why she'll only take Raylon if they're removed again."

"How the system could give them back to that monster is beyond me," Danielle said. As soon as the words left her mouth she saw Jenna pull away.

"She's not a monster," Jenna said. "She loves her kids. She's sick. When she's medicated she's a capable mother doing her best with some hard circumstances."

"Like your mother?" Danielle knew she was on dangerous ground, but she couldn't seem to stop talking. The image of Deon was too haunting.

"Yes," Jenna said. "Exactly like my mother."

"But your mom *isn't* capable, Jenna. She wasn't then, and she isn't now. She hit you just last week. Medication doesn't fix everything."

Jenna snatched the file out of Danielle's hand. "You don't know anything about my mother. You've never even met her."

"I know she hits you, and your sister is afraid to leave the house because half her face is burned off."

Jenna slammed Deon's file on top of the others, then picked up the entire stack and stood. Danielle closed her eyes and stood up.

"Jenna, I'm sorry. I'm trying to understand. It's just—"

"No, you're not. You make your decisions with half the information. You thought I should take Deon and Raylon away before you ever saw this."

"Yeah, and this makes it worse!"

"You know what doesn't fix everything, Danielle? Foster care. Half those people are pedophiles and the other half just want to collect a check. Ladona has problems, big ones, but she loves them, and she's family. I don't pull kids out of everything they know on blind faith they're going to something better. And as far as my mom…" Jenna looked like she might cry, but then she hardened so fast Danielle wasn't sure she'd actually seen it. "I trust you with a couple of stories and you think that's grounds to make assumptions about what a monster she is?"

"Jenna, I didn't—"

"I *love* my mom, okay? And she's not responsible for Callie's burns. I am."

Jenna stormed out and slammed the door before Danielle could put a sentence together.

CHAPTER TWENTY-FIVE

Jenna was still shaking with anger when she made it to her car. She threw her files in the passenger seat and tore out of the parking lot. She only made it a few blocks before the anger subsided, and tears took its place. She pulled over and let them break free.

She couldn't remember the last time she'd shared the details of her life with anyone. The fear of judgment had always paralyzed her. Being judged personally, but also her mom and sister. Opening up to Danielle only to find all her worst fears realized was more painful than she'd even guessed it would be. Maybe it was unreasonable to expect anything else. Maybe everyone would always judge her because she *was* wrong. She hurt Callie, and no amount of remembering she was a kid at the time or that the caseworker should have done things differently made the guilt of that easier to bear.

Her phone lit up with Danielle's name, but she couldn't bring herself to answer. She drove home, but when she got there she stayed in the car. She didn't want to see her family, couldn't stand the evidence of her failures screaming in her face. Her phone lit up again. Jenna stared at Danielle's name. Danielle. How had she gotten under her skin so completely, so fast? She'd been ready to accept a transfer or even give up her job for Danielle. Maybe she'd come to that decision too hastily. She hadn't even managed to tell Danielle before everything had fallen to pieces. Even as her mind started rewriting her answer to Paula, she ached for Danielle's arms around her. And even as she pictured going back, she still wanted to scream at her. Jenna reclined her seat and closed her eyes, falling through the waters of sadness.

❖

Jenna stirred as the chime of her phone sounded. She slowly came out of the disorientation, realizing she was in her car. She'd fallen asleep parked in the driveway. She adjusted her seat upright and stretched, then checked the time. It was only six in the morning. She had three missed calls and a voice mail, all from Danielle. A mixture of warmth and dread made her stomach plummet.

She'd been too harsh. Danielle only reacted to what was a very disturbing photo, and Jenna hadn't given her the time or freedom to go through those emotions. And then she disappeared. She left Danielle to think, well, to think anything. To think it was over, probably.

Jenna put her phone to her ear and listened to the voice mail. Danielle's apology was simple and accompanied by a request for a call. Basic, but her voice was obviously trembling. Jenna called Danielle back, but it went to voice mail. Her stomach twisted. She overreacted, and now the tables had turned. Without taking another second to think, she started her car and drove back to Danielle's.

She ran up the stairs of the apartment complex and knocked on the door. Her heart pounded as she waited for an answer. She jolted, then breathed in relief when the lock turned with a clunk, but it was Brianna who filled the frame when the door swung open. Her eyelids were heavy, and she swayed like she was still drunk from the night before.

"Hey," Jenna said into the dark apartment.

"Hello again." Brianna appeared to wake up the rest of the way as she said it.

"Can I come in?" Jenna asked. "Or could you maybe tell Danielle I'm here? I don't want to intrude."

"Danielle isn't here."

"What?"

"She left about an hour ago."

"At five in the morning?"

"Yep. A little strange," Brianna agreed, shrugging. "Seemed kind of upset. She goes to the gym sometimes when she's like that. You guys done already?"

"No," Jenna said. "I mean, I hope not."

Brianna clicked her tongue. "That doesn't sound good."

"It was just a little disagreement."

"Ah, well, it's probably for the best."

"What do you mean?"

"We've been talking about committing for a while now. This probably simplifies things for her. I think she might have been a little torn."

Jenna felt the color draining from her face. Her palms were sweating but numb, a sensation she'd never felt before.

"I don't take it personally," Brianna said. "I can see why. You're beautiful and smart and everything. But Danielle and I have history."

"What do you mean, history?"

Brianna's eyebrows raised in surprise. "Oh, shit," she said. "She didn't tell you?"

"Tell me what?"

Brianna scratched the back of her neck. "I probably shouldn't be the one—"

"It's a bit late for that."

"We used to be a couple. I thought you knew. It's been a lot more casual than that for a while now, just a night here and there, but we've been tossing around the idea of being exclusive again."

Jenna narrowed her eyes. "I don't believe you."

"Okay." Brianna scoffed. "Did you notice that ring she's been wearing all of a sudden? I gave it to her."

Jenna felt fumes gathering her chest. She could barely breathe. She wanted to shove her way inside and talk to Danielle, but she knew she wasn't there. That much felt true.

"Oh jeez, you still don't believe me," Brianna said. She leaned close to Jenna's ear and mimicked the sound of Danielle's orgasm. Shock rattled through her, and she shoved Brianna away, knocking her a good three paces back. Brianna just laughed as her jostled red locks settled again.

"I wanted to try for a threesome with you that night we all went out, but she didn't think you'd go for it. I think it was a little greedy of her to keep you all to herself, but at least she got you out of her system."

"Fuck you."

The door slammed the second she turned her back.

CHAPTER TWENTY-SIX

Danielle couldn't figure Jenna out. She tried to call Jenna repeatedly from the moment she left the apartment, but hadn't gotten through. When she saw the missed call from her and heard from Brianna that she stopped by, she assumed Jenna must be ready to talk, but then she disappeared again. The silence that stretched across the rest of the weekend was agonizing. Danielle had never been more eager to go to work in her life, knowing she would finally run into Jenna whether she liked it or not.

She pulled into the lot early, grateful to see Jenna's car already there. She nearly jumped out of the driver's seat and power walked inside. The halls were empty, and Danielle had the bizarre thought pop into her head that Jenna might have spent the night here. When she made it to Jenna's office, the door was cracked open and Jenna's back was turned as she looked out the window.

"Hey," Danielle said. Jenna spun. She was in crisp, pressed clothes as usual that had been tailored to her perfect form. Her hair fell in their natural, loose curls, which Danielle loved, but probably meant Jenna hadn't been able to summon the effort to straighten them. Danielle could tell she'd been crying. Her heart ached knowing she'd caused those tears. She'd overstepped in her reaction to the pictures of Deon.

"Hey," Jenna said. Danielle's stomach twisted at the hollowness in Jenna's voice. She didn't know why she expected a warm greeting. Jenna was ignoring her calls. She didn't want to see her, wouldn't see her if she didn't have to. If they didn't work together would it be over just like that?

"Jenna, I'm really sorry," Danielle said. "Can I please come in? Can I talk to you?"

"If you want." Jenna walked toward her desk. She sat on the corner and looked at Danielle expectantly.

"Brianna told me you came by. I thought maybe you wanted to…" Danielle stopped, unsure how to finish.

"I'm surprised she told you."

"What? Why?"

Jenna scoffed and looked at the opposite wall. "She wants you for herself."

Danielle stepped the rest of the way into the office and sat in the chair in front of Jenna, letting her elbows rest on her knees as she leaned toward her. "What are you talking about?"

"Please don't act clueless," Jenna said. "It'll only make it worse."

Danielle felt physically pushed back by the words. What in the hell had Brianna said? Jenna's stare was burning into her, and she knew she had to answer, but she felt no answer would be right.

"She tried something recently," Danielle said. "But it was stupid, Jenna. Nothing happened. She was just drunk. She didn't mean it."

"She meant it," Jenna said. "And according to her, you're interested."

"What?" Danielle felt anger burning through her. "She said that?"

Jenna just nodded. It felt like she was a million miles away. Danielle wanted to reach out and touch her, to fix it, to pull her back, but she wasn't welcome to do so.

"Jenna, that's complete bullshit. I'm not interested in her. She's just attention seeking. She says and does crazy things when she's drunk. You can't take her seriously."

"Is that how you talk to her about me? I'm crazy? It's nothing?"

Danielle stood up, pushing the chair away with the back of her knees, fuming.

"Of course not. I told you Brianna is an alcoholic. I told you she was going to act crazy if we went over there, and now you've seen her pull one of her stunts. Don't let her bullshit get to you. Don't let it screw us up." Danielle walked over to the corner of the desk and touched Jenna's face, searching for some sign of affection beneath her anger and suspicion. Jenna endured the touch for a few seconds, but stayed shut to Danielle, and she pulled her hand softly away, letting it land on her knee.

"That's a nice ring," she said. "New?"

Danielle was disoriented by the subject change. "What? Yes. Jenna, please look at me."

Jenna looked up, her eyes glimmering with the battle between tears and glass.

"Do you really think I'd do that to you?"

Jenna shrugged, and Danielle could feel a crack forming in her heart. "We didn't talk about being exclusive," Jenna said. "I guess I assumed we were, but I can't say it's insane to me that you might be interested in Brianna. She's pretty. You live together. You're obviously close. Just because I thought we were on our way to something doesn't mean you did."

"But I did, Jenna. Please hear me. Brianna just has a certain number of drinks and she starts acting—"

"It wasn't drunken babbling, Danielle. She said things. She knew things."

"What things?"

Voices in the hall made them both pause. Danielle turned to close the door.

"Don't," Jenna said.

"Jenna—"

"Paula talked to me Friday. Someone told her about us. We can't be in here together with the door closed."

"What? How?" Danielle spun. "Who?"

"I don't know."

"Are you kidding me? When were you going to tell me?"

"I meant to Friday night. Remember I said I had something to tell you? But things went off the tracks."

"Is that why you're doing this? You want out, but it's easier for you if you tell yourself I was cheating on you?"

"Actually, I was going to put in for a transfer so we can be together."

"Oh." Danielle's head was spinning. "That's great, if you're sure."

"I'm not sure, Danielle. How could I be sure right now? I have to tell Paula something today, and I have no idea what to do anymore. Brianna tells me one thing; you tell me something else."

"How could you believe her over me?" Danielle fought the lump in her throat. She refused to get dramatic.

"I won't," Jenna said. "I'm going to ask you something, and I'm going to believe what you tell me. But, Danielle, I love my job, okay? I love my friends. I care about my cases. Nashville is three hours away. I'll have to move somewhere between here and there to make it all work. I'll do all that. I'll transfer, and I'll be happy with it if we're for real, but if I throw this away and I find out you were playing me I will never forgive you."

"I swear—"

"How does Brianna know what you sound like when you come?"

Danielle felt like she'd been slapped in the face. The edges of her vision seemed to close and tunnel. She could lie. She could say they were roommates, that Brianna had overheard her with someone in the past. She had the distinct feeling it was the only way she could win Jenna back, but it wasn't the truth, and she'd already hidden it too long. She sighed.

"We used to date."

Jenna looked away and shook her head.

"I should have told you." Danielle gathered Jenna's hands in hers. "I was going to tell you Friday. Remember I said I had something to tell you too?"

"I don't understand," Jenna said. "Why didn't you just tell me right away? Were you considering going back to her?"

"No. That was never part of it, Jenna. I swear. It was just that you already thought I should kick Brianna out when I told you she was an alcoholic. I was afraid if I told you this too you'd be jealous and try to make me throw her out, and I can't do that. She won't make it on her own. It's important to me to help her, but we're not together."

"God, I feel like such an idiot," Jenna said.

"I'm so sorry," Danielle said. She searched Jenna for a hint of what she was thinking. She had to understand. Danielle had to convince her.

Jenna shook her head, waiting for the new voices in the hall to pass. "I can't do this."

Danielle's heart fell into her stomach, and she tried to cover her surprise. She stared into Jenna, but she couldn't penetrate her armor.

"I'm sorry, Jenna. But there's nothing going on with Brianna. There hasn't been in a long time. Please believe me."

"I want to, but this whole time I've been telling you all this stuff about myself, stuff I don't tell anyone. I told you everything about the case, and you judged me. I told you about my family, and you judged them. And this whole time I didn't press you about your past, and now I find out you kept it a secret to control my reaction. I've been risking everything for you, and you wouldn't do it back. You couldn't even trust me to understand you, like I would force you to do something you didn't want to? And now I'm supposed to give up my career while Brianna tells me what you're like in bed? I'm supposed to trust you even more? I can't, Danielle. I'm sorry."

Danielle was shaken. Her throat felt swollen, and her chest burned, but she wouldn't let herself cry. Not in front of Jenna. Not at work. She thought about asking for another chance. She thought about apologizing again. She even thought about begging, but she couldn't do any of that. She made a mess of things, and even though it seemed like too much to end things entirely, it would be better for Jenna. Why beg for a relationship that was going to be a problem simply by existing? How could she expect Jenna to take her up on that?

She just nodded in the absence of her ability to form words. She was shocked how bad it hurt. It hadn't been that long. It shouldn't hurt so bad.

"I understand," she finally managed. She couldn't look at Jenna again. She'd fall apart. She turned and left, straining to hear Jenna's call after her that wasn't there.

CHAPTER TWENTY-SEVEN

Jenna wasted the entire day staring at her computer screen rereading lines she would never focus on long enough to understand. She just wanted to go home and fall apart. The workday was winding to a close by the time she opened a blank email.

Her dead fingers ran across the keyboard in a mechanical flurry as she crafted the letter to Paula Caliery. She passed on the transfer and threw herself at the feet of whatever discipline was deemed appropriate. She was disgusted calling Danielle a momentary indiscretion. She cried as she promised it was over, that she would sign the documents, and that they could work together professionally. And then she hit send without indulging the urge to linger over it. It was done.

She didn't notice Sasha filling her doorway until she pointedly cleared her throat. Jenna looked up, and Sasha came inside and closed the door.

"You okay?" she asked.

"Yeah."

"You've been crying."

"I'm fine."

"You bailed on drinks."

"Yeah."

Sasha sat in one of the chairs on the opposite side of her desk. They were meant for guests, for business, clients, but all Jenna had experienced with them so far was personal drama.

"Door is closed," Sasha said. "You can tell me."

Jenna stared at her lap and shook her head.

"Do they have the room bugged? You under that tight of surveillance?"

Jenna cracked a smile and looked at Sasha, torn between her need for a friend and her suspicion. "Was it you?"

"No," Sasha said, then smiled. "What are we talking about?"

"Someone told Paula."

"Told Paula what, honey? Full sentences. Were you smoking weed in the bathroom or something?"

"About Danielle. I know you knew; you told me not to go there."

"Shit," Sasha said. "Someone told Paula." Sasha's sympathy read genuine, but Jenna still felt beat up by her broken trust with Danielle.

"And I'm your best suspect?" Sasha asked. "You must be hurting for clues."

"You're the only one who knew."

"No, I'm the only one who said something. And I said something because I *didn't* want Paula to find out."

"Who else knew?"

Sasha shrugged. "I'm not sure. No one said anything to me. I just assume if I could figure it out other people could too."

"So, it wasn't you?"

"Of course not."

"If it was, just tell me. Please. I can't handle any more bullshit."

"Jenna Ann Thompson, I'll let you accuse me once, but I'm not prepared to accept you think so little of our friendship that you truly believe I would do that to you."

Jenna felt a tear spill down her cheek, and she let Sasha hug her even though she knew it would open the floodgates. She let a few more tears fall before she pushed Sasha gently away and wiped her cheeks dry.

Sasha checked her watch. "You want to grab a beer?"

"Not really."

"You obviously didn't get fired, so I have to assume the tears are something else. As your best friend, I demand you come out for beer. Or we can go to my place, or yours. Wherever."

Jenna laughed, and as weak and forced as it was, it felt good. She nodded.

"Okay, but wine, not beer. And your place? I don't really want to go out, and Callie just yelled at me for bringing someone over last week. I don't want to deal with another fight with her."

Sasha visibly held back what she wanted to say. "Yep, my place it is, and we're adding that to our list of topics to cover."

"All right, but save it for the second bottle."

"Deal."

Jenna grabbed her jacket and draped it over her arm, then shoved her work laptop into her bag.

Sasha scoffed. "Don't even bother. You're not working tonight."

"It's for tomorrow. I'm working from home."

"I like your style, Thompson. She gets in trouble, and she reacts by cutting out early to drink and stays home the next day."

"Well, jeez, don't talk me out of it."

"I wouldn't dream of it. After you."

They headed for the parking lot together. Jenna felt like everyone was watching her. Every person that passed, she wondered if they knew, what they'd heard, if they were the one who told. She knew in some measure people just liked knowing secrets. They liked to gossip, but she couldn't help but feel at least somewhat personally attacked. Whoever told Paula knew she would get in significant trouble, and they'd done it in spite of that, or maybe because of it.

When they got to the lot, Jenna saw Danielle. She was leaned against the front of her car staring at her phone. She felt Sasha and Danielle both studying her, and she knew her cheeks were coloring under the pressure. It felt like a month since she'd seen Danielle, not a handful of hours. Her insides felt like they were collapsible, crashing into her gut.

"Meet you at your place," Jenna said.

"You sure? We can just go in my car if you want. I'm planning to get you too drunk to drive."

"I'm planning to oblige, but at the very least I'll need to drive home in the morning."

"Okay, see you there then."

When they parted ways, Jenna could feel Danielle scrutinizing her, watching the exchange. Jenna would go crazy guessing at what she might be thinking, so she quickly resolved not to entertain the possibilities. She tried to strike the balance of not walking with her nose in the air avoiding Danielle's eyes, but also not meeting them, where she was sure she'd drown. Jenna's entire body flexed anticipating Danielle saying something, but she didn't.

When she finally pulled up in front of Sasha's house she breathed with relief. She opened the door without knocking, reminding herself how good of friends they were. If anyone could make her feel better, it was Sasha, though she had her doubts tonight.

"Crackin' into it now," Sasha said from the kitchen as she worked on the corkscrew. Jenna sat on Sasha's brown cloth couch. Her whole house felt tan, the walls light tan, the carpets dark tan, the furniture brown or wooden. She'd teased Sasha about it more than once in the past, but it felt warm tonight, comforting. Sasha emerged from the kitchen and handed Jenna a glass of wine, then settled into the chair that was angled to face the couch.

"So?" she said. "Hit me with it."

"Danielle and I broke up."

Sasha raised her hand as she was taking a large gulp of wine. "Pause, don't forget you have to start from the beginning because you haven't been telling me a damn thing!" Sasha scowled at her. "I knew I saw some pretty serious vibes going on between you, but broke up means you were a couple. Did you guys get serious?"

"I don't know. It feels kind of stupid when you say it that way. We didn't even know each other that long. But..." Jenna paused. "Yeah, it was serious."

"I can't believe you didn't tell me this."

"I couldn't," Jenna said. "It was a secret."

"A secret you knew I knew."

"But you didn't approve. I didn't want to make you part of it. And it all went by so fast. I spent the first half of it telling myself it wasn't happening, but it was."

"I'll say."

"Well, that's it," Jenna said. "That's what's going on."

"Jenna, I've known you a long time, and I know you don't get serious with girls lightly. If you're in love with her you can't let this job stop you. It's a good job, but there are lots of good jobs, and your résumé is beautiful."

"You think I should quit my job for her?"

"No, not necessarily, but you could, you know? You'd be okay. I just hate to see you crying at work. It's kind of the poster image for not worth it."

"It wasn't the job that broke us up."

"Oh." Sasha retrieved the bottle of wine, refilling their glasses and keeping the bottle at hand. "What happened?"

"You remember her roommate, the one that came to the party?"

"Yes," Sasha dragged out the word.

"Ex-girlfriend slash roommate slash pining lover."

"Oh God." Sasha put her palm to her forehead. "So, there's something going on there?"

Jenna shrugged, suddenly feeling more angry than anything else. "Hell if I know. Brianna told me there was."

"And Danielle?"

"She says not for a long time, but she also told me Brianna was just a friend. She never fessed up that they dated, not until I made it very clear I already knew. And she has no intention of kicking Brianna out. She says it's important to her to help Brianna with her alcohol problem. Even if Danielle and I can get past this, she'll still be living with Brianna. It would drive me crazy. How can I believe her now? I don't want to be that jealous girl that questions everything out of someone's mouth. I don't like to act that way, and I don't like the feeling."

"I hear you," Sasha said. "If Brianna is really an alcoholic mess I can't believe Danielle is hung up on her."

Jenna shrugged. "Maybe she's not such a mess. Maybe that's a lie. I have no idea what to think anymore."

"You really think it was all bullshit? I saw the way she looked at you. It looked real."

Jenna felt tears tickling the back of her eyes. "I thought so too, but I just don't know, and I had to answer Paula today about what I'm going to do. I told her I ended it. I just couldn't transfer, leave all you guys, for a maybe."

"Dang. Makes sense."

"So that's that."

"I guess so," Sasha said. She hugged Jenna. "You going to be okay?"

"Of course," Jenna said, but she didn't feel it. She couldn't believe how broken she felt, how much she ached for Danielle already. The moments of anger she was able to muster here and there were nothing next to the overwhelming sadness and yearning she felt the rest of the time.

"And I want to know who the hell ratted me out."

Sasha shrugged. "I really can't help you with that, kid. I have no idea."

"Paula wouldn't say."

"Course not."

"Am I hated and I don't know it?" Jenna asked.

"Oh, honey, of course not. You're our favorite."

"Obviously not."

"Did you…" Sasha paused to chuckle. "Did you get affectionate in public? Maybe it was a client?"

Jenna shook her head. "Impossible."

"It could be anyone," Sasha said. "You'll probably never know. And even if you found out you'd just hate them, and you wouldn't be able to do anything about it. It's probably better you don't know."

Jenna sighed. "You're right. It's bad enough I'm going to have to try to act normal working with Danielle. I don't need a war with someone on top of it. I just hate thinking I'm walking around being friends with someone who did that."

Jenna's phone buzzed from the coffee table. Sasha and Jenna both stared at it without moving, then looked at each other.

"Want me to look?" Sasha asked.

"Yes."

Sasha picked up the phone. "It's just Callie. She wants to know when you're coming home to…" Sasha squinted. "To make her dinner? Oh, hell no, why do you put up with this crap, Jenna? She's twenty damn years old."

Jenna grabbed the phone. Sasha tried to keep it, but Jenna wrenched it away. Sasha laughed.

"You better be telling her to get off her ass and eat some cereal straight from the box like every other person on the planet who doesn't want to cook."

"I'm telling her I'm not coming home and to order."

"So she can burn a hole in your wallet instead of your shoes? Seriously, Jenna, cut her off."

Jenna sent the text and threw her phone back on the table. "What do you mean cut her off? She's not the average twenty-year-old, Sash. She can't even leave the house. She's terrified of people. It might be unreasonable, but it's very real to her."

"What does that have to do with going into the kitchen and cooking her own meals?"

"Nothing." Jenna sighed. "She just needs a lot of help."

"No, she doesn't. They're just scars. It's terrible, you know I appreciate that, but she's physically capable. She's taking advantage of you."

"Not intentionally. She just..." Jenna paused. "I don't know, it's like she stopped growing up when the burns happened. She's just stuck in that frame of mind. It's a trauma thing. It's real."

"I know it's real, honey, but it's not okay. You feel guilty about what happened, and she knows that. She uses it to make you wait on her hand and foot. And you let her."

"I know." Jenna sighed.

Sasha opened her mouth, ready to make her next point, but stopped in surprise. "You do?"

"Sure," Jenna said. "I'm not blind. I know it's a problem, and I'm trying to help her onto the right path. Cutting her off or throwing her out or whatever you're suggesting won't fix it, though. Wherever I failed along the way to make her a functioning adult, I need to figure out how to fix it. I raised a girl who has no idea how to make it in the world. It's hardly fair to throw her into that world just to rid myself of a nuisance."

"I think you're simplifying quite a bit."

"Maybe." Jenna shrugged. "But I can't just abandon her."

"No one is saying anything about abandoning her, girl. Just start with making her feed herself."

Jenna fell into a fit of laughter as the absurdity of Callie's refusal to make her own dinner hit her. Her head was swimming with wine. She downed the rest of the glass and stretched out on the couch.

"God, I just want to stop thinking about them. Both of them."

CHAPTER TWENTY-EIGHT

Danielle opened the door to the apartment in a fury, determined to hold on to the feeling even though it was the sadness that really wanted her. Brianna wasn't in the living room for once. Danielle didn't for a second believe that was coincidence. She stormed into Brianna's bedroom and found it was empty too.

Danielle went into the kitchen and poured a rare, stiff drink. If Brianna thought staying out until four in the morning was going to protect her, she was mistaken. She'd have to come home at some point, and Danielle resolved to sit at the dining table staring at the door until she did. She refused to let Brianna avoid the worst of the storm. She refused to give her what she wanted by calming down over time. She should have told Jenna they dated up front, but it was Brianna's lies that shook her trust so deeply, that had planted the possibility of the worst.

It was three in the morning, and Danielle was fighting sleep when she finally heard Brianna's key slip into the lock. Brianna opened the door slowly, emerging through it in a half crouch as if that would somehow make her quieter. She straightened when she saw Danielle sitting at the table, then smiled and stumbled inside.

"Hey, beautiful! I was trying not to wake you." She glanced at Danielle's drink on the table, then at Danielle. She rushed over and hugged Danielle, her forearm sloppily circling her head like a blindfold. Danielle pried her arm off and slung it away.

"Sit down, Brianna."

"Jeez, someone's a mean drunk."

"Why did you lie to Jenna?"

Brianna's face got serious for a fleeting second, but her eyes quickly went back out of focus. She was trashed.

"Who said I lied to Jenna?"

"She told me what you said. Why did you do that? Why did you have to fuck everything up?"

"What?" Brianna took on an expression of shock and slumped into the free dining table chair. "I didn't fuck everything up. We were just talking."

"You fucked it all up. You told her I was interested in you."

"It's not my fault you didn't tell her we dated. How was I supposed to know? I didn't know you were ashamed of me." Brianna teared up, and for the first time ever, Danielle didn't care in even the smallest fraction. Her tears were meaningless, manipulative, and soon to be forgotten.

"I know I should have told her; that's not what we're talking about," Danielle said. "I'm asking why you told her we're into each other. We don't even like each other, Brianna."

"We don't? Well, shit, here I thought we were friends."

"Yes, friends! Barely! You think I'm a boring, prissy little prude, and I think you're a drunk. There's nothing romantic between us."

"Look, we might not have worked out as a couple, but that doesn't mean I need you parading your new girlfriend around in front of me. Have some respect."

Danielle laughed. "You told me to bring her here, you psycho! Did you just want to trick me into doing it so you could sabotage us?"

Brianna pushed her chair back from the table. "'Kay you've called me a drunk and a psycho now. I'm not talking to you while you're like this."

"Like what? Drunk? It's a pain in the ass, isn't it, Brianna?" Danielle stood up and got in her way. "Really sucks when people just say whatever pops into their fucking heads with no regard for the consequences, doesn't it?"

"Get the fuck out of my face, Danielle!"

"She asked how you know what I sound like when I come. What the fuck did you say to her? What did you do? How could she even…" Danielle held her hands up, feeling them shake with rage.

Brianna smirked. "Is that what you two are all twisted about? Jesus, get over it. I was just playing around. You know how I am. She wasn't supposed to get all riled over it."

"I don't believe you. You knew what you were doing. Upsetting her was exactly what you wanted."

Brianna shrugged and tried to pass again, but Danielle was still in the way and Brianna was too tipsy to navigate around the furniture. "Move!"

"Do you even care that you broke us up? Do you have a conscience at all?"

"You know what, Danielle, if Jenna was so into you and you guys were so perfect, she'd have heard you out, and she'd have gotten over it. You were dating for two seconds. She could have given you another chance. You want to know the truth? She was out of your league, and she didn't like you that much. She's sexy, has a good job, and she's *fun*. She was taking shots with me at the bar that night we went out. She didn't freak out like a giant baby like you did when I threw up; she told you to chill. What does she need with someone like you? She's like me. It was a matter of time before she got bored with you, just like I did."

"Is that what this is all about?" Danielle asked. "You wanted her, and you didn't get why she wanted me, so you had to ruin it?"

"Please, I don't care about either of you."

"That's not how you acted when you talked to Jenna."

Brianna's eyes were pools of confusion, unable to focus. She was clearly no longer following the conversation. Danielle felt like she witnessed the exact moment Brianna lost track of what was going on. She'd have to start completely over to make her way to the point. Danielle finally let her pass. Brianna tripped on the shoes she had taken off seconds before and stumbled onto the couch. She put her head down and resolved to just stay there.

"Don't think you can talk to me in the morning just because you sobered up," Danielle said, and headed for her bedroom.

"Huh?" Brianna's head shot off the couch as if she'd just woken up. "Danielle?"

Danielle shook her head and flexed her muscles with frustration. Brianna would be completely confused by Danielle's refusal to speak with her by morning. She could say anything she wanted, and it would be forgotten. Part of her wanted to abuse that fact, but the other part felt completely powerless because of it.

"Danielle!" Brianna said. "Help me get to bed. I can't walk."

"Fuck you."

CHAPTER TWENTY-NINE

Jenna insisted on driving home at seven in the morning when Sasha got up to go to work, but everything ached with heaviness. When she got home, she went directly to her bed and flopped down again. She'd barely closed her eyes when her reminder to give her mom her medication dinged on her phone. She opened up a text to Callie and asked her to do it, but thirty seconds from the time it showed she'd read the message, Callie was barging into her room.

"When did you get home?"

Jenna groaned and rolled over. "Just now."

"You stay out all night ignoring everything here and you want me to do you favors?"

Jenna put the pillow over her head. "Not today, Callie."

"Do you even care about us anymore? Don't you care if Mom gets her medication?"

"Yes, that's why I asked you. Some people might even call it you doing your share, you know? Not a favor."

"What is going on with you, Jenna? You're not acting like yourself anymore. Ever since you met that girl."

Jenna scoffed and pulled the pillow tighter over her head. "Seriously, not right now."

Callie sat on the edge of her bed. She yanked the pillow away. Jenna slapped the bed and sat up.

"What?"

Callie recoiled from the harshness, surprise filling her face and stopping her in her tracks.

"Are you okay?"

"No, Callie. I'm really not."

"Do you need…" Callie paused as if she'd never offered help in her life, as if she had no idea how to end the sentence. "Something?"

"I need you to give Mom her meds."

"But she doesn't listen to me, Jenna. I can't talk her into it like you can."

"Fine." Jenna flung the covers aside and stood up.

"Jenna—"

"I'm doing it."

"Jenna, wait, what happened? What's going on?" Callie grabbed her arm, spinning her back around.

"Nothing is going on. I don't feel well. I just want to go to bed."

"Bullshit. You've been acting weird for weeks. You're always out with that Danielle. You don't take care of anything around here anymore. You've barely even noticed Mom losing control. If Danielle is telling you—"

"Do you want me to hang out somewhere else so you don't have to see people or do you want me to be here, Callie? You can't have both. You can't force me not to have friends. And Danielle isn't telling me anything. We broke up. I know you're thrilled."

"Oh," Callie said. "I'm sorry."

Jenna shook her head. "No, you're not."

"I'm sorry it's hurting you," Callie said. "You can do better, though, Jenna."

"You didn't even know her."

"No, but she kept you away. She didn't understand our situation here, or she wouldn't have done that."

Jenna paused. Callie was both completely wrong and a little right. Danielle hadn't kept her away from home, not any more than any girlfriend would, but she did feel like Danielle didn't completely understand her family situation.

"Did it ever occur to you that maybe I would have been home more if you'd been more welcoming to her?" Jenna asked. "If you'd let her get to know and understand us and be in our home without being attacked?"

"So, it's my fault? Is that why you're being so shitty to me? I'm sorry, Jenna. I'm sorry I was a bitch that night you brought her over, and I'm sorry you two broke up."

"I—" Jenna felt blindsided by the apology. "Thanks."

"So, what happened?"

Jenna shook her head. "It's a long story."

"You'll find someone else," Callie said. "Someone better."

Jenna laughed lightly. "It's not that simple, Cal. Connection doesn't just happen every day."

Callie shrugged. "You'll still find it. You're amazing. You could have anyone."

Jenna's heart felt heavy. She couldn't imagine doing better than Danielle, and even if she theoretically could, she still wouldn't be able to just brush Danielle off as casually as Callie wanted to. She couldn't even picture someone better. Danielle was perfect. Kind, smart, motivated, deep, gorgeous. Their connection had been so easy, so instant. But she had to be able to trust her. She refused to be an insecure, jealous lover, and she didn't think she could be otherwise with Danielle right now. The whole time she thought they were effortlessly sharing all of themselves, Danielle was holding back. She was only now realizing how much she didn't know about Danielle. Maybe she'd been falling in love alone.

Danielle made her way to Mr. Borden's office. It was a few doors down and across the hall from Jenna's. She'd seen it, and Mr. Borden, in passing, but the email she received that directed her there this morning had perplexed her. She knocked on the half-open door as she stuck her head through the opening.

"Danielle, come on in," Mr. Borden said. Danielle tentatively entered and sat down. Mr. Borden had a lumpy appearance. He had a fat neck, and his hair was the plainest of browns. He wore a button-down checkered shirt that was one size too small and would be hard-pressed to sell as business casual, let alone formal. Combined with the set of golf clubs in the corner, Danielle doubted Mr. Borden did much work. Danielle cringed at the moisture on his palm as she shook his hand.

"Call me Chuck."

"Sure," Danielle said. "Chuck."

"I called you in here just to touch base, get to know each other a little. I like to have a little face time with all my crew members."

Danielle knew she was doing little to cover her dread and horror. "Your crew? I'm sorry, are you saying I'm on your team now?"

"Yep," Chuck said. "Welcome."

"I was on Jenna's team," Danielle said. "She didn't quit, did she? Or…"

"Oh no," Chuck said. "She's still here. We just had to rearrange things. I'm sure you understand." Chuck seemed like a nice enough guy. He somehow managed not to be offensive when he tilted his head at her, communicating that they both knew exactly why Danielle couldn't be on Jenna's team anymore.

"Do I get to talk to anyone about this?"

"You get to talk to me." Chuck bent his wrists so that both of his hands showcased his face as he beamed at her. Danielle got the impression that his caricature style gestures were his go-to attempt at humor. "I'm not so bad. I promise."

"No, it isn't that," Danielle said. "I'm sorry. I didn't mean to be rude. It's just that Jenna and I were working really well together, and I don't think we necessarily need to be rearranged. We're both professionals."

"I'm sure you are."

"Did she ask for me to be moved?"

"I don't have or need many details," Chuck said. "But the impression I got was that it is non-negotiable. You could maybe try to get put on a different team, but not hers."

"No," Danielle sighed. "I wouldn't do that. It isn't you."

"Great! Well, I just want you to know as far as I'm concerned, we're starting with a clean slate here. None of your coaching notes with Jenna will be carried over, and the issue between you and Jenna is a matter that's being handled over my head, but I was led to believe it will have no further impact on you."

"Her notes on me aren't being carried over? The warning I received for the whole dead body thing?"

"Nope. All thrown out."

"Why?"

"Well, she's not exactly a credible source on you anymore."

"But…" Danielle paused, perplexed. "But her disciplining me is proof that she *was* a credible source, if anything, isn't it?"

Chuck grimaced. "We're on some testy ground. I can't really go into details on the decisions surrounding Jenna."

"I guess I don't understand why not. I was an involved party. Shouldn't I give a statement or something?"

Chuck shrugged. "Over my head. I know that's not a very satisfying answer, but if I could give you some advice, it would be to let it go. The higher-ups would like to sweep it under the rug, and it benefits you to let them. They're very happy with your work outside of this."

Danielle finally sat down, deflated.

"I was familiarizing myself with your cases," Chuck said. "I see you have a visit with the Clarks scheduled today. I was hoping you could update—"

"What?"

Chuck looked up, showing his first signs of annoyance. "The Clarks. You have a visit today?"

"I don't. Jenna does."

Chuck slipped on a pair of reading glasses that looked ridiculously small on his large, round face and looked at his computer screen again. "Nope, I'm showing it's your case."

"That's a mistake. Jenna has been working that case for years. I was just training with her on it."

"Supervisors don't have cases, Danielle. She was assigned to it in a training capacity, but you've been released from training. It's your case."

"She'll need to supervise the visit," Danielle said.

"If you need a supervisor to accompany you for some reason, it would be me now. Why do you need a supervisor?"

"What? No, I don't need *a* supervisor. Jenna is the only one those boys will talk to. They'll chew me up and spit me out if I show up there without her."

"I understand it will be a transition," Chuck said. "But it's time to make it. Jenna is not permitted to accompany you on visits or supervise you in any fashion. She is to have nothing more to do with the Clarks. I could see about reassigning it to another caseworker if you have some kind of unresolvable issue with the boys, but—"

"No," Danielle said. "No, don't do that. That would be even worse."

"All right, then," Chuck said. "It's settled. As I was saying, if you could give me an update when you get back."

Danielle stood, knowing she was again failing to carry herself professionally or even with plain old kindness. She was interrupting and disrespecting her new supervisor, and she couldn't seem to stop. She could be in much deeper trouble for her hidden relationship with Jenna, and instead of gratitude or relief, all she could feel was anger and resentment. Even as she thought it through she couldn't muster up the ability to thank him and leave with grace. She just huffed out of the office.

Once in the hallway, she couldn't help but stare at Jenna's door. It was half open too, the way it usually was when she was inside working. She glanced back at Chuck's door, then rushed into Jenna's office. Jenna looked up abruptly, confused. There were papers on the floor behind her like they'd been thrown. Danielle saw the picture of Deon among them.

"Jenna, I'm so sorry. I told them it should be your case. I tried."

Jenna leaned back in her chair. "You shouldn't be here. You'll get in trouble."

"I'll tell them it wasn't your choice. I'll make sure they know you wanted to be there."

Jenna nodded slowly. She looked exhausted, not sleepy, just worn out.

"Thanks."

Danielle heard voices coming down the hall and looked at Jenna, paralyzed. Jenna stood up and passed her. Her shoulder brushed Danielle's gently, and her smell circled Danielle and made her knees feel weak. Her closeness felt so right. She just wanted to pull her into her arms. Jenna glanced into the hall and turned back.

"Safe."

Danielle nodded, staring into her. *Forgive me, Jenna. Please.* Her mouth was dry, and she couldn't make the words come out.

"I'll take good care of them," Danielle said. "I promise." She walked into the hallway and away from Jenna's office at the fastest pace she could pass as normal.

CHAPTER THIRTY

Danielle sat in the Clarks' apartment parking lot trying to figure out what she was going to say to the family. She'd been observing their visits for weeks, but she'd barely said a word. It hadn't bothered her at the time, but she realized now Jenna had made almost no effort to pass the case to her. She never wanted to do it. And now the boys weren't ready for her to be in charge any more than she was. More than that, she was afraid of what she might find inside. The decisions were hers now, and her first instincts had almost never been the same as Jenna's.

Her argument with Jenna had shaken her. She had always been confident in her reasoning, in her judgment, but Jenna attacked hers. She hadn't been impressed with Danielle's brand of logic, and she'd made some points that made Danielle doubt everything. But she couldn't do her job with doubt. She had to be able to make decisions and own them, or the job would drive her crazy. She had to make choices she could live with, but she also desperately wanted to honor Jenna's wishes.

She took a deep breath and got out of the car. Step one. She made her way to the apartment door. Step two. But she couldn't seem to make it to step three. She had to knock. She had to really do it. Finally, she tapped, part of her hoping they wouldn't answer.

No such luck. Ladona flung the door open. Her hair was wild, and Danielle felt a twinge of nervousness as she tried to weigh if that meant Ladona was having one of her volatile days. Her face filled with confusion.

"Who are you?"

"My name is Danielle Corey, Ms. Clark. We've met."

"Right," Ladona said. "Of course, we have. You're right. Come on in."

Danielle heard feet stampeding down the stairs, but Deon and Raylon halted halfway down when they saw her.

"Come on down," Danielle said. They continued down the stairs at a walk. "I'd like to have a quick chat with everyone if we could gather down here."

"Where's Ms. Thompson?" Raylon asked.

"She wanted to be here."

"Is she sick?" Raylon was beside her now, his innocent round eyes gleaming up at her.

"Have a seat," she said to all of them. Ladona and Raylon sat, but Deon stayed in the corner with his arms crossed.

"Deon?"

"Where's Jenna?"

"Ms. Thompson," Ladona scolded him.

"Where is she?"

Danielle took a deep breath. "She wanted to be here, Deon."

"She's not coming back, is she?"

"I'll explain everythi—"

"Just answer the question!" Deon yelled.

"Deon, you better mind your manners, boy," Ladona jumped in.

"Your case has been passed on to me," Danielle said. "Ms. Thompson is not going to be coming back."

Ladona's attention snapped from Deon back to Danielle. "She's not coming back at all?"

"She was promoted a little while ago," Danielle said. "She wanted to continue to work with you, but it was decided that it was inappropriate, as she's no longer a caseworker."

"Oh." Ladona's face crinkled with a frown. "I guess that makes sense."

"Is she going to say good-bye?" Raylon asked.

"No, dummy," Deon snapped. "She's seen this coming for weeks, ever since this one started showing up." Deon gestured at Danielle.

"Nuh-uh," Raylon said. "She said nothing was different."

"Yeah, well, she ain't here, is she?" Deon stormed upstairs.

"I'm really sorry, you guys," Danielle said to Ladona and Raylon. "I know you've been working with Jenna for a long time. I know you're close."

Ladona waved her away. "I don't suppose you all are here to be our friends. I'll talk to him," she said. "He'll be fine. You've just got a job to do."

"Yes," Danielle said. "I do want to talk about how things are going to go moving forward."

"What do you mean?"

"I'm familiar with this case," Danielle said slowly. "Both from the files and from talking to Ms. Thompson."

"I would hope so."

"I know the three of you and Ms. Thompson have operated a certain way, had certain understandings."

"I'm not sure what you mean, Ms. Corey."

"Ms. Thompson didn't always report everything," Danielle said. "She told me that, along with everything that's been going on here."

Ladona looked away, her jaw clenched. "Raylon, go on upstairs with your brother." Ladona watched until he reached the top of the stairs, then turned back to Danielle. "I don't know anything about that."

"I'm not trying to trick you," Danielle said.

"You trying to intimidate me?"

"No. I'm not taking any action about any of that. It's all behind us. I just need you to understand that I don't work that way. I'm not hiding anything for you."

Ladona scoffed. "You know you look like a damn teenager? You're a child, sitting there, so eager to be a robot."

"I don't—"

"You could learn a thing or two from Ms. Thompson, sweetheart. She knew how to use her brain, and her heart. Life isn't all about reports."

"I want you to be successful, Ms. Clark. I'm not telling you this to threaten you. I'm telling you this so you don't have the wrong expectations."

"The wrong expectations? I think I've got it, Ms. Corey. There will be no exercising of common sense from you."

"It's not—"

"You know what, I want to talk to your supervisor," she said. "What kind of way is this to start a visit? I don't know you. We don't know you. And you want to jump off trying to intimidate me? Trying to tell me someone did me some kind of favor in the past letting me keep my children? You're just sitting there waiting for reason, aren't you? Isn't that what you're telling me?"

"Not at all." Danielle's heart was racing, but she tried to hide it. "If you really want to talk to my supervisor I can—"

"The hell with your supervisor. You get Ms. Thompson back here. She's the only one out of the lot of you that's a damn human."

"She can't come back."

"Bullshit."

"I'm your—"

"I think you need to leave," Ladona said. "I'm not comfortable with your insinuations. I want someone else."

Danielle sighed. Jenna filled her mind, the things she'd said when Ladona raged at her. Ladona didn't always like Jenna. It didn't have to be a disaster that she was upset.

"Ladona, Jenna and I were close too. It's why she told me everything she did. She trusted me. If you can find a way to trust me too, I promise I care very much about you and your family. I'm more invested than some other random caseworker will be."

"That's not how you're talking."

"I just want you to understand that I have to be able to live with the decisions I make here. If either of your sons got hurt on my watch, I wouldn't be able to forgive myself."

"There's nothing hurting those boys."

"Okay," Danielle said. "But if anything ever does, you need to know it's going into the paperwork. That's all."

"Fine. You done?"

"I'd like to talk to the boys for a minute."

"You're brave."

Danielle laughed lightly. She didn't feel brave. She knew Deon hated her, and she guessed Raylon was well on his way. She walked up the stairs and went to Deon's room, pleased to find Raylon inside with him. She didn't bother asking if she could come in, knowing she'd be in an impossible spot if he said no.

She walked in and sat next to Raylon on the bed, across from Deon, who was in his desk chair like the last time she'd been in his room, with Jenna. Her heart ached. Jenna should be here. She couldn't begin to replace her.

"Hey, guys," she said. "Can I talk to you for a minute?"

"Guess so." Deon glared at her.

"Jenna didn't lie to you, Deon. She meant it when she said she was going to keep coming."

"What happened, then?"

"She got in trouble," Danielle said. He couldn't hide his new interest.

"I thought you said she got promoted."

"She did, a few weeks ago, but she was able to talk them into letting her keep coming for a while. When she got in trouble they wouldn't let her do it anymore."

"In trouble for what?" Raylon asked.

"I can't really talk about it," Danielle said. "And I don't want to tell you to keep secrets from your mother—"

"We won't tell her," Deon said.

"I shouldn't really tell you any of this," Danielle said. "But Jenna trusted you, and I need you to know she cared about you two like family. She would die if you thought she doesn't care."

"She get in trouble because of us?" Deon asked.

"No."

"She seemed to like you," Deon said. "I guess you must be cool."

Danielle smiled. "Think you can give me a chance?"

"Yeah, I guess so." Deon smiled like he was trying not to, an expression so endearing Danielle felt like she was seeing him as Jenna must have. A kid trying to be the man of the house, ill-equipped to do so in many ways, and succeeding in so many others.

CHAPTER THIRTY-ONE

Even a week later, Jenna still felt sick picturing Danielle's visit with Raylon and Deon without her. Especially Deon. She knew he'd feel betrayed, and she was twisted up by the guilt of what he might do. She hated thinking of him skipping school again, fighting with his family, pushing everyone away. She hoped she had overestimated her own importance in his life, but she knew she hadn't. She wanted to text Danielle and ask how it had gone, but there were so many reasons she couldn't.

The reminder for her mom's meds brought her back to her own home, her own family. She wouldn't bother trying to get Callie to help. Every time she let Callie whine her way out of something she heard Sasha's voice in her head, scolding her, but as much as she meant to take a hard stance with Callie, she somehow never seemed to be able to follow through. She always wound up somewhat agreeing with Callie. Her mom *did* respond better to her. She knew that was because Callie never stepped up to do her part, and that maybe it would change over time if she forced her, but forcing her just never seemed quite worth it.

She grabbed her mom's pills out of the kitchen and knocked on her bedroom door. Her mom was sitting cross-legged on her bed, staring at static on the television as it crackled loudly through the room. It was unnerving the first time she saw her mom doing something like that, but it was more or less routine now.

"No signal?" Jenna asked.

"I like it," her mom said. "It feels fuzzy. Drowns out the noise a bit."

Jenna went in and sat by her. "Time for your pills."

"I don't want them."

Jenna took an extra breath. It was exhausting fighting with her mom about pills every day, and her sporadic successes weren't enough. Her mom had to take them as prescribed, but patience was key. The angrier she got, the more her mom thought she had some sinister motive for wanting her to take them.

"All right," she said. "Why don't we just chat for a bit."

"I'd like that," her mom said. She looked over at Jenna and put her hand on her face. "You're such a sweetheart, Jenna. You know I love you, right?"

"I know, Mom. I love you too."

"You've always been my favorite."

Jenna smiled, but her skin crawled with discomfort. "You shouldn't say that."

"I know. I know. We're not supposed to say these things. But I'm only human. You've always taken care of me, Jenna, even when you were little. You've always been so good, so sweet to me."

"Callie was just too young to know how, Mom, that's all. She loves you too."

"No, she doesn't. She just thinks I'm a lunatic."

"That's not true."

"Yes, it is, honey. You don't have to lie for her. I know. It's always been me and you. Your dad never did either of us a bit of good. Your sister never wanted to lift a finger. Always me and you."

Jenna squeezed her mom's hand and hugged her. "I'll always make sure you're okay."

"I know." Her mom smiled. "I need to tell you something, Jenna. It's going to be hard to hear."

"What is it?"

"Your sister has turned against us. It's just us now."

"Turned against us? What are you talking about?" Jenna felt shaken by the subject change. She thought she'd been talking to her mother in a state of lucidity, and it made her stomach turn to realize it was delusion based.

"She's with them, Jenna. I heard her."

"Heard what?"

"She reported you. She's giving them information." Her mom's eyes were like saucers as they stared at her, round and worried but not panicked.

"Giving who information?"

"I don't know." She paused. "She made a phone call, and a machine answered. It was talking about endangered persons. Then she said she wanted to report something anonymously."

Jenna grabbed her mom's hand. "You mean like a recorded message? Those are pretty common now, Mom. It could have been anything."

"She saw me standing there and threw me out after that. I tried to listen at the door, but it was hard to hear. But she said your name, Jenna. She said it more than once. She said she had to report you. She's trying to get rid of us both. I know it."

Jenna tried to picture who Callie could have been calling. Almost everything was under her name, so she could easily have said Jenna's name to pull up an account. Maybe her phone or the cable company. But she had to admit, Callie wasn't one to take initiative on fixing those issues.

"I'll ask her about it."

"No!" Her mom leaned forward. "Don't tell her you know, Jenna. It's your only upper hand."

"Callie isn't the enemy, Mom. She couldn't get by without us. She wouldn't try to get rid of us."

"I know what I heard, Jenna. It wasn't the voices. I heard it with my own ears. She reported you."

"That just doesn't—"

"Promise me you won't tell her I told you. Just watch her. You'll see."

Jenna didn't want to agree, but she knew her mom wouldn't let her out of the room until she did.

"If I say yes will you take your pills?"

Her mom looked her in the eye for a long time. "They make me foggy, Jenna. I can't think on them. I won't be able to help you. You'll have to look out for yourself. I have to know you're looking out for yourself. You have to believe me about Callie. She's talking to someone about you. She's lying about you to the government. I know it."

"Okay," Jenna said. "I'll look out for myself. I promise."

Her mom took the pills from her palm and popped them into her mouth. Jenna waited until she was sure the pills would dissolve in case her mom was trying to cheek them. When Jenna left the room, she expected her mom's accusations to stay behind, but Jenna found the words swirling through her mind again and again. A machine talking about endangered persons. Her sister reporting something anonymously, saying her name. Callie wouldn't need to be anonymous for any of the logical possibilities she could come up with.

Her mom had made plenty of unfounded accusations in the past. She thought everyone was talking to the government, that everyone was out to get her. But she didn't usually get so specific. She didn't usually make sense.

Jenna went to the kitchen to find some food. Callie was lying on the couch watching TV. She didn't look up when Jenna came in. Jenna eyed her cell phone sitting on the dining table while it charged. It was right there.

She shook her head. She didn't need to snoop through Callie's phone. It was ridiculous to subscribe to her schizophrenic mom's suspicions. She opened the fridge and stood in front of it for a full minute before she realized she wasn't processing anything. She finally grabbed a container of grapes and took them to the dining table. She stared at Callie's phone as she popped a grape in her mouth. She glanced over at Callie on the couch. She wasn't moving a muscle. She might even be asleep.

On impulse, Jenna grabbed the phone and opened it. She went into the call history and scrolled. Jenna was the last several outgoing calls, followed by outgoing calls to two phone numbers with no names attached to them. The first was the phone number for CPS. Jenna quickly dismissed it, assuming Callie had tried to call her at work when she hadn't answered her cell. The second looked vaguely familiar, but she couldn't place it.

Jenna fished her own phone out of her pocket and punched in the number. She closed Callie's phone and went upstairs before she did anything with it. When she closed her bedroom door she hit send, and Paula Caliery's name popped up on her screen. She hit end, feeling her blood drain.

Callie called her boss. Callie called her boss and said she wanted to report something anonymously. Jenna felt sweat gathering on her palms. A stone formed in her chest, and she felt it might drag her to the floor. She'd called a week and a half ago, the day before Paula had pulled her into the office to tell her someone informed her she and Danielle were having a relationship. It wasn't Sasha. It wasn't some mystery coworker. Her own sister turned her in. Her own sister nearly got her fired. And part of her couldn't believe she hadn't seen it coming. Callie hated Danielle. She hated that Jenna was spending her time anywhere but home, with anyone else.

Her mom was right. Callie had turned on her.

CHAPTER THIRTY-TWO

Jenna's phone buzzed. It was subdued, barely enough of a vibration to move it across the surface of her slippery desk. She didn't have to look to know who it was, but she still did. Some part of her was enjoying watching Callie's name light up, linger, and disappear. She'd never ignored Callie before. No matter how angry or stressed she was, she always bent to her, imagining some horrific scene if she didn't. But Callie was an adult now. They both were. And she finally felt more like a sister, a friend, even an enemy at the moment, than a mother. It was time for Callie to see the results of hurting people.

She couldn't pretend it was all tough love, though. She wasn't just teaching Callie a much-needed lesson. It hurt. Callie's betrayal hurt her to the core. Text messages flooded her screen. A few words jumped out and registered, but she wouldn't read the full thing. Where. Fuck. Answer. She got the picture.

Jenna's desk phone rang, and she shook her head before she picked up.

"Thompson."

"Hi, Ms. Thompson. I've got a young lady on the line asking for you."

"Could you take a message, please?"

"Yes, I saw that you're unavailable, Ms. Thompson. I'm sorry, but she's called several times, and now she's saying it's an emergency."

Jenna felt her jaw tighten. She wanted to accept the transfer and immediately hang up, but Callie would call back and she couldn't afford to make a scene.

"Go ahead and put her through," she said. The young receptionist told Callie she was connected, and Jenna waited until she heard the click of her disconnecting before she spoke.

"Do you honestly have no regard for my work at all?"

"I tried your cell a billion times."

"Which should have been an indicator that I'm busy. I'm working, Callie."

"Don't you even care what the emergency is?"

"You not liking the food in the fridge isn't an emergency. Nor is running out of serum, wanting a milkshake, or being pissed I didn't answer on the first ring."

"It's Mom, ass."

"I'll talk to her when I get home. I have to go, Callie."

"She's on her way to your work."

"What?" Jenna stood up.

"Told you it's an emergency. She's probably almost there by now since you wouldn't answer."

"Why didn't you stop her?"

"Right, just tackle her and drag her to the basement and lock her up?"

"Talk her down, Callie. Be *kind*."

"You can't honestly think it's that simple."

"I do it all the time, Callie. It *is* that simple."

"Well, she's already gone."

Jenna felt an angry groan rumbling in her chest.

"I'm sorry you don't like having a freak show of a family, Jenna, but you do."

"I don't mind freak shows. I mind selfishness and laziness." Jenna slammed the phone on the receiver. She looked out her office window into the parking lot and searched for the Volkswagen. When she didn't spot it, she hurried out of her office, hoping she could catch her mom in the parking lot.

When she reached the ground level she heard her mom's voice and grimaced in dread.

"Jenna Thompson!" her mom screamed at the receptionist. "Where are you keeping her? What have you done to her?"

Jenna circled the corner. "Mom," she called out. Her mother spun. She looked wild. Her face was contorted with fear. She ran over and wrapped her arms around Jenna.

"Sorry, Ms. Thompson." Jenna recognized the receptionist's voice who had just transferred Callie to her. The poor thing had been berated by two of her family members in a matter of minutes. "She doesn't have an ID. We didn't want to—"

"It's okay." Jenna wrapped her arm around her mom, guiding her away from the desk. "Mom, what are you doing here?"

"I woke up, and you weren't there. And your sister…" Her mom checked over her shoulder. "I know she had you taken away. I told you she's been scheming. She lied about you and they came to get you."

"No one came to get me. I'm right here. I just had to work."

"They didn't come?"

"No, Mom. No one's coming."

"But your sister, I heard her, Jenna. It wasn't the voices. *I* heard her."

Jenna sighed. "I know you did. She did call, but just my boss. Nothing bad is going to happen."

"Your boss? Here?"

"Yes."

"That's it, then. We have to get out of here before it's too late."

"These people aren't dangerous, Mom. They're not going to hurt me."

"Oh, Jenna, don't be naive. They follow you everywhere. I see them more and more. They watch the house. Your sister told them where to find us. She's a traitor."

Jenna tried to urge her mother down the hall, hoping to make their way outside eventually, but it was a long corridor and her mom would only be moved a few inches at a time.

"Callie is your daughter," Jenna said. "She loves you. She loves both of us. She was just mad at me. It's not serious. She's just young."

Her coworkers seemed to be passing by in record numbers, something she knew wasn't a coincidence. Word was spreading, and they all wanted to watch. She wanted to yell at them, but she couldn't draw her mom's attention to them. That would make things much worse. She had to focus on her mom. She had to calm her down.

❖

Danielle threw her jacket in her locker and glanced at the empty door where Jenna used to keep the picture of the gorgeous model. She glanced at the supply closet where they'd stolen their forbidden kisses. She was running out of ideas, out of ways she wanted to apologize, out of reasons to stumble into Jenna's office, and out of certainty they belonged together. What if Brianna was right, and she simply wasn't Jenna's type?

Danielle looked at the ring her brother had given her. For when she felt alone. She certainly felt alone now. She'd wanted to be the only one in charge of her opinions and decisions about Brianna, but it resulted in painful isolation. All she had now was Brianna, who was hardly the sort of company she needed.

The door to the locker room open and a group of people melted inside in a fit of weak-kneed laughter. Danielle glanced over and found Val's face among them.

"What's so funny?" she asked.

"Jenna's mom is flipping shit in the lobby."

"She's here?"

"Oh, yeah. She ripped the front desk a new one. Thinks we kidnapped Jenna and brought her here."

Danielle slammed her locker shut. "That's not funny."

Val turned serious. "Oh, come on. Jenna's with her. She's in good hands."

Danielle passed them. "Not funny," she repeated.

Val grabbed her arm. "Don't get involved. It will make you both look bad." Val tried to maintain eye contact to emphasize her insinuation, but Danielle wouldn't have it and pulled her arm free.

"She likes to handle her own business anyway," Val said. "You'll just embarrass her."

"Embarrass her?" Danielle said. "You mean like having people laughing at her would?"

Danielle left the locker room and headed for the lobby, not sure what she planned to do when she got there. The yelling was clear and loud from two rooms away. She turned the last corner and saw Jenna standing a few feet away from a woman, her mother, who held a lamp poised to strike. Danielle's breath stopped in her chest.

"They got you!" the woman screamed. She was the mirror image of Jenna, appearing closer to her age than she possibly could be. The whole family shared a striking resemblance. "They brainwashed you, didn't they?"

Jenna tried to approach, but her mother swung the lamp, sweeping it horizontally between them, catching only air.

Danielle saw the receptionist pick up the phone out of the corner of her eye and rushed over. She clicked the receiver to disconnect the line.

"I'm supposed to call the cops for this kind of thing." The receptionist couldn't be a day over nineteen, and the scrambled emotions ran through her face like a parade.

"Did Jenna ask you to call them?"

"She's a little busy." The young girl gestured at Jenna.

"Okay, we're not calling the cops," Danielle said. "Call Tina Richards."

"Who?"

"From the fourth floor. In the directory under mental health counselors. Tell her it's for Jenna."

A loud crash sounded, and Danielle looked up to see Jenna's mom had thrown the lamp, but she wasn't sure if it connected. If it did, Jenna barely flinched. Her hands were still in front of her, her voice still soft, her focus absolute. Danielle doubted Jenna even knew she was there.

"I'm calling the cops," the receptionist said.

"Tina Richards," Danielle snapped. "Now."

The girl shook her head and dialed. She was only on the phone a moment before she hung up, and the woman who must be Tina appeared seconds later from the elevator.

She was in her forties and had a small, unassuming frame, but she walked over with an air of steadfast confidence. Surprise swept through Jenna's face when she noticed Tina by her side.

Jenna's mom looked around the room, trying to spot a new weapon.

"Who the hell are you?" she screamed. "You're not taking me away!"

"My name is Tina," she said. "We met a few years ago. I'm not taking you anywhere you don't want to go. I just want to know what's going on."

The words were simple, but her tone was soothing, soft and sure. It had a relaxing effect on the entire room. Danielle could see Jenna's mom try to place the woman, then finally vague recognition. She looked calmer by a degree, but her gaze bounced from face to face, landing on a few that weren't there.

"What are you all looking at?" she yelled.

Danielle gently grabbed the receptionist's arm and pulled her into the next room. "Let's give them some space."

The girl was annoyed, but went with her. Danielle knew this was probably the highlight of the girl's month and couldn't work out why she was so keen to pretend to be put out. Once they were around the corner, the yelling died out instantly, and it was only another few minutes before they heard the voices fade and the front door close. When Danielle looked around the corner again, she could see Jenna through the glass doors. She was hugging her mom, then she helped her into the Volkswagen that was parked on the sidewalk. It was the same car she'd seen at Jenna's house. Tina circled the car and got in the driver's seat, then drove off, leaving Jenna standing on the curb.

Danielle couldn't believe the turnaround and understood why Jenna had said Tina was the best. She wanted to check on Jenna, wanted to know if she was hurt, what Tina had said to calm her mother down, whether she was taking her home or to some sort of facility, what Jenna was feeling, but none of that was any of her business anymore. She couldn't go wrap her arms around Jenna the way she wanted to. She turned and left before Jenna could spot her.

Chapter Thirty-three

Danielle was so focused on charging through the parking lot she didn't notice Sasha until she was plowing her over. Danielle stepped on her foot and bumped her hard enough to send her backward and make her drop her papers.

"Whoa, shit," Sasha said.

"I'm so sorry," Danielle said. "I wasn't watching." Danielle crouched and started gathering Sasha's papers.

"It's okay," Sasha said and chuckled. "You okay?"

"Sure."

She could feel Sasha studying her without looking up.

"You sure?"

"Yeah," Danielle said. "Just on my way to see the Clarks."

"Oh," Sasha said. "How's that going?"

"About like I expected," Danielle said. She forced herself to look up. "No, that's not true. It's actually going okay. It just feels wrong."

Sasha nodded. "There's a lot of pressure taking over for someone else, but you're good at what you do. Can't be as bad as finding that body, right?"

Danielle laughed lightly remembering her own history with Sasha. She should feel closer to her, but knowing how close Sasha and Jenna were made it hard to imagine Sasha didn't hate her. "No, not as bad as the body."

They finished gathering the papers and stood up.

"Hey, we're all going out tomorrow if you want to come," Sasha said.

Danielle laughed.

"What?" Sasha asked. "Is that such a crazy idea? You've been looking down lately. We're pretty good at picking up peoples' spirits."

"Does 'we' include Jenna?"

Sasha looked taken aback and stumbled for words. "I...hopefully. She's invited. She seems like she needs some cheering up too. Is that a problem?"

"We don't have to do this thing where we pretend like you don't know," Danielle said. "You're her best friend. I know you know."

Sasha chuckled. "Okay, but still, does that mean you guys can't be around each other? You don't think you'll stay friends?"

"Maybe one day." Danielle fought the ache forming in her chest at the idea. She didn't want to be friends.

"Okay," Sasha said. "But if you change your mind we'll be at Big J's at eight."

"Thanks." Danielle nodded and started for her car again. She slipped into the safety of her car, feeling tears welling up. Nothing made her remember how hurt she was like trying to pretend she wasn't. She choked down the tears. She had to check on Deon and Raylon today, and she had to embody Jenna's calm and safe presence when she did it. She couldn't have a red, puffy face.

Danielle parked in front of their complex and launched out of the car before she could think too much about it. As she approached the apartment building she heard yelling, but it took her all the way to the Clarks' door to be certain it was coming from their apartment. There was a booming male voice screaming inside and loud bangs as if he was throwing things.

Danielle leaned closer and stood perfectly still. She strained to hear better and finally made out a small whimper, but the high-pitched voice could be female or child. She debated whether or not to knock, looking over her shoulder as if the answer would somehow be back in her car. Just as she decided she should call the police, things went quiet. She held her breath. Voices started up again inside, closer to a normal volume, and she knocked before she could second-guess herself. She hated the idea of standing outside waiting while someone might be getting hurt, while the boys might be hurt, when her presence alone would probably stop everything. The moment her knuckles hit the door the talking abruptly stopped, then resumed in hurried whispers.

"Coming," Ladona said. Danielle guessed it had been her voice she had heard, which relieved her in at least some measure. Several seconds went by while Danielle stood outside. The door opened, but stopped violently just inches later when it caught on the chain. "Oops." Ladona closed the door, removed the chain, and opened it again. "Ms. Corey," she said.

"Ladona."

"I'm so sorry to keep you waiting out here. Come on inside."

Danielle cautiously stepped inside, surveilling the room. She expected to see the owner of the male voice immediately, but he wasn't in sight. From the sounds seconds before, she expected to see toppled furniture, but everything was in place.

"How have you been since we last saw you?" Ladona asked.

Danielle slowly turned, puzzled by the attempt to pretend such an obvious disturbance hadn't just happened. "Ladona, who else is here?"

"Just me and Deon."

Danielle paused again, trying to gather her thoughts. "You and Deon?" Deon was growing up fast. He seemed to mature every time she saw him, but she couldn't believe for a second his voice had turned into that of a forty-year-old man's over the week.

"That's right," Ladona said. "Raylon had a school project he had to take care of today with some classmates. I hope that's all right since it's school and all. I tell you that tutor Ms. Thompson recommended has done wonders for both of them."

"Who was in here yelling just now?" Danielle asked. She couldn't stop spinning, checking every corner of the room, afraid he'd spring out.

"Yelling?" Ladona spun like she was also looking for the culprit. "There's no one yelling in here."

"Ladona, I heard it. You remember what I said the last time we met, about how I have to report everything? If I don't know what—"

"Oh, you know what it must have been, I had a friend over watching football. He gets a little worked up sometimes. We weren't arguing or anything."

"Where's your friend?"

"He's, uh…" Ladona turned. "Carl, come on out here and meet the social worker." Ladona turned back and leaned closer. "I'm so sorry about all this. He just thought I'd get in trouble if you knew I had someone over because that boyfriend I used to have wasn't so nice. He was just trying to look out for me. There's no yelling, though, Ms. Corey. I promise."

Danielle scrutinized Ladona for bruises or red marks, but couldn't see any.

"Carl!"

Footsteps stomped through the kitchen and a man appeared in the door frame, taking up nearly all of it. He was a tall brick of muscle with a temper, and Danielle couldn't help but feel uncomfortable around him, but she couldn't just leave. She had to ask questions. Questions that might piss him off.

"Nice to meet you." Carl held out his hand. Danielle tentatively shook it, checking his knuckles for injury and finding nothing. "I live just a few apartments down," he said. "We like to get together and watch football now and then."

"Who's playing?"

Carl's bright smile faded from his face. "Just about everybody," he said. "Games on all day."

"Right," Danielle said. Silence stretched, and Ladona started to fidget and shift her weight while Carl seemed to try to be even taller than he already was.

"She says she heard you yelling," Ladona finally broke the silence.

"Oh," he said. "Sure, I might have. These refs get me kind of fired up sometimes, no cause for concern."

"Yes, that's what she was saying," Danielle said. "Carl, I don't mean to be rude, but since you live just a few doors down, if I could ask you to step out for the time being. We do need to get through this visit, and it's typically better if it's just the family."

"Right," Carl said. "We're not going to have any problems, are we?"

"I'm not sure what you mean."

"About the yelling."

"I certainly hope not."

"What do you mean by that?" He leaned closer. "You're either going to make it a problem or you're not."

Danielle's heart pounded as his shadow swallowed her. She stood up straight and held her ground. "It's just a routine visit, Carl. There are rarely problems. If you won't leave, though, I won't be able to finish the visit. Then my supervisor will have to come by."

Part of Danielle wanted to lie her way through this, say whatever she had to just to get the man out, but she also knew making eager promises would ring false, and she wanted to avoid implying it would depend on what the family said, knowing that could put them in a dangerous position. Carl stared at her for a long time before he finally broke out into another smile.

"I'm just messing with you, girl. Of course, I'll step out. None of my business how a woman raises her kids. Ladona, you just come knock on my door when you're finished here, and we'll get back to the game."

Ladona nodded and watched him go. Danielle felt them both take a breath of relief when the door closed, but the silence continued for another minute. Danielle turned back to Ladona.

"You want to tell me what happened?"

"I don't know what you mean. He just—"

Danielle held up her hand. "Don't say he was watching football. I know that's a lie, and if you lie to me I can't help you. Is that the guy that hit Deon?"

Ladona looked paralyzed. Danielle could see her trying to work out the best story to tell. She rubbed her face, trying to sort out her own thoughts. The man had a temper, that much was obvious, but there was no damage to the house, no marks on Ladona, and she hadn't been able to hear his exact words when he was yelling. She could let it go, but it didn't feel right. Would Jenna feel right about that?

"Where are the boys?" Danielle asked.

"Deon is in his room. Raylon is at a school thing like I told you."

"You better get him home."

"What? Why?"

"I need to see that he's okay."

"That's ridiculous, of course he is. He wasn't even here."

"I need to be sure of that."

"You calling me a liar?"

Danielle's patience was starting to wear and she struggled to keep the expression on her face professional. "When I came in here you told me it was just you and Deon. It wasn't. That was a lie."

"Oh, you just think you're something else, don't you?"

"I'm going to talk to Deon."

"I'm right here." Deon's voice sounded lower, sadder than usual. Danielle spun. She could see he'd been crying, but he otherwise looked okay. Danielle walked over to him.

"You want to get some air and talk?"

Ladona appeared at her shoulder in an instant, and Danielle felt her stomach twist. Ladona didn't want her to be alone with Deon, which meant she was hiding something.

"We're just going to step outside and have a word," Danielle said.

"The hell you are," Ladona snapped. "I don't like the way you're treating us. You can see that boy is fine, and you can talk to him right here. I don't want you filling his head up with nonsense and pressuring him to say what you want to hear."

Danielle fought the urge to snap, to tell Ladona exactly what she thought. That would be traumatic for Deon, feeling like he had to choose an allegiance between them, feeling pressured to lie by his mother, pressured to betray her by Danielle. She didn't want to do that to him. She couldn't. And asking him a single question, even asking him to step outside with her, would force him to choose. She had to be the adult. She had to choose. Jenna's voice rang through her head, telling her to give Deon a voice, but this wasn't the way.

She looked at Deon's face. She could see him fighting his lip, desperate not to let it quiver. She turned back to Ladona.

"All right, we'll stay right here. Ladona, I need you to either have Raylon come home right now or tell me where he is. I'm not leaving without seeing he is in good health myself."

"You better find a comfortable place on the floor, then, because he's spending the night at a friend's house working on a project, and I'm not bringing him home. He's doing well in school finally. He doesn't need this."

"This is not optional, Ms. Clark."

"What are you going to do, then?"

"If you refuse to let me check on Raylon, I'm taking Deon with me right now and getting the police involved to help find Raylon. I'll start the paperwork to remove them both from your care right now, Ladona. Don't think I won't."

"He's in his room," Deon muttered.

"Deon!"

Danielle spun. "Excuse me?"

"He's not at a friend's house. He's upstairs."

"You spoiled, selfish, little piece of shit. You mangy—"

"That's enough!" Danielle yelled and took her phone from her pocket. She texted Chuck that she needed him for an emergency removal. She didn't want to hurt Deon or Raylon, or Jenna for that matter, but as much as Jenna might be able to relate to Deon's relationship with Raylon, Danielle knew what being called names by a parent did, and she couldn't allow it. She couldn't allow the lies or the yelling or the emotional abuse. A knot formed in her throat as she hit send. The message should be going to Jenna. Not even that, Jenna should be here. She should be seeing this. She should be making this decision.

"Do you want to come upstairs with me?" Danielle asked Deon. He sheepishly nodded. Danielle could feel Ladona staring at her back as she started up the stairs. Each step felt like a marathon. She wanted to hurry, to help Raylon as fast as possible, but she was also terrified to see what was wrong with him, why they'd tried to hide him. She turned down the hall and found his door.

"Can I go in first?" Deon asked.

"Sure." Danielle nodded, but she touched Deon's shoulder before he opened the door. "That was very brave," she said. "Telling me he was here."

Deon shrugged.

"You know it was the right thing to do, right?"

"He's going to be mad at me. Everybody is."

"That's not true," Danielle said. "Raylon will understand when he gets older. I'm proud of you. Jenna would be proud of you. She told me you'd know when it was time, and she was right."

Deon looked confused at first, but then he nodded. "It's time."

Deon twisted the knob and entered slowly, like he was trying not to wake Raylon up.

Hey," he said. "Ms. Corey is here."

"What? No." Raylon whined and his voice broke into a cry. Danielle felt her eyes well up, but she pushed it away. She had to be strong for them. Deon pushed the door the rest of the way open, and they both walked inside. Raylon was curled into a ball on the floor, leaning against his twin bed. The entire right side of his face was purple. Danielle felt her muscles flexing, and she fought to stay upright, to keep a straight face. Deon sat beside him as tears poured down Raylon's face. Danielle sat on the floor facing them.

"Don't let her take me away, Deon." Raylon wrapped his arms around Deon's waist and buried his bruised face in Deon's armpit. Deon hugged him, and with Raylon's face safely crushed against him, Deon cried too.

"We have to go, Raylon. There's nothing anyone can do anymore. Not me, or Mama, or Jenna, or Ms. Corey. We have to go."

"But I don't want to go," Raylon said. "I want to stay with you."

"You have to go to Aunt Audrey's," Deon said.

"What about you?"

Deon looked at Danielle. "What about me?"

"I'll talk to your aunt," Danielle said. "I'll see if she's changed her mind."

"She won't."

"If she doesn't, you'll go to a group home for a little while until you get a foster family. They're nice people. They'll take care of you."

Danielle could see Deon didn't believe that for a second, but he wouldn't say so in front of Raylon. Danielle wanted to reassure him, but Jenna's opinion about foster families kept circling through her head. She didn't want to promise him something that wasn't true, even though she desperately hoped he would be lucky enough to end up in a loving home.

"We're going to take you to a doctor first," Danielle said to Raylon. "We're going to have them check on your face and make sure you're okay. They'll check on both of you."

"What do they need to check on me for? Nothing happened to me," Deon said.

"Just a checkup," Danielle said. "To make sure. Then we'll get you both situated."

"Can I still talk to Deon?" Raylon asked.

"Of course," Danielle said, but Deon shot her a skeptical look.

"Aunt Audrey doesn't like me," he said. "She won't let him."

Danielle's heart sank. She didn't know why she didn't see it coming. Jenna wouldn't have fought so hard to keep them in their home if the threat of devastating and complete separation wasn't very real, yet she found it shocking their aunt would be so cruel. Nothing should shock her after seeing Raylon's purple little face. She couldn't imagine what it had felt like for him to be hit so hard.

"Who did this to you?" she asked.

Raylon looked at Deon. When he nodded, Raylon muttered, "Carl."

"He lives a couple of doors down?"

Deon shook his head. "Nah, they just say that. He lives here now."

"Since when?"

Deon shrugged. "Week or two."

Danielle heard footsteps approaching. When she looked over her shoulder, Chuck was standing in the doorway with a solemn look on his face. Raylon and Deon clung to each other, their fearful eyes pleading with her.

"Just another minute?" she asked.

"Of course," Chuck said. "Meet you downstairs."

Danielle opened her arms, and Deon and Raylon both lunged into a tight hug. "It's going to be okay," she said. "It's going to get better."

CHAPTER THIRTY-FOUR

Her mom's very public breakdown was the last thing Jenna needed following her scandal with Danielle, yet she couldn't bring herself to apologize for it. She could barely hear Paula talking, could barely follow the movement of her lips. All she could think about was how she'd forgotten her phone in her office. She shouldn't be answering it in a meeting anyway, but worrying about whether Tina got her mom safely home and whether or not Callie would behave during Tina's impromptu visit was more distracting than her phone would have been. She caught the word "probation" and looked up.

"Probation?"

"For an additional six months," Paula said. She looked sympathetic.

"You're putting me on probation?"

"Well, you're already on it," Paula said. "Six months is standard in a new position, but in light of recent events, they'd like to extend yours to a year. It's cautionary."

"Cautionary." Jenna knew the heaviness in her chest must mean she cared, but it didn't feel that way. She felt like she was melting into the chair. Disappearing. "All right."

"Don't let that make you feel like you can't ask for help," Paula said. "We're here to support you. Anything you ne—"

"Sure." Jenna stood up. "I understand. I suppose I should get back to it."

Paula's eyebrow raised in surprise when Jenna stood, but she nodded and let Jenna leave. Jenna walked as fast as she could down the hall to her office. She closed her door and fished her cell phone out of her desk drawer. When she unlocked it, it opened straight to her text messages, and she saw Callie had read her message that Mom was on the way home with Tina, but she hadn't responded. When she backed out of her texts she saw two missed calls and a voice mail.

Jenna hit play and put the phone to her ear, expecting to hear that her Mom was home safe, but she instead felt the adrenaline she thought she was too depressed to feel come surging from her fingertips into her chest. Tina's voice was shaky, a failing attempt at calmness as she explained there had been a car accident. Jenna pulled the phone from her face and called Tina back. She answered on the first ring.

"Jenna, you got my message?"

"Some of it, you broke up at the end. Is everyone okay?"

"Mostly," Tina said. "No serious injuries except your car."

"What happened?"

"Your mom got spooked on the way home. I must have said something wrong. She grabbed the steering wheel, and we went into oncoming traffic. No one was going too fast, thank goodness, but your mom got out and ran off."

"What?" Jenna heard her voice raise in what must sound like anger, though she didn't blame Tina.

"I'm sorry, Jenna. I would have gone after her, but my knee is bothering me from the crash."

"Oh my God, where are you?"

"I'm on Dexter, but there's no use coming here. They're already towing your car out of traffic. I'm going in to have them check my knee in just a minute, and your mom took off a while ago. I called your sister and told her what happened. You might want to touch base with her."

"I'm so sorry, Tina. This is my fault. Do you need help getting to the hospital?"

"No, I'm sure it's nothing. Go on and look for your mom."

Jenna disconnected the call and grabbed her keys as she tried to call Callie. It went to voice mail as she stormed out of her office. She nearly ran Chuck over, but she barely muttered an apology as she raced for the parking lot. Her heart was pounding as she imagined where her mother could be by now. She should have gone back to her office for her phone when she realized she forgot it. The hell with her meeting. She should have taken her mom home herself. She knew she should go with them, even though Tina discouraged it.

She should have answered Callie's calls no matter how mad she was. Fear of this exact type of situation had always made her do so in the past. It seemed exceptionally cruel that it actually happened. She should know by now that Callie didn't pick up her slack when she was busy; she just let things go unhandled. She'd been mad at her sister, but her mom would pay the price. Anything could happen to her while she was wandering around. She wouldn't know where she was, and she'd be afraid of everyone. Picturing her mom in that kind of terror made her throat turn to fire.

She tried Callie again as she slipped into her Acura. Voice mail. Her stomach lurched as she was seized with concern for her sister too. Callie always answered the phone. Had she gone out looking for their mom? Had her mom shown up at home and freaked out on Callie?

Jenna scoured the streets as she sped home even though the odds of coming across her mom that way were slim to none. She screeched into the driveway and jogged through the front door.

"Callie!" She surveyed the room for signs of a disturbance. Everything was in order. She went to her sister's room and burst inside. Callie was lying on her bed with headphones in. She yanked them off when she saw Jenna.

"What the hell, Callie?" Jenna yelled.

Callie jolted up. "What?"

"You can't answer your phone?"

"I had headphones in."

"You didn't think to keep your phone close by? We're kind of in the middle of a crisis here. It didn't occur to you someone might call? That we might need your help? How can you even listen to music right now?"

"What are you talking about? Mom is always in crisis."

Jenna was dumbfounded. "Tina called you, right?"

"Yeah."

"She told you they were in a car crash? That Mom ran away?"

Callie rolled her eyes. "Yes."

"What the fuck, Callie?"

Callie sat forward, as if Jenna had just finally captured her interest. "What?"

"Mom is out there convinced people are trying to kidnap and kill her. Anything could happen to her, and you don't go look for her? You don't answer your phone? You don't even pause your fucking music? What is wrong with you?"

Callie shot to her feet. "Look for her? Are you serious? What part of I don't like to leave the house do you not understand?"

"What are you, five? I don't like to do a lot of things, Callie, but I do them anyway. That's what you do for family."

"Oh really? You do them anyway? It doesn't seem like that to me. You don't do anything anymore. You want me to do everything now."

"I have done everything around here our entire lives, Callie! I pay the bills. I cook the food. I take care of Mom. I take care of you. You don't know how exhausting it is. I need help sometimes."

"You should have thought about that before you blew half my face off!"

Jenna felt as if she'd been physically slapped. "I should have thought about it first? What, you think I did it on purpose?"

"Of course not, stupid, but it still happened."

"And you think that means you never have to lift a finger? I have to do everything because I'm responsible for your face, is that it?"

"Yeah," Callie said. "That's exactly it. I don't feel bad for you, Jenna. I don't feel bad that you have to work that job that I know you love anyway. I don't feel bad that you have to take care of Mom who loves you more anyway. Your problems are stupid next to mine. I'll never have a normal life."

"That's not true, Callie."

She snorted. "Which part?"

Jenna shook her head. "All of it. Mom doesn't love me more. You—"

"Hah!" Callie interrupted. "Are you dense? Mom absolutely loves you more!"

"No, she doesn't," Jenna said. "It's just when her illness gets out of hand she gets paranoid. You know that. It has nothing to do with not loving you."

"That's great. She loves me; she just also thinks I'm a government agent stabbing you two in the back?"

Jenna shook her head with fury. "Yeah, why could that possibly be?"

"What?"

"Where would she get the idea you were stabbing me in the back, Cal?"

"Maybe she saw my secret CIA bunker under the house. What the hell are you getting at?"

"She heard you talking to my boss. That's why she thinks you're setting me up."

Callie froze in surprise, scrutinizing Jenna's face. "I don't know what she thinks she h—"

"Don't," Jenna snapped. "I know what you did. You called my boss, and you told her about me and Danielle. You wanted to break us up."

Callie locked eyes with her. The seconds felt like hours. "Fine," she said. "I did."

"Did it occur to you I could get fired? You know that's food out of your own mouth, right?"

Callie scoffed. "Please, they'd never fire you. Even if they did you'd have a new job the next day."

"So you just wanted to break my heart?"

"Oh, just stop," Callie said. "Knock it off."

"What?"

"I don't feel bad for you, Jenna," Callie said again. "I don't feel bad about any of your stupid fake problems, and if you whine about your amazing life one more time I'm going to fucking hit you. So I cost you a girlfriend. I'm sure there are a million more where she came from dying to get in your pants. No one will *ever* want to be with me. I'm fucking disfigured. Forever. It was *your* fault, Jenna, and you get off scot-free. And then you want to complain?"

"Fucking cry me a river, Callie," Jenna said. Her hands were shaking, and she felt that same urge Callie described, to grab her or shake her or hit her.

"Fuck you!" Callie screamed.

"No, no more bullshit. You can have a normal life. You can have friends. You can fall in love. You can do anything anyone else can,

Callie. They're just scars. I am not responsible for you refusing to live your life."

"Excuse me?" Callie said. "How dare you? They're just scars?"

"You're not paralyzed, Callie. You're not in a wheelchair. You didn't lose an arm. There's nothing stopping you except yourself."

"Oh, really? You think people don't look at me in disgust? You think they don't think I'm a freak?"

"No, Cal, I really don't. You're not disgusting."

Callie snorted and shook her head. "You have your head so far up your ass, Jenna. Just leave me alone. Leave me and Mom behind, and go get laid. That's what you want to hear, right? Fine, do it. I should take care of Mom because I don't have a life anyway, right? So go get Danielle back and shut up. Get laid for both of us."

"I didn't lock you up in this little tower of yours, Callie! If you want to get laid so bad, do it!"

"I can't!" Callie screamed. "Clean out your fucking ears and listen! My face is disgusting. No one wants to be with me."

"No one wants to be with you because you're a bitch!" Jenna yelled. "You think it's your face, but it's not. It's *you*. You're awful to everyone because you think they're going to be awful to you, but they're not."

A knock sounded at the door. Hard, crisp knocks. Jenna and Callie stared at each other, paralyzed and disoriented for a second. They finally broke free of each other's gazes and headed for the door. Jenna jogged down the stairs, praying someone found their mom. She opened the door and lost her equilibrium again when she saw a police officer standing there.

"Jenna Thompson?" he asked.

"Yes? Did you find my mother?"

"Yes. Were you planning to report her missing?" The officer had an imposing frame, only a little taller than average, but built in a way that suggested he spent as much time at the gym as he did at work.

"Of course." Jenna only managed to mask her irritation a little. "I just got home a few minutes ago. I was hoping she came back here and thought I should check before I called."

He cleared his throat. "Someone else called to advise she was missing and gave this address as her residence."

"Tina," Jenna said.

He nodded. "In any case, we found her in Crescent Hill."

"That's great," Jenna said. "Where is she?" She craned her neck to see the police car, but couldn't see anyone in the back. "Is she on a mental health hold?"

"She's in custody."

"Meaning what?" Jenna felt Callie brush her shoulder as she approached and shared the doorway with her.

"She attacked someone," he said. "Hurt them bad."

Jenna covered her mouth. Heat crawled up her neck.

"Are you saying she's in jail?" Callie asked.

"Yes, ma'am. She was arrested for attempted murder."

"Attempted murder?" Callie and Jenna spoke in unison, but Callie's voice covered hers. "She's schizophrenic. She wasn't trying to murder anyone; she's terrified. And she needs to be in a hospital, not a jail."

"The victim has life threatening injuries," he said. "That was the charge. If you want to dispute it, that will happen in court."

"But what about now?" Jenna said. "She's right. Our mom needs to be in a hospital. She needs care. She doesn't belong in jail."

"She'll speak with mental health professionals in jail."

Jenna was dumbfounded. She could hardly put up a fight when the officer handed her some papers.

"This has all the information you need." He darted off the porch before she could say another word. She slowly closed the door and turned to Callie. Her fingers felt numb. She couldn't feel the papers in her hand, couldn't recognize the squiggles on the page as letters and words. She felt like she was breathing through a straw, and the image of their mom sitting on a concrete jail floor ripped her throat and chest to pieces. Just as tears were coming to her eyes, Callie took the papers. She scanned over them, then looked up.

"We need a lawyer."

CHAPTER THIRTY-FIVE

Danielle stepped over Brianna's sleeping body. She passed out on the floor more often than not ever since Danielle stopped bothering to help her to bed. She kept strange hours, sleeping all day into the early evening, then going to work as a bartender at a rowdy bar, which afforded her the ability to drink on the job and make more money in five hours than most people did in eight. Danielle knew her shift ended at two, but she usually stumbled in around six after partying the remainder of the night away. Seeing Bri that way tore her down the middle even though she was still livid. In a way, it was evidence she was right all along. Brianna would not figure things out if forced. She just crash-landed. And in another way, she saw she was also wrong. While Brianna didn't straighten out, the world didn't end because she slept on the floor, either.

When she tried to set her foot down on the other side of Brianna, her toe caught an empty plastic vodka bottle and sent it skidding noisily down the hall. Danielle sighed and scooped it up, then added it to the pile of bottles she'd started saving. Beyond that, Danielle couldn't focus on Brianna long. It was Raylon's bruised face that haunted her now. His blue and purple cheek had found its way into her dreams, and Brianna's drunkenness could barely touch the impact a hurt child made.

Danielle grabbed her keys and the copies she made of the photos of Raylon's face. She made them for Jenna, but now she couldn't decide whether or not to show her. She didn't know if Jenna even knew the boys had been removed, but she would eventually. She couldn't stand the idea of Jenna thinking she casually pulled Deon and Raylon from their home, that she hadn't cared what Jenna had explained to her, what she'd shared. She wanted to explain what happened, to prove she'd made the right call, but she also had an inkling that might be a selfish thing to do. The images would crush Jenna. They could even make her feel responsible. Was it a gift or a burden to show her?

Danielle spent the entire day flip-flopping on her decision to show up to Sasha's gathering at all. When she received the invitation, she hadn't even considered it, but so much happened so quickly. She had to talk to Jenna, yet some part of her still wondered if she was lying to herself, if it wasn't more that she simply *wanted* to talk to Jenna. After all the back and forth, now she was pulling into the parking lot at Big J's, trying to spot Jenna's car and feeling the undeniable flutter in her stomach when she did.

Danielle threw the car in park and got out. She left the file with the pictures in the passenger seat. Her feet crunched on the gravel, and she couldn't resist glancing toward the row of parking spaces they'd disappeared into to sneak their first illicit kiss. Her stomach twisted as the memory of Jenna's commanding touch flooded her mind.

Danielle spotted Sasha and Adam at a table on the small fenced-in patio. Sasha noticed her just a second later, and her face lit up as she waved Danielle over.

"You made it!" Sasha said.

Danielle threw her legs over the waist-level, wrought iron fence and took the empty chair, noticing the lack of familiar faces.

"Am I the only one?"

Adam laughed. "Are we not good enough?"

"Most of them are inside," Sasha said.

"Jenna's here," Adam said. "She's having a night."

"What do you mean?" Danielle surveyed each of their faces.

"I mean she's back." Adam drew out the word with glee while he danced in his chair. When he saw she was still confused he chuckled. "They're doing shots at the bar. Lots of them."

"Oh." Danielle inferred that Jenna had friendly company. She remembered how they'd alluded to her wild ways more than once, but she'd never seen much of it. The idea she might be about to see

Jenna tangled in someone else's arms made her desperate for an exit strategy. Sasha smacked Adam on the chest.

"It's not even like that," she said. "I'm actually really worried about her. It's not fun. It's not partying. This is, I don't know. I've never seen her so down."

Danielle's her heart plummeted into her stomach. "She heard then?"

"Heard what?"

"About Deon and Raylon."

"I'm not sure," Sasha said. "I guess that means *you* haven't heard."

"Hold on, I'm getting confused," Adam said.

"About her mom," Sasha said.

"Oh, about her showing up at work?" Danielle asked.

Sasha frowned. "After that. Jenna's mom got arrested for attempted murder. And I think something happened with Callie."

"What?" Danielle stood up and looked over her shoulder at the door, trying to see through to the bar. She looked back to Sasha, who shrugged.

"I can only get bits and pieces from her," she said. "Go on in and try."

Adam grimaced. "Are we sure that's a good idea? After the whole break up thi—"

"What, you know now too?"

"Honey, everyone knows now."

"Fantastic." Danielle went through the door to the bar without pausing to second-guess it. It took her a second to spot Jenna, but soon she saw Jenna's long dark wavy hair. As if seeing her somehow turned on the volume in her head, she heard Jenna's laugh at the same moment she saw her. She was surrounded by a group of women, three, four, maybe five of them. It was hard to tell who was part of the group and who was just passing through. She didn't recognize any of them. They weren't from the office. Danielle wondered if this was what everyone had been talking about, how Jenna usually operated. Was she the type that showed up with friends but inevitably flew away on the breeze like a dandelion seed?

There was a blonde standing too close to her, pressing her thigh into Jenna's, gazing at her with an intensity that begged to be special, but Jenna seemed unaware of it. She was laughing with the bartender as the boyish young woman poured a row of shots. When Jenna glanced over and their eyes met, Danielle lost her breath. Suddenly, her mouth was dry and her legs didn't work, but she walked somehow. She pushed through the crowd, determined to make it all the way into Jenna's space without being intimidated by her company.

"Didn't expect to see you tonight," Jenna said.

"Did you not want to?" Danielle tried to read Jenna, tried to judge if she knew about Raylon and Deon or not. If she did know, she had to explain, but if she didn't, it was hardly a good time to add to her list of sorrows. Jenna's gaze traveled up and down her and Danielle felt a shiver crawl through her.

"I always want to," Jenna said. The ease of her honesty surprised Danielle. She hadn't expected any warmth from her. Jenna grabbed two of the shot glasses, offering one to Danielle.

"No thanks," she said.

Jenna smiled as if to herself. The blonde that had been all over her moments before appeared at her side again, slipping her arm around Jenna's shoulder as she reached across with the other arm for the shot Danielle refused.

"Another?" She clinked her glass against the one Jenna was already holding. Jenna glanced at Danielle. She thought she saw a moment of discomfort pass through her, but Jenna looked away and took the shot, returning the empty glass swiftly to the bar. The blonde allowed her arm to linger around Jenna's shoulder.

"You want to shoot some pool?" she asked. Danielle hated her even though she knew she had no right. Jenna wasn't hers, and the woman wasn't being obscene or obnoxious about what was a completely fair advance, but Danielle wanted to yank her off of Jenna by her earrings all the same.

"Can I talk to you?" Danielle asked.

Jenna's eyes shot up and locked on hers. Danielle found she couldn't breathe as both she and the blonde waited for an answer.

"Of course."

"Outside," Danielle said. Jenna looked over each of her shoulders like she was trying to spot some reason why they should leave. "Please," Danielle added.

Jenna nodded and stood up, following Danielle through the bar without another word to the blonde. Danielle took that to mean they'd just met and soaked in the relief. She didn't come here to get Jenna back. She just wanted to make sure she was okay, to explain what happened with the case, but seeing someone else touch her was unbearable.

Danielle felt a rush of calm when they went out the door into the night air and the oppressing chatter bouncing off the walls fell away. It was like a pressure inside her head was relieved. She could breathe and think again.

"What's up?" Jenna asked.

Danielle turned. "Are you okay?"

Jenna laughed. "You brought me out here to ask if I'm okay?"

"Yes," Danielle said. "And no. I…"

Jenna waited, offering no help. There was a slight sway in Jenna's stance and Danielle realized how many drinks she must have had.

"Are you drunk?"

"Oh yeah," Jenna said.

"Oh," Danielle said. "I guess we'll talk tomorrow."

"What?"

"If you're too drunk—"

"I didn't say I'm *too* drunk. I just said I'm drunk. What did you want to talk about?"

"I didn't know if you heard—"

"I did."

"About the boys."

"Yeah." Jenna sighed. "I heard about that."

"Chuck?"

Jenna laughed. "God no."

"Paula?"

"Nope, on her shit list too."

"Then…"

"Ladona."

"Oh." Danielle pulled away in surprise. "I guess I didn't realize she had your number, or that she would call, but of course she does, would. That makes sense."

"She just called my office," Jenna said. "It's not like she comes over for Thanksgiving dinner."

"I didn't mean that," Danielle said, suddenly feeling flustered. "What did she say?"

Jenna shrugged. "Same stuff everyone says after their kids are taken away. You're baby snatching devils. Give them back."

"I'm so sorry," Danielle said. "Jenna, I tried. I'm so sorry you were blindsided by that. I didn't mean—"

"I know," Jenna said. "I'm sure only a quarter of what she said was true, and even that was enough for me to piece together that you did the right thing."

"I want to explain. I have pictures if you want to see them."

"Pictures?"

"Yeah, from the case file."

"That's against the rules." Jenna playfully tsked.

"I know," Danielle said. "But it's important to me. I want you to feel good about this, as much as you can. I want you to know I didn't just go in there and change everything all around. I didn't ignore what you said."

Jenna's eyes watered. "I'm sorry, Danielle."

"What?"

"I never should have made you feel like you owed it to me to do things a certain way with them. It wasn't right, especially when my way wasn't even always by the book. You knew how to do the job the day you walked in."

Danielle shook her head. "Every case is different, and you know that one inside and out. There's nothing wrong with wanting consistency for them." Danielle watched Jenna try to fight off tears. "Do you want to see the pictures?"

Jenna stared at the ground. "How bad is it?"

"Pretty bad."

"Both of them?"

"Just Raylon."

Tears spilled over. "Sweet little Raylon. Deon is going to feel bad about that for the rest of his life."

"Deon? It's not his fault."

"Of course not, but he's going to wish he asked to leave sooner, or that he intervened somehow. You were right all along, Danielle. I shouldn't have let them have a say. I don't know what I was thinking, letting my experience as a kid have anything to do with how I do things. It's not like we turned out well. I don't know why I've been walking around thinking I was mature enough to make those kinds of decisions at that age, like anything would have been different with a different caseworker. How could I pretend to know that? Maybe we would have done everything exactly the same. Maybe it's all an excuse I've been telling myself, and I would have made the same mistakes no matter what." Jenna walked over to the bench a few paces away and slumped onto it. "Callie hates me."

"What are you talking about? Callie loves you. You're everything to her."

Jenna shook her head. The moonlight bounced off her fair skin and made her look like some kind of mystical creature.

"No," Jenna said. "I used to think that, but all this time she's hated me for what I did to her face. She's the one who told Paula about us."

Danielle felt the words blurring and swirling together in her mind. As if she suddenly realized how drunk she was, Jenna quickly sat forward and put her head in her hands. Danielle waited, trying to judge if she would be sick or not, if her emotions were going to flip to something else the way Brianna's always did, but nothing happened.

"Why would she do that?" Danielle asked.

"Because she fucking hates me." Tears rolled down Jenna's face. "She wanted to break us up. She didn't even say she was sorry. She thinks no one will ever fall in love with her, so she doesn't want me to have it either. My mom heard her talking to Paula and told me, and oh God, my mom." Jenna fell into a fit of sobs, and Danielle couldn't stop herself from reaching out and wrapping her arms around Jenna, pulling her tight against her chest.

"I just heard," Danielle said. "I'm so sorry, Jenna."

"I should have just taken her home myself." Jenna pulled away and Danielle released her.

"You couldn't have done that," Danielle said. "She was suspicious of you. Tina was doing much better. That's why you let her do it, not because you weren't willing."

Jenna looked over in surprise, and Danielle saw understanding wash over her.

"You called Tina? She said someone did, but I couldn't figure it out."

Danielle nodded. "You said she was the best, the only one who was ever any help."

"That was thoughtful of you."

"And it turned out horribly, so if you want to blame someone, you can blame me."

Jenna shook her head. "That's ridiculous."

"Well, now you know how you sound. It wasn't your fault, Jenna."

Jenna still couldn't shake the layer of tears, and the angles of her face reflected the night light with a soft clarity that put everything in focus.

"It was my fault, though," she said. "I should have gotten Callie out of there when we were little. I should have gotten her help. She is the way she is because of me. All this time I've been wondering why she won't help me out, why she won't help make sure Mom stays on her meds. It's because she hates us both, and we deserve it. If I'd have just told the social worker the truth Callie would be living such a different life, and Mom would be getting the care she needs in a facility. The only one who benefitted was me. All this time I thought I was sacrificing I was really just being selfish."

"Jenna." Danielle put her hand on Jenna's knee. "I know I jumped to conclusions before, and I'm sorry. Please tell me what really happened to your sister's face." Danielle's heart beat faster as she waited. She wouldn't be a bit surprised if Jenna refused to tell her. What right did she have to ask? What right did she have to know? But Jenna took a deep breath and looked at the sidewalk again.

"It was the Fourth of July," Jenna said. "Callie was eight years old, and she'd never seen fireworks. Mom was too afraid to leave the house, and she didn't want us going out without her, so we were stuck at home."

"She wouldn't let you out of the house?"

Jenna shook her head, still staring at the ground. "Not really. Just for school, and some days she wouldn't even let us do that. We missed enough that the school got concerned about why, but we lied our way through it. Pretended we were ditching a lot to protect Mom, but that's beside the point. We had a few friends that lived in the neighborhood, and we had a big backyard, so sometimes if we could get them to come over Mom would let us play in the back. I decided it was time Callie had a proper Fourth of July, so after school I stole some bootleg fireworks from one of those little stands and brought them home, had our friends come over."

Danielle could already imagine how the rest went, but she'd made the mistake of making assumptions once already, so she waited.

"My mom used to be really fun," Jenna said.

Danielle smiled watching Jenna remember it.

"Schizophrenia can come along pretty late, you know? I had all these memories of her when she was fine, just a great mom." Jenna choked up again. "There was this time when I was younger that my mom bought bottle rockets for the Fourth. Her friends and she would light them while they held them between their fingers. I begged her to let me do it, and eventually she did. She held her hand on mine, and she lit it, told me to hold it loosely. It shot right out of my fingers. No big deal."

Danielle nodded. She'd seen people do a million things with bottle rockets.

"It was this great moment for me, my mom showing me how to do that, the anticipation, the elation when it happened. I always remembered her holding my hand like that, the way she was smiling when I looked over. I just thought she was the coolest person alive." Jenna smiled softly. "I wanted Callie to have that. She doesn't remember Mom like I do. It's why they're not close. By the time Callie was having real, meaningful memories, Mom was already changing."

"So you showed her?"

Jenna nodded. "Yeah, I showed her. She loved it. She looked at me the way I looked at Mom. I felt like a million bucks."

"So what happened?"

"Our friends came over, saw what we were doing. They were my age, not Callie's. They'd done that a million times already. They suggested we have a bottle rocket war, start shooting them at each other. We did. We were all running around the backyard like lunatics, using ashes as war paint, trying to hit each other with them. Callie was so much smaller than we were, but no one treated her that way. She wasn't my kid sister. She was just part of the group."

Jenna sighed and finally leaned back on the bench again, breaking her gaze at the ground and looking at Danielle. "We never had much money in those days. When I went to the fireworks stand I had to steal them, and I couldn't exactly spend a lot of time picking stuff out. I just shoved whatever I could in my pockets and ran. I didn't realize it at first, but they weren't all the same. When we ran out of bottle rockets, I just went on to the next ones. I thought they were just a different brand or something, didn't think much of it, but they were a lot bigger. I don't know how I didn't give it more thought. I didn't even read the label, couldn't even tell you what it was." Jenna shook her head, disgust taking over her face. "We were all so caught up in the fun. We just didn't want it to end. I don't think I actually hit anyone once with the bottle rockets, but wouldn't you know the very first of the bigger ones I shot off hit Callie right in the face."

Danielle found she had leaned forward as she stared at Jenna, waiting. Jenna opened her mouth, but nothing came out the first time. She closed her eyes for a second, then tried again.

"Callie fell to the ground and started screaming bloody murder. There were sparks flying all over the place still, even when she was already on the ground. I was so scared. I just knew it was blasting farther and farther into her face trying to shoot forward. It was horrifying. Our friends didn't even realize what happened at first, but somehow from all the way inside the house, Mom did. I ran over to Callie. Mom came flying out the back door. Callie's face was all these colors, bright red, white in some places, black in others. She was crying so hard. I've never heard someone cry like that."

Danielle let a few seconds of silence pass before she spoke. "How old were you?"

"Old enough."

"What do you mean?"

"Old enough to know better, if that's what you're wondering. I was thirteen."

"That's young, Jenna. Really young. I know you had to grow up fast, but you were still a kid. And you were trying to help your sister experience the magic of childhood. You were trying to be a stand-in parent. That's a big job for a thirteen-year-old."

"Callie screamed at me yesterday that I blew her face off. I was trying to yell at her for not helping me more around the house, with Mom, and she told me I had no right because I blew her face off. And you know, I couldn't think of a single thing to say. She's right. How stupid do I sound talking about taking the trash out when I blew my little sister's fucking face off? What does she care if I'm having a hard time? Or if Mom is? It wasn't just that it happened, either. We didn't get her proper care."

"What?" Danielle said. "What do you mean?"

"That's why she scarred so badly. She would have anyway, but they could have maybe made her look better, but we didn't take her in for a lot of her follow-ups."

"Why not?" Danielle felt the life draining from her limbs. Jenna nodded, seeming to witness it happen.

"The school already knew something wasn't right. They'd been itching to intervene, but we knew the right things to say, and before that there wasn't anything physical for them to go on. Once Callie turned up with those awful burns they were able to get CPS involved." Jenna spun her fingers through her hair and pulled. "We were terrified of them, Danielle. The school, the hospital, the social workers, all of them. They didn't explain things to us, so we just had our imagination and what Mom said."

"What did your mom say?"

"That they'd take us away. We wouldn't see her anymore, might not see each other anymore. That we could end up with people we didn't like. They were government entities, and that was the scariest thing you could say about someone in our house. And the doctors, Mom thought they wanted to experiment on Callie or something. When they peeled away the dead skin, Mom told us they were harvesting her flesh for clone research. They released Callie back to us after the initial treatment with instructions to come back for follow-ups, but like hell we wanted to go."

"But didn't they ask questions about why she missed appointments?"

"They did, at first. We were forced to go to a couple of mandatory visits, but some of it wasn't required. Some of it was cosmetic, not covered by insurance, things like that. Things Callie deserved but didn't get, that they couldn't force us to do. Mom thought it was all so sinister. I helped her through the visits, told the social workers it was all fine. I told Callie what to say. All I wanted was to keep Mom from getting in trouble. I knew she was sick, but I didn't want to leave her. I was the one who burned Callie's face, not her, so it was easy to tell myself we should stay with her. I lied my way through everything until CPS went away, and now Callie lives with terrible scars and shame because of me. I orchestrated this huge lie that cost everyone."

"Jenna, it wasn't your—"

"Please stop saying that. Mom was too sick to do otherwise. Callie was too young. I was the capable one in that house. I was the only one who could have made things go differently, and I didn't. And now Callie has finally admitted she hates me for it." Jenna took a deep breath and wiped away a tear. "When I heard you removed Deon and Raylon, it broke my heart for them, of course, but honestly, I give up on my judgment. I'm not sure it's ever done anyone any good. If you came here because you think you owe me something, you don't."

"Jenna, don't do that to yourself. You were just a kid. You made the best decision you could with skewed information. And there's nothing wrong with your judgment now. You were right. I was too hasty before. It was the right call to remove Deon and Raylon now, but not before. My family abandoned me the second they didn't like what I was doing with my life. I was gay, so they ended it. I'm not used to seeing a family fight for each other, but that's how it should be. You're great at what you do, and you made me better at it too."

Jenna smiled weakly and surveyed her surroundings, seeming to come out of some sort of haze. "I'm sorry to keep you out here so long," she said. "You probably want to get back to Brianna."

Danielle felt slapped and disoriented by the words. "What?"

"I take it you guys worked it out?"

"We're not speaking."

"You're not?" Jenna's brow crumpled in confusion.

"No," Danielle said. "I can't begin to forgive her for what she did. I probably couldn't even if she asked me to, but she's been too drunk to even do that."

"Why the ring, then?"

Danielle was every bit as confused as Jenna looked. She glanced down at her hand, the ring her brother gave her.

"What the hell are you talking about?"

"Why wear her ring if you can't forgive her?"

"This?" Danielle held up her hand. "This has nothing to do with Brianna. Did she say that?"

Jenna nodded. "She said she gave it to you when you decided to try to work things out."

"What?" Danielle shot to her feet, feeling her blood boiling up her spine. "I told you we were never going to work anything out. That was all fabricated."

"I know you did," Jenna said. "But..." she paused. "I thought you changed your mind or something, I guess."

"No, Jenna! I don't want her. I never wanted her. I wanted you!"

Jenna stood up too now, stepping closer. Danielle felt her pulse pick up as she tried to anticipate what Jenna could be doing. She still had a slight sway when she tried to stand upright. Danielle remembered again how much Jenna had to drink. She carried herself much better than Brianna did, but the small things still gave her away.

"What is it then?" Jenna asked.

It took Danielle a second to trace the question back to her ring. "My brother gave it to me, as a reminder that he still loves me even though he can't talk to me. He said my mom gave it to him, so we both like to think it's from her too. It's easier thinking my dad is the only one who wants nothing to do with me."

Danielle expected to see shock on Jenna's face, but her surprise was much more subtle, deeper. Danielle could feel that she believed her finally.

"Wow," she said. "I'm sorry about your family."

"Don't be sorry about that," Danielle snapped. "Be sorry for not believing me."

"I wanted to," Jenna said. "But—"

"But I didn't tell you the truth right away, so how could you? I know. And then I insulted you on top of it, talking about the case, about your family, and Callie would obviously rather ruin your career than see you with me. It's all fucked. I get it."

"You sound pissed."

"Yeah." Danielle felt the energy drain out of her as she admitted to it. "It just never should have happened." She sighed. "We never should have happened. It was a bad idea from the start."

Jenna stepped closer. "I keep telling myself that too," she said. "I can't seem to feel it, though."

Jenna slowly touched her face. Her palm was warm against her cheek, and she stared into her with an intensity that made her tremble beneath its weight. She could step into Jenna's arms, take back what was meant to be hers, but she couldn't seem to move. Jenna leaned forward, but her breath smelled like liquor, and Danielle pulled away before she knew what was happening.

"You're drunk," she said.

Brianna's words circled in her head, her argument that Jenna was like her, not like Danielle, and she knew now as much as she did then that Brianna was right. Jenna was the gorgeous, fun, free-spirited life of the party. As fun as it was to be around, it wasn't who she was.

Jenna pulled back too. The heat in her gaze disappeared.

"You think I wouldn't do this sober?" she asked.

"I think I can't date another alcoholic."

Jenna snorted and laughed so immediately Danielle knew it was an automatic response, something she hadn't intended to do, but Jenna didn't come down from her obvious resentment.

"Are you kidding?" she asked. "You think I'm an alcoholic? Because you've seen me drunk once?"

"Your friends talk about what a party girl you are all the time."

"And you think that means I drink too much? Do you even know if I drink at all these parties? Do you think that's the only way to socialize?"

Danielle felt her cheeks flush as self-doubt crawled through her. "No," she said. "I guess I don't know. I just know I don't like this. I don't like seeing you like this. And the last time I ignored that I ended up with Brianna."

Jenna shook her head. "Fine," she said. "I don't know what I was thinking anyway. You're right. We never should have happened."

CHAPTER THIRTY-SIX

Jenna woke up to an alarm sounding on her phone. Her heart tumbled to the floor when she recognized it as the reminder to give her mom her medication. It had been a hassle, a daily nuisance for most of her life, and after just a day without it, she felt disoriented and empty. She would give anything to go argue with her mom about her pills now.

She slowly registered the clatter of dishes from downstairs, a sound that brought her back to early childhood when she used to wake to her mom making breakfast, or late at night when she'd been sent to bed but was still wide-awake. She hadn't heard that sound in years. She rolled out of bed and made her way downstairs to find Callie cleaning the kitchen. Jenna stopped in the doorframe at the bottom of the steps. Callie spun and smiled.

"Morning," she said.

Jenna squinted, trying to muddle through the morning and hangover blur. She couldn't remember the last time she'd seen Callie smile. Or do chores. Especially after she'd spent the night out.

"Morning," Jenna said.

"You want some coffee? You look like shit."

Jenna shuffled to the dining table and sat down. "Uh, sure."

Callie poured her a cup of coffee and slid onto the chair next to her. "I called that lawyer you liked."

"What?"

"I saw your list of lawyers on the computer," Callie said. "You had a bunch of stars next to one of them, so I called him."

"I…" Jenna looked around the room as if it would somehow clue her in to Callie's new demeanor. "Really?"

"Yeah," Callie said. "He needed some money to talk to me, so I gave him the emergency credit card. I hope that's okay."

"Of course," Jenna said. "It's definitely an emergency."

"Yeah." Callie frowned. "Anyway, I told him what's going on, and he's really confident he can help. He wants to talk to you too, of course, but he said from what he heard there's no way attempted murder is going to stick."

Jenna was floored. She could barely put two thoughts together. "Thank you, Callie. That's amazing."

Callie shrugged. "It was just a phone call."

Jenna timidly sipped her coffee, afraid to speak, afraid to fall back into the chaos that had been their last conversation, worried that speaking would break some sort of spell or maybe just wake her up from a dream. Callie leaned forward and grabbed her hand. Jenna was startled by the gesture and met Callie's eyes.

"I'm sorry," Callie said.

It was so simple, but her throat tightened as tears threatened to crawl up. She felt like a battered pulp, a walking bruise with skin thin enough to rip at a touch. She shook her head.

"I'm the one who should be sorry."

"You've been sorry for years," Callie said. "It's time for you to stop being sorry. And it's time for me to stop being so horrible to you."

"I should have never called you a—"

Callie held up her hand. "Let me get this out real quick, okay?"

Jenna exhaled until her lungs were empty and her muscles relaxed.

"Okay. Shoot."

"It did shake me up when you called me a bitch. Later, I realized that's because you're like a mom to me, and you've never done that before. When all this stuff happened with Mom…" Callie paused. "I've never seen you like that. It was like you couldn't move, like you didn't know what to do. You always know what to do. I knew I should feel like that too, but I didn't. And I realized again, it's because you were my mom. It's different for me. I love her, but she doesn't feel like a parent."

Callie paused to take a breath, but motioned for Jenna to continue waiting. "I don't think I ever told you how much I appreciate you being that for me. I can't imagine taking care of a kid now, let alone when I was thirteen. You are an amazing big sister."

"Thanks, Cal. I wish I could have been better."

"You know, after the accident with the fireworks, you were so upset," Callie said. "I think you were more upset than I was. I wanted you to be okay, so I kept telling you *I* was okay. And then we both got better, and it didn't seem right to bring it up, but I was angry. It started coming out in ways you didn't deserve."

Jenna felt a tear roll down her cheek. She cried so much last night she wasn't sure she could handle any more. Her face felt swollen and sensitive, and her eyes didn't want to stay open.

"Tina called me," Callie said. "She wanted to talk about the Volkswagen and insurance and all that. She called me because it's my car, but I didn't really know anything about it. She thought that was weird, of course, and we got around to how I don't use it and my scars. She says I need to talk to someone. I thought it was stupid at first, but then you and I fought, and it all started to fall into place. She's right. I'm a mess. I don't even know who my own car insurance provider is. It was embarrassing. Then when you were such a mess about Mom, it was the first time I ever felt like *I* could step up for *you*. So, I called the lawyer." Callie sipped her coffee. "It actually felt really good to be the strong one for a second. It made me want to do more."

"I don't know what to say, Cal. I'm so proud of you. And I'm so sorry I hurt you."

Callie hugged her, squeezing her tight and jostling her until she finally laughed, something she thought she wasn't capable of anymore. Callie returned to her seat and interlaced her fingers.

"So."

"What?" Jenna asked.

"You want to talk about it?"

"Which it?"

"Whichever one kept you out all night and had you coming home crying."

Jenna felt her cheeks flush. "You heard that?"

"Of course," Callie said. "And you look like shit. Something tells me it's not just Mom."

Jenna felt her lips tighten into a sad smile. "I got too drunk last night," she said. "Makes you emotional."

"Okay," Callie said. "But about what?"

"You don't want to hear that stuff."

"Danielle?"

Jenna nodded numbly.

"I don't get it," Callie said. "If you love her so much, go get her. I know I screwed up work for you, but I meant it when I said I knew you could get a new job tomorrow. You could. If it's making you that miserable not to be with her, forget the job."

"It wasn't just that," Jenna said. "There was a whole thing with her ex. Her roommate."

"She went back to her?"

"No. I thought she did. Maybe. She…" Jenna stared at the table. "It's complicated."

"I think I can follow."

"It doesn't even matter," Jenna said. "I tried last night. She's not into it anymore."

"She said that?"

"She said she can't date an alcoholic." Jenna heard the bitterness in her own voice.

"What?" Callie said. "You're not an alcoholic."

"I know." Jenna sighed. "It's complicated."

"Sounds stupid."

Jenna smiled and playfully swatted her. Callie beamed and dodged it as Jenna's phone lit up on the table. She glanced at the caller ID and saw it was from work.

"Jeez, here they go already." Jenna picked up the phone. "Thompson."

"Hi, Ms. Thompson. I just wanted to pass on the message to you that Danielle won't be coming in to work today. She asked me to get in touch with her supervisor directly since it's such late notice."

"Danielle Corey?"

"Yes, ma'am. She said she has to help her roommate move out. She said it was a sensitive situation that needed her immediate attention. She apologizes for the late notice."

"Oh." Jenna was dumbstruck. "Uh, thanks, but she's actually not on my team anymore. She's been transferred. Chuck Borden is her supervisor now."

"Oh, gosh, really? They must not have updated it in the system yet. I'm sorry to bother you so early for nothing."

"No problem."

Jenna disconnected the phone and saw Callie gazing at her with comical intensity.

"I heard that," she said. "Your phone is way too loud."

"What difference does it make?"

"Um, hello? Did you not just tell me the roommate was your other thing?"

"Yeah."

"Roommate gone. Problem solved. Call her!"

"It *was* the problem," Jenna said. "I already got over that problem. She's the one with the problem now, Cal."

"You're telling me my beautiful, amazing, smart, charismatic sister got rejected and is just going to take it lying down?"

Jenna laughed. "It's *complicated.*"

Callie rolled her eyes. "No, it's not, Jenna."

CHAPTER THIRTY-SEVEN

Danielle watched Brianna attempt to get all the makeup she'd fallen asleep in off her face. The dark smears from her eyeshadow were the war paint of a woman on a mission to self-destruct. They'd barely spoken a word to each other since their fight, and though Danielle had the ammo to go another round now that she knew Brianna lied to Jenna about the ring on top of everything else, she didn't mention it. It wasn't what mattered. It offered her clarity. It pushed her over the edge with Brianna, but would only serve as a crutch and distraction in her hands.

With her face finally clean, Brianna emerged from the bathroom, heading for the kitchen. As she passed Danielle she paused, taking the eye contact they'd gone weeks without as an invitation.

"Rough night?" Brianna asked.

"Yeah," Danielle said.

"What happened?"

"I decided you need to move out."

Brianna froze. She slowly turned to face Danielle, putting off the trip to the refrigerator. Instead, she came and sat by Danielle on the couch.

"That's a little drastic," she said. "I'm really sorry for what I did, Danielle. I really didn't think it would break you two up."

"Brianna."

"Okay, I did, but I'm sorry. I had a psycho jealous moment. I don't even know why, Danielle. I don't have the hots for you. I really don't. I'll make it right. I'll talk to Jenna, whatever you want."

"It's too late for that, Brianna."

"Don't say that. We've been friends for years. We can get past this. Let me make it right."

"You did it because you were drunk," Danielle said. "I know you don't want me. You were drunk, and you did something impulsive."

"Exactly."

"But you're always drunk, Brianna. It's not about Jenna. You need help. You can't keep going on like this."

Brianna scoffed. "Oh, please! You think everyone's a drunk! It's just because you're a saint and never touch alcohol."

"You pass out on the floor more often than you make it to bed."

"So?"

"You need a drink the second you wake up, all day long, before bed. I've even heard you wake up in the middle of the night just to take a couple shots, then go back to sleep."

"That's—"

Danielle grabbed the duffel bag at her feet, turned it over, and let the dozens of empty vodka bottles she'd collected fall to the floor. The hollow plastic bottles plunked into each other and scattered. She'd been gathering them with this purpose in mind. She'd had no idea when she would actually use them, but after hearing Brianna had dared to lie to Jenna about her ring, she couldn't wait another day. It wasn't really any different than any of Brianna's other lies, but it felt worse somehow. The ring felt sacred, and Brianna's story felt like blasphemy.

"I found these," Danielle said. "All over the house. Did you know you had that many?"

Brianna traced the scattered bottles across the floor. "But that's from who knows how long."

"It's a month's worth."

"How—"

"Because I cleaned out all your hiding places last month and threw them away."

"You've been keeping track?"

"Yes," Danielle said. "And these are just the ones you hide. Plenty more end up in the regular trash." Danielle was careful to keep her voice even and soft. She didn't want to make Brianna angrier than she had to.

"It's not as serious as you're making it look," Brianna said.

"Why do you think you hide them?" Danielle asked. Brianna's brow crumpled. "I know you drink a lot. You know I know. We're not together; you don't answer to me. So why hide them?"

"I don't know. I think I just leave them around when I'm drunk."

"They're not just left around. They're hidden, in backpacks you don't use, in the vacuum cleaner bag, in the corners of the closet, behind the washing machine. You hide them when you're drunk. I think it's because you know it's a problem and it's hard for you to see how much you're drinking. I think you're hiding them from yourself, not me."

"Okay, Freud. What else?"

"Nothing," Danielle said. "I just think you need help, and I think that's okay, but I'm not qualified."

"This is fucking bullshit. So, what, you're throwing me out onto the street? You think that's going to get me sober? You want to see me really drink just wait until you see that."

"I called a rehab facility. They have an opening, if you'll go."

"Fuck no. I'm not going to fucking rehab. Just because you want to get rid of me and get your stupid girlfriend back? Fuck you."

Danielle put her hand on Brianna's knee. "Brianna, I care about you. I really do. This isn't about Jenna."

"Like hell."

"The way you acted with her helped me see how bad it's gotten, that's all, but I'm not trying to get rid of you for her, or at all."

"If you cared about me you wouldn't do this." Brianna's anger dissolved, replaced by tears. "I don't have anyone else, Danielle. If you abandon me, I'll be alone." The word abandon hit her square in the chest, and when she met Brianna's expectant eyes, she realized it was designed to. Her blood drained. She'd been manipulated. For how long she couldn't guess, but it stopped now.

"Brianna, I'm not abandoning you. If you won't go to rehab, I'll have you evicted, and you *will* end up on the street. And our friendship will be over, but that's not what I want. If you do this, you won't be losing me. I'll come visit you in rehab. I'll call you to check in. I'll support you through every step, and we can still be friends. But we can't go on like this anymore. This drinking, it's killing our friendship, and it's killing you."

Brianna's face was red and puffy. Danielle couldn't remember the last time she'd seen Brianna so stripped down, so raw.

"I don't want to go." Brianna sobbed. "Just give me another chance, I can quit on my own."

"No," Danielle said. "You need help, Brianna. If nothing else, you need help to detox. It's dangerous to just quit. Will you at least go there for that? Talk to them? Do that much. Then see how you feel."

Brianna shook her head more and more fervently as the tears came down. "Don't make me do this. Don't do this to me."

"Brianna, you're like family to me. You were there for me when my real family wasn't. I know you know that. And I know deep down somewhere you know I wouldn't be a real friend if I let you let this kill you. Please let me take you to this place. They're the best in the state."

Brianna put her face in her palms and started crying harder, but she slowly started nodding her head. Danielle rubbed her back.

"Yeah?"

"God!" Brianna sobbed. "Yeah! Fine!"

Danielle smiled and stood up.

"Now?" Brianna yelled.

Danielle nodded. "Yes, before you change your mind."

"Can I have a last drink?"

"Yeah," Danielle said. Anything to just get her there.

"And I need to pack."

"I packed a bag for you. You can only take a handful of things. They gave me a list and I took care of it."

"Are you fucking serious?" Brianna broke down into another wave of sobs.

"It's going to be okay."

Brianna went into the kitchen and grabbed her bottle of vodka. "Let's go, then," she said. "I can see you're eager to get rid of me."

"It's not—"

"Yeah, yeah, whatever. Let's go."

Danielle grabbed the bag she'd packed for Brianna and followed her out the door. Brianna tipped the bottle to the sky and downed what was left of it. Danielle's stomach turned watching her, but she didn't say anything.

The drive was silent. Brianna brooded, slamming her feet into the floor and crying every few minutes. Danielle pulled up front. When she looked to Brianna, her jaw was clenched, and her sadness had turned to anger.

"I'll walk you in."

"Fuck you." Brianna opened the car door, grabbed the backpack, and slammed the door. In just a few long, angry strides, Brianna disappeared through the automatic doors.

Danielle waited for a few minutes to make sure she didn't come back. Brianna was almost never in her car, yet it felt empty without her after just the few minutes she'd been there. Part of her was afraid her apartment would feel hollow when she got back. She wondered if she'd get lonely in all that quiet. Her family was gone. Brianna was gone. Jenna was gone. But she felt tremendous relief all the same.

Just as she pulled away, Danielle's phone rang. She looked down and saw a number she didn't recognize. She assumed it was the rehab center and answered.

"Hello?"

"Is this Danielle?"

"Yes."

"This is Callie."

Several seconds passed as Danielle tried to process the words.

"Hello?" Callie asked.

"Yes, hi, I'm sorry. Is Jenna okay?"

"She's fine," Callie said. "I mean, relatively. I mean, because of..." she paused. "I'm rambling. She's fine. I wanted to talk to you if you have a second."

Danielle pulled away from the front of the rehab building and parked in the lot. "Sure."

"I wanted to apologize for the way I acted the night I met you," Callie said. "I know it's been a while, and you don't even see my sister anymore, so I probably sound a little weird right now, but it's been bothering me. I was so wrong to act that way toward you, and I'm really, truly sorry."

"Oh," Danielle said. She couldn't shake the feeling that she'd just rolled down a hill. She felt dizzy, like the world was just a swirl of colors.

"It's okay," Danielle said. "You don't need to torture yourself about it. I have pretty thick skin. It's nice of you to call, though."

"Okay," Callie said. Time drew out awkwardly, and Danielle searched for a way to end the conversation, but came up short.

"I don't mean to put my nose where it doesn't belong," Callie said. "I know you're not even with Jenna now, but if you ever came by the house again or whatever, I just want you to know I wouldn't be like that. Don't let me be a reason to not come over."

"Did Jenna—"

"She has no idea I'm calling."

"I see."

"It's not like, a secret," Callie added, her discomfort as obvious as Danielle usually felt hers was. "I owed you an apology."

"Consider it accepted."

"All right then," Callie said. "So, uh, see you. I hope we see you."

"Right," Danielle said. She'd already disconnected the phone by the time she realized that was probably an odd answer. She hated talking to people she didn't know, on the phone even more so. As she sat in her car in the silence it sank in more and more. Things she should have said popped into her head, but it was too late. Callie had called her. Jenna's sister. The same sister who hated her guts.

She didn't imagine Jenna was the type to push her to do that, and she didn't imagine Callie was the type that could be pushed, so what had made her call? Had Jenna told her about the night before? Last she'd heard, Jenna and Callie weren't getting along at all, so what could have made Callie want to do her a favor suddenly? Maybe it really did have nothing to do with Jenna.

After her conversation with Jenna at the bar, she'd chosen to preoccupy herself with putting her foot down, with demanding excessive drinking take an immediate exit from her life, even if it meant losing Brianna. Even if it meant losing Jenna. She'd focused so much energy on finding a reputable rehab center for Brianna, working out how to present the opportunity, that Jenna had fallen to the back of her thoughts. But Jenna was always a force lingering in the back of her mind that would sooner or later hit like a sledgehammer, and it was happening now.

Jenna tried to kiss her. Jenna poured her heart out and tried to kiss her, and she'd pulled away. Jenna did exactly what Danielle spent the last month wishing she would do, and she'd stopped her.

Danielle glanced in her rearview mirror at the rehab center, then at the brochure for it in the passenger seat. She'd practically memorized it while researching for Brianna. She hadn't even thought to run Jenna through the list of indicators. So many of the signs she couldn't possibly know, intense cravings to drink, drinking alone, hidden stashes of alcohol, withdrawal symptoms if they stopped, increased tolerance. She didn't know if Jenna experienced those things.

She did know Jenna didn't black out, didn't forget what they'd talked about the next day like Brianna always did. She hadn't lost an interest in the other parts of her life. She never smelled like alcohol. She never appeared drunk at work. She didn't have flushed skin or bloodshot eyes. Come to think of it, the only time she'd seen Jenna drink was the two times they'd been at the bar together with everyone, and even then, she'd been composed. She hadn't felt the need to drink at her own house, or at Danielle's.

Danielle felt a tingle of panic glide across her skin as she tried to pinpoint a single damning symptom. Why had she been so sure Jenna was out of control? It was just one night, and even though that kind of intoxication made Danielle uncomfortable under any circumstance, the circumstances were understandable. Most of her concern had simply come from Jenna's reputation among her friends as a party animal, and Jenna was right, they hadn't even said she got wasted. She'd been the one to connect partying with crazy drinking. She'd done that because of Brianna.

Her stomach twisted into a painful knot as she replayed Jenna's surprised and hurt face when she'd pulled away from the kiss she so desperately wanted, as she'd rejected the very reconciliation she'd gone crazy longing for. What had she done?

CHAPTER THIRTY-EIGHT

Jenna liked being at work before everyone else. The early morning light calmed her restless soul as she drove to the office. Something about not having to keep it together for everyone made it easier to keep it together. It was something she discovered when things started falling apart, and even though Callie was finally finding her way, she suspected she still had plenty of keeping it together to fight through.

The lawyer they hired to defend their mother was expensive but effective. He all but promised the charges would be drastically reduced. The man her mother attacked was healing faster than expected and seemed to want his medical bills covered more than vengeance, a price that would cripple her financially, but that she was happy to pay for her mother's freedom. As well as it seemed to be going, though, she wouldn't be able to relax until it was final. The worry was so incessant the only way she found she could breathe was to sit in her empty, silent office before the day started.

Jenna parked up front, a right reserved for management that she seldom took advantage of. She struggled to balance her files in one arm, her coffee and jacket in the other, and lock the car without losing control of everything. The parking lot was nearly empty, with only a couple of cars scattered throughout. That seemed to be the case even when absolutely no one should be there.

Before she made it to the front door, Sasha's silver Mazda sped up the street. Jenna smiled as Sasha rounded the corner going at least forty before she turned sharply into a parking space and hopped out.

"Morning," Jenna said and smirked. "In a hurry?"

Sasha beamed. "Training up for my drag racing career."

Jenna waited while Sasha caught up.

"What are you doing here early?" Sasha asked.

"Just getting some paperwork done before the office chatter starts."

"That your way of saying you don't want to talk?"

"No." Jenna laughed. "We can talk all the way up the stairs."

"Message received." Sasha laughed. "That's too bad, because I think it's going to take longer than that to get the story from the other night out of you."

"What story?"

"The bar. You and Danielle. You were outside together forever, and I remember what that meant the last time." Sasha winked. Jenna felt like she'd been jabbed in the chin.

"No story this time."

"What? Really?"

"Really."

"I thought for sure. The way she was asking about you. The way she looked at you."

"Pretty sure that look was disgust."

Sasha shot her a puzzled look. "Okay, I can't read minds, but it was definitely not disgust."

"I don't really want to talk about it," Jenna said. She rounded the corner into the stairwell and jogged up the flight. She appreciated all the sudden support from the very people who had resisted the idea most, but she couldn't listen to another person tell her to go back to Danielle when she had already tried and been rejected. She came to work early to avoid thinking about her problems, not to rehash every detail of her humiliation.

"Okay," Sasha said.

"What brings you in early?"

"Same. Catching up on paperwork. I may or may not have cut out early every day last week."

"Sash," Jenna playfully scolded her.

"Shh. Don't tell the boss."

"You're killing me."

"I'm here early making up for it, aren't I?"

"All right, but I better not see you out of the office until you're caught up."

"Aye-aye."

Sasha veered over to her desk in the common room the caseworkers used. They weren't cubicles, but the small workstations were arranged close enough together it felt the same. When Jenna received an office she thought she would never need so much room and that it would look mostly empty forever. That had been so very wrong.

"Catch you later." Jenna continued down the hall that led to her office a couple hundred feet away.

She fumbled for her keys, trying again to stack her belongings in a precarious tower propped between her left arm and her body. She fit her office key in the door and turned it while pushing it open with her toes. She flipped on the light switch, then felt something against the back of her head.

"Don't scream."

Jenna started to turn, but the hard, probing object at the back of her head pressed harder, and Jenna's stomach dropped as she realized it must be a gun.

"Ladona?"

A hand pushed her forward and sent the items in her arms scattering to the floor. The door closed with a thud. She turned and saw Ladona standing between her and the door with a pistol raised, pointed at her face. Ladona's hair stood on end, scraggly and disheveled. Her large frame blocked the way so completely Jenna didn't think she could try to run for it even if the door were open, but Ladona wasn't taking chances; she locked it.

"You took my babies away."

"No."

"Yes, you did."

"I'm not in charge of your case anymore, Ladona."

"Exactly!" she snapped. "You gave it to that other girl, that judgmental little bitch. Don't act like you didn't know what would happen."

Jenna raised her hands slowly. Her throat was dry. There were a million things she wanted to say, but as the reality of the gun pointed at her set in, she wasn't sure any of them were right.

"Ladona, put the gun down, and we'll talk about it. If anyone sees you with that you'll never get the boys back."

"Oh, now you want to help?" she said. "It's a little late, don't you think? They took them away. I'm not even allowed to know where they live. Not even Raylon. He's with my own sister, and even she won't tell me. You people ruined my life. You said you were there to help. You told us you would keep us together. You promised!"

"I promised to do my best," Jenna said. "I didn't make you any guarantees. I told you there are certain things we can't—"

"Shut up!" Ladona said. "We trusted you. My boys trusted you, and you just up and left. Got yourself a fancy office, huh? Just move along with your life? Do you even care that you let them down? Does it even bother you that you ruined our lives?"

"Of course, it does," Jenna said. Ladona stepped closer, like she'd forgotten she had the gun and had to resort to fighting. Jenna took a step backward, her gaze bounding around the office in a panic. No one even knew what was happening. Sasha was just down the hall, probably working on her reports, clueless. No one else would be in for at least half an hour. She discreetly brushed her hand across her pocket, feeling for her phone, but it wasn't there. She spotted it on the floor, mixed in with the papers that had fallen from the folders she'd been carrying.

"How did you get in here?" Jenna asked.

"What, you think I'm too stupid to break into your office?"

"No," Jenna said. "It was just locked."

"So? You think we're all just uneducated morons, that it? Think just because we're poor we can't do anything? Can't even raise our own kids?"

"No, Ladona," Jenna said. "You know that's not what I think."

"I think you're the one that's terrible at your job. Useless bitch. Don't know shit about life, do you?"

"I never wanted this for your family, Ladona. I did everything I could to keep you all together."

Ladona laughed. "You did everything you could? Please. You couldn't even be bothered to show up. You pawned us off on someone else like we were nothing."

"I didn't have a choice."

"Bullshit."

Jenna forced herself to take a breath. She kept peeking at the gun no matter how hard she tried not to look at it. She didn't want to remind Ladona she was holding it, didn't want her to feel like she had to use it, but the pull was strong.

"I'm sorry," Jenna said. "I really am."

"That's not good enough."

"What do you want?"

"You're going to rewrite that report," Ladona said. "That new bitch said you're a supervisor now."

"Yes."

"Good, so fix it."

"It doesn't work like—"

"The hell it doesn't. Don't give me that shit. Fix it." Ladona jabbed the gun at her and hit her in the forehead. The impact wasn't hard, but it still hurt. Jenna didn't want to know how it would feel if she actually took a swing at her with it. "Now!"

"It's not my case anymore. I don't have access."

"I don't believe you," Ladona said.

"I didn't want off the case," Jenna said. "I wanted to keep working with you. I swear. They locked me out of it because they knew I might keep reading the notes, and I was expressly told not to have anything else to do with you."

"You're fucking lying." Ladona's face was full of rage that threatened to tip.

"I'm not."

"If you can't give me my kids back, I'm going to fucking kill you, bitch. You get the picture? You can fix it, or you can pay the price for destroying my family."

Jenna glanced back and forth between Ladona and the computer. Everything she'd said was true. Since Danielle was moved to Chuck's crew, she'd been locked out of their information. She didn't even know how to pretend to do what Ladona wanted, but she eyed the computer like it might whisper an idea to her. If she got on the computer, maybe she could send out an email to someone, get someone to call the police.

"Okay," she said. "Fine. I'll amend the report. I'll say you were in a car crash and that's why Raylon was hurt. I'll say it was an overreaction to remove them, that it was enforced prematurely without all the information. If I—"

"I don't care what you do," Ladona said. "Just fix it."

Jenna nodded and slowly circled the desk, her hands still half raised. She slid into her chair and turned on her laptop. She waited for it to boot up, her heart racing as she tried to picture the fastest way to get word out. Email was hardly a reliable way to reach people quickly, but she did have a work group set up. If she sent it to everyone she'd have a chance someone would see it fast. She would open the message and tell them not to come to work, and to send police. Maybe that was too long. Maybe she should just type 911. They would see her work email; surely they'd check here. The home screen finally came up. Jenna's heart jumped as she anticipated her next move, but Ladona circled the desk and stood over her shoulder. The life drained out of her as her plan went out the window.

"Well?"

Jenna scanned the folders on her desktop as she tried to think of a way to appear to be helping. She remembered she had some old documents from the Clark case saved in her own files and clicked into them. She scrolled to the bottom, trying to be quick enough Ladona wouldn't read the specifics, but slow enough she'd see the correct names. She made it to the comments section at the bottom, highlighted, and deleted them. The notes had been unremarkable, but she imagined the visual of something disappearing would be satisfying.

"What was that?" Ladona asked.

"That deemed you an unfit parent. I'm going to rewrite it and resubmit."

She could feel Ladona's eyes burning into her back. "Move slower."

Jenna nodded. Her palms were sweating. She felt the gun at the back of her head again.

"No tricks."

Jenna opened the online database. If she brought up the list of cases she had access to, Ladona would see that her name wasn't there. That could be game over. Instead, she opened a new document and titled it, "Amendment." It would make no sense to anyone who looked at it. It wasn't the way things were done, but Ladona didn't know that. With the new case created, she entered mindless information about the Clarks. Their names, address, dates of births, then attached the document she'd just rewritten. She moved her mouse over the submit button and glanced over her shoulder.

"I'm sending it now," she said. Ladona nodded, and Jenna hit submit. Ladona closed her laptop, then circled the desk. She sat in the chair across from Jenna, resting the pistol on the desk, aimed at her. Jenna shifted and glanced around the room again.

"Well, that's it," she said. "It's done."

"Good."

The silence stretched as Jenna tried to figure out what she wanted now.

"How long until they're here?" Ladona asked.

"What?"

"My boys."

"I…" Jenna paused. "I'm sorry, what?"

"My boys, stupid. The reason we're doing all this. When will they be here?"

"They're not going to come here. They'll contact you at home."

"No, I want them brought here. I'm not letting you go until I know you did this for real. Jesus, you really do think I'm some kind of dimwit, don't you?"

"No, not at all, but they're not going to bring them here."

"And why the hell not?"

"It's just not the way things are done. They'll come contact you at home, apologize profusely, and make arrangements to bring the boys back."

"Make arrangements?"

"Yes."

"That's some bullshit if I ever heard it. You all are the ones who fucked up. I want my boys *now*."

"These things take time. They'll have to pull them out of the homes they're in now. They have to file a bunch of paperwork."

"You just did the paperwork."

"I changed the report," Jenna said. "They still have to do paperwork to remove them from foster care and place them back in your care."

"Tell them that's not how you want it done. You're the big bad supervisor."

"I don't think it's a good idea to handle this in an unusual manner," Jenna said. "You're holding me at gunpoint. If anyone finds that out they'll take your boys away for good, and you'll go to jail. This is already unusual; we can't raise any more red flags."

"And I'm supposed to just believe you? What stops you from deleting everything you just did the second I walk out of here?"

"What stops me from doing that even after you have the boys?" Jenna jolted at her own words, wishing she could take them back.

Ladona's surprise melted into a scowl. "You saying I should kill you after I get my boys? To make sure you don't ruin it again? You're probably right."

"No," Jenna said. "You don't have to do that." Jenna's mind scattered in a million directions, and for the first time she felt the real possibility that she might die. It had been there all along, of course, but that ridiculous human arrogance, that delusion of immortality kept it from sinking in. She had to think faster. She had to be better.

"I've always thought your sons belonged with you," she said. "You know that. You've seen me manipulate the system for you before. You know I'm willing to do that. Please believe that I didn't want to be taken off your case. It wasn't my choice, and I wouldn't have handled it the way Danielle did. I don't have a problem returning your kids to you, Ladona. I'm just trying to help you do it in a way that won't get them taken away again the next day."

Ladona seemed to fall into deep thought, and she slowly nodded.

"I'll believe you when you bring my sons to me," she said.

"You have a gun on you. How—"

"No one knows that except us, and if you change that you'll be the first to catch a bullet."

Jenna sighed and rubbed her face. "Okay." She picked up her desk phone. Ladona jerked forward and jabbed the gun at her.

"What the fuck do you think you're doing?"

"I'm making the call," Jenna said. "To bring them here."

"No," she said. "No way. Do it online, where I can watch."

"It could take all day for them to respond that way."

"My schedule is clear." She leaned over again to watch Jenna type. Jenna felt frustration building as yet another chance to get help disintegrated, but as soon as it had gone, another idea came to mind. She could email now. She'd only be able to send it to one person, not a list. Possible names scrolled through her mind. Sasha would be the most likely to see it immediately since she was definitely on her computer in the next room, but that also ran the risk of bringing her into the office, into danger.

She opened a blank message, her mind frantically reaching for language that would explain what was happening that Ladona wouldn't catch. An email telling Sasha to bring Deon and Raylon to the office to be released to Ladona immediately would in and of itself catch her attention. Sasha knew she would never send that message to anyone, let alone her.

She put Sasha's name in the "to" field, her stomach twisting as she did. She couldn't change it now. Ladona would be too suspicious. She had to find a way to keep Sasha from coming into her office. She typed out instructions to bring the boys in, peppering the document with words to tip her off. She pretended to be outraged at Danielle's behavior, demanded that Sasha pull the trigger on disciplining her, hoping she'd catch the gun reference. She pressed the importance of Deon and Raylon being taken to office one thirty-two and no other, knowing Ladona had no idea that was the security office.

She hovered over the send button in dread. She couldn't stand the idea that Sasha might come check on her, that she could be blowing her cover and putting her best friend in danger all at once, but she believed in Sasha. She had to have faith she would recognize the email as more than a random absurdity, that she would catch the clues.

"Who is that?" Ladona looked at Sasha's email address like it was a cobra.

"The head of endangered child placement." Jenna made up the title. She could feel that Ladona was suspicious, but what could she do? She clicked send before she could be told otherwise. Her pulse pounded in her ear, and she waited in dread, praying Sasha wouldn't send some smartass email back to her without thinking it through.

Jenna thought she heard a shuffle in the next room, but Ladona didn't flinch. Maybe she imagined it. Her paranoia was raging. She couldn't take a chance. She couldn't let Sasha walk into this. She had to make the danger obvious.

"When this is all over, you better take better care of them." Jenna spun her chair around to face Ladona.

"Excuse me? Don't fucking tell me how to raise my kids." Ladona raised her voice a little, and Jenna felt a twinge of hope.

"I'm a good mother," Ladona said. "They were always safe with me. Fucking baby snatchers. All you care about is your commission, no matter who you have to destroy."

"Oh, you're a good mother?" Jenna smirked. "Please."

"You better shut your mouth, little girl." Ladona shoved the gun in her face, pressing the muzzle into her cheek. Jenna heard something in the hallway, and this time she was sure. They were footsteps, but Ladona obviously didn't hear them. She thought they were alone. Jenna had to raise Ladona's voice like a flag for help, and she had to do it now.

"Good mothers don't let their fat, ugly, drug dealer boyfriends beat their kids," Jenna said.

The slap of the gun came hard and fast and knocked her almost out of the chair. Her vision was watered and blurry. She tried to focus again, almost in a panic, like she was afraid she'd gone blind. She felt warmth on the side of her face where the gun had impacted her, but she refused to give Ladona the satisfaction of seeing her check for blood. She knew it was there.

"Or was it you that hit them?" Jenna asked. She prepared for another blow.

"Fuck you!" Ladona yelled. "You sell babies for a living, you fucking demon! Don't you dare judge me!"

"I don't sell babies." Jenna spoke quietly now, hoping to bring the rage in the room back down. She was sure Sasha must have heard what she needed to, enough to steer her the other direction, but she wasn't sure she could calm Ladona again now that she'd wound her up.

"I swear to God, bitch, if anything goes wrong, whether it's your fault or not, I'll fucking kill you."

Jenna nodded. "You better let me clean myself up then," she said. "People are going to start showing up for work soon. I probably shouldn't look like this."

"If you think you're leaving this room you're stupid."

"Fine."

"Use your spit."

Jenna laughed and licked her fingers, then dragged them down her face. A pain that went to the bone pulsed in her temple and cheek as her fingers touched the edges of the rip in her skin and the thick blood. Jenna glanced up at Ladona and saw her realizing she couldn't make the cut disappear, piecing together the fact that the people who were supposedly bringing her children back would have more than a few questions about how it happened, that her entire plan was in danger. Jenna saw the muscles in her face twitching as emotions fought for control. A knock sounded at the door, and she whipped around to point the gun at Jenna again.

"Who the fuck is that," she whispered.

Jenna shrugged. "I don't know. People do work here. I'm sure it's nothing."

"Get rid of them."

Jenna started for the door, but Ladona pulled her back.

"Your face."

Jenna raised her shoulders again. "What do you want me to do?"

Ladona's eyes darted back and forth in a panic.

"I'll tell them I was in an accident," Jenna said.

"Another accident? Is that the only fuckin' lie you know how to tell?"

"Fine, I fell," Jenna said.

The knock sounded again more urgently. "Ms. Thompson?"

Jenna was relieved to hear a male voice. She didn't recognize it, but at least it wasn't Sasha.

Ladona motioned for Jenna to open the door and hid to the left of it. Jenna breathed, and opened the door. Two security guards stood in the entryway. Their expressions went from bored to high alert as they absorbed the wound on her face. Jenna glanced to the left to tip them off, confident as security guards they'd know better than to let on to her cue.

"Ms. Thompson, we got a carbon monoxide alarm from this floor. I'm afraid we're going to have to evacuate everyone until the fire department gets here. If you could please come with me."

Two gunshots rang out in succession, and the security guards dropped into a crouch, their arms covering their heads as if that could offer any protection. Jenna's ears rang from the shots, and she evaluated herself for pain, unsure who the intended target was. An arm wrapped around her, circling her neck and pulling her backward. Ladona's arm crushed her throat and cut off the air. The muzzle of the gun jammed against the cut in her face, sending excruciating lightning bolts through her head.

"Back the fuck off!" Ladona screamed. The guards scrambled backward, and Jenna was relieved to see they looked uninjured. "Get the fuck away, or I swear I'll shoot her!"

The guards scrambled away from the door, and Ladona slammed it shut.

Chapter Thirty-nine

Danielle dug in her pocket for her vibrating cell phone while she pulled into the work lot. When she saw Sasha's name, the weight of disappointment made her shoulders sag. She'd been hoping to see Jenna's name, hoping Jenna hadn't given up on her. She shook away the sadness. She'd see her in five minutes, and she would make it right. Even though Jenna tried to kiss her just days ago, she couldn't seem to muster any certainty she would still want her. She felt so stupid realizing she'd been the one pulling away even though Jenna was the one with the most to lose. As much as she wanted Jenna, she was the one who had failed to trust.

She glanced at Sasha's name again. At first, she planned to ignore the call, but curiosity crept up.

"Hello?"

"Danielle, it's Sasha. Listen, something is happening. Something bad. Don't come to work."

"What?"

"Ladona Clark is in the building with a gun. She shot at the security guards, and she's holding Jenna hostage."

"What?" Danielle yelled as she pulled into the lot. She felt like all the air was being ripped out of her. She hit the gas and careened around the median, speeding for Sasha's car. "I'm pulling up right now, where are you?"

"Shit, no, go away, Danielle! Get away from the building. The cops are on the way."

Danielle spotted Sasha yelling into her phone and pulled up next to her, disconnecting her cell phone.

Danielle jumped out of her car. "Are you crazy? I'm not leaving if Jenna's in there."

"It's Ladona Clark," Sasha said again.

"Of course, it is," Danielle said.

"Didn't you take her kids away last week?"

"Yes."

"So you are the last person that needs to be here right now," Sasha said. "I'm sure she's got it in for you."

"Exactly," Danielle said. "I can't run away and leave Jenna here to deal with my mess. What if she gets hurt?" Danielle felt panic boiling in her throat. What if Jenna got hurt? What if she got killed? Ladona had nothing to lose now, and she already shot at security. What if this was it? What if she would never get to tell Jenna how much she loved her?

"Where is she?" Danielle asked.

Sasha's eyes went wide, and she shook her head. "No. Absolutely not. I'm not helping you make the worst decision ever."

"The decision is already made. Just tell me where they are so I don't bump into her without meaning to."

"Let the police do it, Danielle. That's what they do. They have vests and guns."

"Yeah, well, they're not here yet, and Jenna could be shot any second. That bullet would be meant for me!"

"You're not thinking—"

Danielle turned and stormed for the front door.

"She wouldn't want you to do this!" Sasha yelled.

Danielle ignored her and ran into the building. Sirens were approaching, but it didn't change her mind. They would take too long. They always sat outside of hostage situations for hours before anyone actually did anything, and she wouldn't, couldn't, wait for that.

She passed through the automatic doors and crouched as she dipped into the hallway to her immediate left. The doors to the various offices were inset from the walls, allowing her the perfect landscape. She could race up the hall, then hide in the small alcoves while she listened for Ladona. She made her way up the hallway in a flash, probably too quickly, but her heart told her Jenna was in her office. It was no accident Ladona took Jenna hostage. She'd gone after her specifically, and where better to look for her than her office?

Danielle rounded the corner into the stairwell and climbed to the third floor, their floor. Her heart started pounding as she reached the door that would let into the open area of the main office. She'd have plenty of desks to hide behind in there, assuming Ladona wasn't watching the door. That was a big assumption. It all felt real the moment she put her hand on the doorknob. Ladona Clark had a gun, and she would almost certainly love to shoot Danielle. But the love of her life was behind that door. She couldn't possibly not open it. She put her ear to the door and listened, but heard nothing.

She slowly turned the doorknob, then pushed and tried to peek inside. The office was empty. The lights were on. That was the only thing that would indicate anything unusual, but it was enough. She was right. They must be in Jenna's office. Danielle surveyed the room. She could make her way to the supervisors' hallway easily enough, but from there she'd be confined to the narrow passage.

She opened the door just enough that she could fit through and crawled to the closest desk. Her arms were shaking, and she was covered in a cold sweat. She listened, heard nothing, and crept forward to the next desk. She glanced around the room, trying to spot something that could serve as a weapon. She remembered Chuck's stupid golf clubs and smiled as she crept toward his office.

A muffled yell made her freeze in her tracks. She couldn't make out the words, but it wasn't Jenna's voice. That meant it had to be Ladona's. Just as she picked up her hand to crawl forward again, another voice sounded, this one through a megaphone from outside. She slowly stood up against the wall and peeked out the window. On the same side of the building as Jenna's office, there were five police cars outside now. One officer was speaking into the megaphone.

"Come out with your hands up!"

"Bring me my sons!" Ladona screamed. Her voice traveled well through the office, enough to surprise Danielle and make her check over her shoulder to confirm she wasn't coming down the hall, but she wasn't. The window Danielle was looking out was opened just a crack, and the sound came through easily. She made sure to stand out of view. The last thing she needed was the police bringing attention to her.

"Release the hostage, and come out with your hands up!"

"You can have her when you bring me my kids!"

Danielle heard a phone ringing down the hall, likely in Jenna's office. There was a slam and Ladona screamed out the window again.

"Just bring me my kids!"

Danielle felt shaken by the volume of Ladona's voice. She was escalated, enraged.

"This is your fault!" she screamed. Danielle's stomach twisted in fear as she pictured Ladona losing control with Jenna at the wrong end of a gun. She ran the rest of the way to Chuck's office and pulled the driver from his golf bag. She crept down the hall to Jenna's office. It was only three doors away now.

"What did you do?" Ladona screamed. Danielle gripped the golf club harder, preparing to attack.

"I didn't do anything," Jenna said.

"Bullshit. Who did you send that report to? Is there a panic button in here? What the fuck did you do? They didn't just show up here for no reason!"

Danielle kept her back plastered to the wall, trying to figure out how she could look around the corner without getting caught. She needed to know exactly where Ladona was if she was going to hit her faster than Ladona could shoot.

"You've been yelling," Jenna said. "Other people work here, and it's getting late. Someone probably came in and heard you. Or maybe security really was here over a carbon monoxide alarm. We can still get through this, though. Just stay calm."

Jenna did sound calm. She sounded in control. Danielle couldn't tell if she was misreading Ladona's level of escalation or if Jenna was just unshakable.

"Don't fucking lie to me," Ladona said. "Quit treating me like some moron you can manipulate. I'm not a child. I know there's no getting out of this."

The office phone rang, and Danielle felt all three of them go still even though she couldn't see in the office. It rang again. It sounded so much louder now, piercing the tension, than it ever had before. Danielle heard a muffled voice through the megaphone outside again, but couldn't make out the words. It sounded like they'd closed the window.

"It's probably them," Jenna said.

"No shit," Ladona said. "Lord, what did you do to me? I told you if you didn't get my boys back to me, if you didn't fix this, I would kill you, and I meant it. I just wanted my babies back."

"That can still happen," Jenna said.

Ladona laughed and snatched the phone off the receiver as it started its third ring. "What?"

Danielle's heart jolted as she realized Ladona would have to be by Jenna's desk to answer the phone, which meant she should be able to glance around the corner from the hallway without her seeing. Danielle leaned forward, not daring to breathe. She couldn't see Ladona at all and could only catch a glimpse of part of Jenna's back. She didn't dare lean forward any farther.

"Bring me my sons," Ladona said into the phone. "That's the only way you're ever going to see this one alive again. You bring them to me now!" She slammed the phone down. When it instantly rang again, she swiped it up. Silence stretched before she spoke.

"They're here?"

Danielle risked a glance into the room again. She still couldn't see Ladona and could still only make out part of Jenna's back. She desperately wanted to get her attention, to pull her out of there, but she couldn't figure out how to alert Jenna without alerting Ladona too.

"Fine." She hung up the phone again. "They're here," she said to Jenna. "Let's go."

"Go?"

Panic seized Danielle, and she scrambled to move out of the hallway without making noise.

"I'm not looking out this window," Ladona said. "Dirty fuckers will probably shoot me. Let's go."

Danielle stood and ran down the hall, ducking into the next alcove up. She tried to keep her footsteps silent, but speed was more important, and she couldn't be sure if she succeeded. All she could hear was her own pulse thundering in her ears.

"This way," Ladona said. They were in the hallway now. Danielle gripped the golf club harder, feeling it wanting to slide in her sweaty grasp. She couldn't predict which way Ladona would go, but if it was toward her, she would have no choice but to attack. She envisioned what she would have to do, the level of aggression she would need, but the footsteps went away.

"Fuck." Danielle mouthed to herself. A few seconds later, she couldn't hear anything. She'd lost track of them. She glanced around the corner and saw the hallway was empty. She crept down the hall, passing Jenna's office. There was blood on the carpet by her desk. Danielle's heart sank. She hadn't had a real look at Jenna, but when she'd seen her standing, she'd ridiculously assumed she wasn't hurt. She couldn't let this go on another second. She powered down the hall. Ladona's voice shattered the silence.

"Why the fuck are they in bulletproof vests?"

The volume of her voice alone made Danielle flinch in fear, but she pushed forward. They were in the main office, by the windows on the left.

"They think I'm going to shoot my own fucking kids?"

"Ladona, I'm sure it's just a precaution," Jenna said.

"They think I'm a danger to my own babies! You did that! I would never hurt them. I love my children, but you made me look like a monster, and now I'll never see them again. You fucking bitch!"

Danielle turned the corner just as Ladona raised the gun at Jenna. Danielle lunged and swung the golf club down on Ladona's arm with all she had. The gun veered downward as the shot sounded. Danielle's vision felt narrow. All she could see or think about was the gun. She raised the golf club again and struck Ladona's wrist once more, loosening the pistol from her grip. The gun tumbled and bounced a few feet across the carpet floor, away from all three of them. Danielle swung a third time, at Ladona's head this time, and sent her sprawling to the ground.

Ladona gripped her head in pain and tried to spring back to her feet, but struggled to right herself. Danielle spun to find Jenna. Half her face was caked in blood and she looked paralyzed with shock, but she was here. She was alive. Danielle lunged toward her, grabbed her arm, and pulled her toward the entrance of the office. Ladona's hollow howl rang through the room. It felt animal. Pure and raw and dripping with pain.

"Damn you!" Ladona said. "You ruined everything! You ruined my fucking life! What do I have now?"

Danielle's temples felt tingly as she focused on her hand around Jenna's arm, around the realness of her. It was all that mattered. She pulled Jenna around the corner of the entrance, but the second they rounded the corner, Jenna turned into an immovable wall, stone. Danielle turned and met her frantic eyes.

"Come on!" Danielle said. "We have to go."

"She'll kill herself," Jenna said.

"What?"

"She'll kill herself if we go!"

"She'll kill all of us if we don't!" Danielle tried to pull Jenna again, but she didn't move.

Ladona's wails filled the room and leaked into the halls. "I just want my sons back. All I ever wanted was to take care of my babies."

"I have to do something," Jenna said. "I can help her. I can calm her down!" Jenna tried to go back into the office, but Danielle wrapped both her arms around Jenna's chest in a tight bear hug and pulled her back with all her strength.

"She just tried to shoot you! You can't calm her down."

"I can!" Jenna said and pulled again. Danielle was plastered to Jenna's back, holding on to her. She pulled backward and tried to drag Jenna to the floor. She didn't care what it took; she couldn't lose her. She couldn't let her go on a suicide mission.

"Please!" Danielle yelled when she felt Jenna gaining leverage. "You'll die!" Jenna managed to drag herself to the doorway. Danielle lunged on top of her and drove her weight down to keep her from going any farther. She looked up, trying to spot Ladona, trying to weigh their danger.

Ladona was looking out the window now, at her sons in their ballistic vests. She put the gun to the side of her head and pulled the trigger. The sound rang through Danielle's entire body. Blood and brain sprayed from Ladona's head, and she thumped to the ground.

CHAPTER FORTY

Jenna felt the life drain out of her when Ladona hit the floor. Danielle's arms were still wrapped around her shoulders as they both stared, paralyzed, at the body.

"Fuck," Jenna said. Danielle's arms loosened. Her weight lifted. Jenna found her feet and cautiously approached. She stopped the moment she was close enough to peer around the desk that blocked her view. Blood was pooling on the floor and dripping down the back of Ladona's head.

"Fuck." She turned away from the body and wiped tears from her face. She left the office nearly in a jog, desperate to get away from the blood, the body. Danielle's feet were thudding behind her, keeping pace with her as she made her way to the stairs. She realized she wasn't even breathing and stopped to lean against the cold stairwell wall.

"Fuck," she said again and gripped her head.

"I'm sorry," Danielle said. "I didn't mean for…"

Danielle was standing frozen a few feet away, watching with a hollow look, like she thought Jenna was mad at her. She was when Danielle was holding her down, but it had disappeared the moment the gun fired.

"It's not your fault. You were right," Jenna said. "She didn't hesitate at all. Her mind was made up. What would I have even said? She was right. She was never getting her kids back, not after this."

"I heard you," Danielle said. "For a while before I could figure out how to get to you. You said everything you could."

Jenna looked at the floor and shook her head. "Doesn't feel like it."

"You did," Danielle said. Danielle's gaze was so intense it pulled her back to life.

"What the hell are you even doing here?" The words jumped out of her. "Are you crazy? She would have shot you for sure if she had the chance. What was your plan?"

"Just what I did," Danielle said. "Search and rescue, I guess. Save you."

"You're insane," Jenna said. "You risked your life. You..." It hit her. "You saved my life."

"I couldn't lose you, Jenna." Their voices felt full and strong in the solid stairwell, but she knew they both felt paper-thin inside.

Danielle stepped closer and pulled Jenna into an embrace. Jenna stiffened in surprise when Danielle's lips met hers with a certainty she'd never felt before. All the doubts and complications that plagued them before felt meaningless now. All that mattered was kissing her. She melted into Danielle, welcoming her soft lips and strong arms. Danielle gently pulled away, loosening her grip but not letting go.

"I love you, Jenna," she said. "I was an idiot the last time we talked, what I said, when I left."

"You sure that's not the life-or-death moment talking?"

"It's not," Danielle said. "I mean, thinking you might die, it was the worst thing I've ever felt. It puts things in perspective. But I was already on my way to tell you this when I heard about Ladona. Please tell me we can fix this, Jenna. I want to be with you. I'm so sorry for everything that happened."

Jenna looked into Danielle's eyes. The sincerity, the love she saw there made her feel like all her bones had disappeared from her body. She touched Danielle's cheek.

"I want to be with you too. I love you, Danielle."

Jenna leaned in and touched Danielle's lips with her own, feeling the relief wash through her. She pulled Danielle into a tight embrace like she was trying to melt into her, like she would never let go.

A voice faintly pierced the stairwell from outside, the blurry roar of the megaphone. Jenna and Danielle jolted apart.

"Shit," Jenna said. "I have to talk to Deon and Raylon. I have to tell them what happened. How am I going to do that?"

Danielle grabbed her hand and squeezed. "You're the one they'll want to hear it from."

Jenna sighed. "I know. We better go."

When they made it to the front door of the building, the cops all had their guns raised as they screamed commands. They kept their hands in the air as three officers in full gear swept in and guided them away.

"She's dead," Jenna said, but they pulled her away in the same speedy manner as if she hadn't spoken. When they were behind the cop cars in the area the officers deemed safe, they finally looked her in the face. Danielle's hand slipped back into hers.

"What happened in there?" the officer asked.

Jenna recounted the story, trying to balance speed with detail, but she could barely focus as she swept the parking lot for Deon and Raylon. Instead, she spotted Callie, who was running toward her full speed.

"Jenna!" The officers let her by, and Callie blasted into her arms, knocking her several feet back. Callie's arms squeezed around her neck tight enough to hurt a little, but Jenna smiled and hugged her back. When Callie finally released her, she planted both hands on Jenna's shoulders.

"Are you okay?" she asked. "Jesus, that's a nasty cut."

"I'm okay," Jenna said. "I'm glad you're here."

"Of course, I'm here." Callie hugged her again.

When she pulled away, Sasha was next to her and reached in for a hug too.

"Fuck, Jenna," she said. "That email…"

"I didn't know what else to do."

"It was great. I thought you were messing with me for a second, but when I really looked, everything was there. Then I heard you in your office, and God, I was so scared for you. What happened? Is she still in there?"

Jenna shook her head slowly, surveying her surroundings again for Deon and Raylon. She looked back to Sasha.

"She's not coming out," Jenna said. "Where are the boys?"

"They're in the car over there."

Jenna glanced at the officer for permission. He nodded. Jenna started slowly toward the vehicle. Callie and Sasha were chirping excitedly at Danielle behind her, but it faded as her mind tumbled through the things she had to say to the boys, to the clichés everyone used, to the graphic details she could never tell them, the impossible questions they might ask.

As she approached the car, a short, plump woman stepped in front of her, blocking the way. Her resemblance to Ladona was obvious, and Jenna knew this was the aunt who wanted nothing to do with Deon. A woman who just lost a sister.

Jenna held out her hand. "You must be Mrs. Jorgenson."

"Yes. Audrey."

"My name is Jenna Thompson. I—"

"Oh, I know who you are."

"I'm not sure if that's good or bad," Jenna said. "But I want you to know I care about your family a great deal."

The woman nodded. "I heard that," she said. "At one point. The boys adore you."

Jenna smiled. "That's good to hear."

"You were inside with her?" she asked.

"Yes."

"And?"

"She was very distraught," Jenna said. "When she saw the boys in vests, when it looked like she'd never get them back…"

"She shot herself?"

Jenna nodded.

"Heard it from here." She wiped a tear from her eye. "We all knew it would happen someday. She talked about it a lot."

"I didn't know that."

"Scared us all to death, but what do you do?"

Jenna shifted her weight, trying to figure out what to say. "It's a tough situation."

"I'm sure afraid of what it's going to do to those boys. I'll tell you that."

"Audrey, I don't mean to overstep, but have you considered giving Deon one more chance?"

Audrey scoffed and shook her head. "Of course, I have," she said. "No one wants to put a boy in foster care. But he was too much last time. He was awful to me. I have health problems, Ms. Thompson; I can't do it. It'll be the death of me. And I won't have him leading Raylon astray."

"He cares about Raylon more than anything," Jenna said. "It's the only reason that's ever been good enough for him to act right. I'm afraid of what will happen to Deon without him."

"And what about Raylon? Do you care what happens to him being around a brother who's halfway in the street life already?"

"Of course, I do," Jenna said. "But I also worry what will happen to Raylon if he loses his brother and his mother in the same month."

Audrey shook her head again. "Hell of a time to bring this up. I have to plan my sister's funeral, you know?"

"I know," Jenna said. "I thought that might be easier as a family."

Audrey scanned Jenna with an appraising stare. Jenna could see her struggling with the idea.

"Just one more chance," Jenna said. "Foster care isn't going anywhere if it doesn't work out, but this might be your only shot to keep them both on track."

Audrey's eyes burned into her, and she finally waved her hand. "Fine," she said. "One more chance. One."

Jenna smiled and hugged her. Audrey felt like iron in her arms, but she squeezed her before she let go anyway.

"Tell them I'll be in the car." She walked away muttering under her breath, then looked over her shoulder. "And tell them what happened, if you think you can. You know better than I do."

Jenna took a second to prepare before she started back toward the police car with the boys. She was ecstatic to tell them they were going to live together, but the reality was still horrible. She wasn't sure how she was going to say those awful words; your mom is dead. It felt impossible.

She reached the car, and the door opened from inside. Raylon's head popped out. Deon was in the shadows on the other side.

"Ms. Thompson?" Raylon said.

"Come on out, guys."

Raylon climbed out instantly. Deon got out on the other side and walked around, moving slowly. He kept looking between Jenna and Raylon like he already knew. Like he was daring her to crush his poor little brother. The scene around them said it all. The cops had put back their rifles and shields. Bystanders were taking selfies with the mob of cops in the background. Everyone was smiling again. And Ladona was absent. Deon knew. How could this look to him? All this relief? All this happiness, when his mom was gone? Watching them both struggle with the awkwardness of the vests, knowing it had sent their mom over the edge put a burning sensation in her chest.

Jenna waited for Deon to make his way around the car even as it took so long Raylon was coming unglued with impatience. She let Deon decide when this would happen, and eventually he made his way over to her and leaned against the car.

"Is our mom going to jail?" Raylon asked.

Jenna grabbed each of their hands. "No, sweetie. Your mom…" She knew she couldn't use a platitude with a child his age, not that she ever cared for them anyway.

"Your mom isn't coming back. She died."

"She died?" Deon asked. "What do you mean she died?" His voice was sharp and harsh, the way it always was when he detected the slightest measure of someone patronizing him. He knew the words "she died" didn't quite say it.

Jenna fought the passivity that wanted to take over. "She killed herself." She looked at each of their faces, waiting for a reaction, but none came from either of them. "She was really upset," Jenna said. "And she wasn't well. But she loved you both so much."

Silence stretched, and finally, tears began to roll down Raylon's face. Jenna knelt down and hugged him. When he pulled away and she stood again, Deon still looked like a statue. She hugged him.

"I'm glad you're okay." He was scrutinizing the side of her face where she knew she had bled badly. She was disoriented by the comment. It felt off topic, beside the point. She guessed he wasn't processing it yet.

"Do you want to talk about it?" she asked.

He shook his head. His stone demeanor betrayed just a glimpse of grief and rage.

"It doesn't matter," he said. "We weren't going to see her anymore anyway."

Jenna tilted her head and looked into his eyes. "You can be mad at her and still love her," she said.

Deon returned her stare and finally nodded like he didn't want to.

"It might take some time to figure out how you feel about it," Jenna said. "You can always call me. Even if it's way later."

Deon nodded and wrapped his arm around Raylon.

"When do I have to go back?" Deon asked.

"You don't," Jenna said. "You're going home with your aunt."

Raylon broke into a beaming smile, and Jenna felt warmed by his innocence, the ease with which he could smile, even now.

"Really?" Raylon asked.

"Really."

"Today?" Deon asked. "I don't have to go back at all?"

"Well, I'm sure you can go get your stuff."

"I don't want it. I want to go now. Can I go now?"

"Yes," Jenna said. "You can go now. I'll take care of the rest."

CHAPTER FORTY-ONE

Good as new," Dr. Williams said. Danielle leaned over to get a look at the laceration on Jenna's head where Ladona Clark had hit her with the pistol. There was a pink mark where her skin had split that would soon be a scar, a reminder, and nothing more.

"How do I look?" Jenna smiled at her.

"You look beautiful."

"Callie!" Jenna said. Callie pulled back the curtain and came in with a candy bar between her teeth.

"What?" she said with a full mouth.

"Look, I have a scar now too."

Callie laughed and covered her mouth, trying not to spew chocolate everywhere. "Yeah, rugged."

Jenna hopped to her feet and turned to the doctor. "So that's it?"

"That's it," he said. "You're free to go."

Jenna lead the way through the halls and into the parking lot, moving at a fast, excited, pace as if she'd been in the hospital for months, not the hour she actually had been. Danielle couldn't stop smiling as she watched. She'd spent every single day with Jenna since the shooting, and she couldn't believe she still felt more in love every day.

"Lunch?" Jenna asked.

"I have to go to work," Callie said.

"Dinner?"

"I, uh, have plans."

Danielle and Jenna raised their eyebrows at each other and shot Callie a look.

"Plans?" Danielle asked.

"Yes," Callie drew the word out.

"With a gentleman caller, perhaps?" Jenna asked.

"A gentleman, yes. I'm not sure he's a caller."

"But he might be?"

"He might be." Callie shrugged and looked down to hide the smile that crept across her face.

"All right," Jenna said. "Have fun."

"I will."

"Don't forget we visit Mom tomorrow," Jenna called after her.

"So not staying out all night," Callie said.

"Just in case."

Callie shook her head, but she was smiling as she walked away. Jenna turned to Danielle and wrapped her arm around her shoulders.

"Just us, then," she said.

"That's always okay with me," Danielle said. "Just a few more days before you have to go back to work. Let's make the best of them."

Jenna's smile faded.

"What?"

They reached the car and got inside. Jenna turned to face Danielle without starting the engine.

"I've been thinking a lot about that," she said.

"Okay," Danielle said. Jenna seemed full of nervous energy. She looked anxious, like she was afraid of what she might say. "What is it, baby?" Danielle asked. "Are you worried about the transfer? I told you, you don't have to if you don't want. I'll find another job. Really."

"No," Jenna said. "No, please don't. Actually, I've been thinking I'm the one who needs a new job."

"Really?"

"I know this is going to sound crazy," Jenna said. "I talked so much about how I loved my job and everything, but I don't think I do. Not really."

"Is it about what happened? I'm sure they'll give you more time off if you need it."

"It isn't that," Jenna said. "Everything that happened with Deon and Raylon, the way I wanted to keep them together so bad, the way I went as far as not reporting things sometimes…"

"You never put them in danger," Danielle said. She'd seen Jenna go through many phases of guilt, and it her hurt to witness it when she knew how much good Jenna had really done for them.

"I know," Jenna said. "But I hate breaking up families. I really hate it. Even when I know it's the best thing, it just rips me apart. And I've been thinking a lot about Ladona."

"Ladona?"

"Yeah," Jenna said. "And my mom. When Ladona was about to kill herself, I wanted to help so bad. After it was over I realized I wouldn't have even known how to help, not really. I wouldn't have known what to say. I would have just gotten myself shot. Even with my own mom I didn't really know what to say. Tina's been talking to me about how I should deal with Mom's delusions. I was doing it all wrong. So much of what happened with her was because I didn't know how to help her better."

"You can't blame yourself for that, Jenna. You spent your whole life taking care of her. You did the best you could. And you did everything possible to make what happened right again. You practically bankrupted yourself paying that man's medical bills, and he's okay now. And your mom will be transferred to a facility soon. She'll get the help she needs. You're an amazing daughter."

"I know," Jenna said. "It's not about blame. I think I want to be a mental health counselor. Like Tina. I always admired what she did so much, but it never occurred to me that I could do it too. I want to know what to say next time. All the times I've worked with mentally ill parents I saw my mom in them. I saw the love for their kids underneath the rest of it. I want to help them. And I want to be able to take care of my mom properly at home someday." Jenna finally looked up at her. "If that's okay with you, of course," she said and smiled.

Danielle leaned across the car and kissed her. Jenna met her lips with a certainty and warmth that made a tingle ripple through her skin. Danielle hooked her hand behind Jenna's neck and pulled her deeper into the kiss. Jenna's mouth opened to her, and she moved closer, leaning across the center console until their bodies were touching and a gentle moan sounded from Jenna's throat. Danielle shivered with longing.

"Home?" Jenna said, their lips barely parting.

"Yes."

Jenna kissed her one more time before she pulled away and started the car.

"I think it's a great idea," Danielle said when the swirling in her head settled. "All of it."

A huge smile spread across Jenna's face. "No more secret dating at work?"

"No more secrets at all."

About the Author

Nicole is a lifelong storyteller with a passion for exploring the hidden corners of life. She lives in Denver, Colorado, where she is a collector of jobs that inspire her writing. She has worked as a 911 operator, police dispatcher, EMS dispatcher, and martial arts instructor. Most recently, she and her wife started a music video production company and love working together as producer and director.

Books Available from Bold Strokes Books

Against All Odds by Kris Bryant, Maggie Cummings, M. Ullrich. Peyton and Tory escaped death once, but will they survive when Bradley's determined to make his kill rate one hundred percent? (978-1-163555-193-8)

Autumn's Light by Aurora Rey. Casual hookups aren' t supposed to include romantic dinners and meeting the family. Can Mat Pero see beyond the heartbreak that led her to keep her worlds so separate, and will Graham Connor be waiting if she does? (978-1-163555-272-0)

Breaking the Rules by Larkin Rose. When Virginia and Carmen are thrown together by an embarrassing mistake they find out their stubborn determination isn't so heroic after all. (978-1-163555-261-4)

Broad Awakening by Mickey Brent. In the sequel to *Underwater Vibes*, Hélène and Sylvie find ruts in their road to eternal bliss. (978-1-163555-270-6)

Broken Vows by MJ Williamz. Sister Mary Margaret must reconcile her divided heart or risk losing a love that just might be heaven sent. (978-1-163555-022-1)

Flesh and Gold by Ann Aptaker. Havana, 1952, where art thief and smuggler Cantor Gold dodges gangland bullets and mobsters' schemes while she searches Havana' s steamy Red Light district for her kidnapped love. (978-1-163555-153-2)

Isle of Broken Years by Jane Fletcher. Spanish noblewoman Catalina de Valasco is in peril, even before the pirates holding her for ransom sail into seas destined to become known as the Bermuda Triangle. (978-1-163555-175-4)

Love Like This by Melissa Brayden. Hadley Cooper and Spencer Adair set out to take the fashion world by storm. If only they knew their hearts were about to be taken. (978-1-163555-018-4)

Secrets On the Clock by Nicole Disney. Jenna and Danielle love their jobs helping endangered children, but that might not be enough to stop them from breaking the rules by falling in love. (978-1-163555-292-8)

Unexpected Partners by Michelle Larkin. Dr. Chloe Maddox tries desperately to deny her attraction for Detective Dana Blake as they flee from a serial killer who's hunting them both. (978-1-163555-203-4)

A Fighting Chance by T. L. Hayes. Will Lou be able to come to terms with her past to give love a fighting chance? (978-1-163555-257-7)

Chosen by Brey Willows. When the choice is adapt or die, can love save us all? (978-1-163555-110-5)

Death Checks In by David S. Pederson. Despite Heath's promises to Alan to not get involved, Heath can't resist investigating a shopkeeper's murder in Chicago, which dashes their plans for a romantic weekend getaway. (978-1-163555-329-1)

Gnarled Hollow by Charlotte Greene. After they are invited to study a secluded nineteenth-century estate, a former English professor and a group of historians discover that they will have to fight against the unknown if they have any hope of staying alive. (978-1-163555-235-5)

Jacob's Grace by C.P. Rowlands. Captain Tag Becket wants to keep her head down and her past behind her, but her feelings for AJ's second-in-command, Grace Fields, makes keeping secrets next to impossible. (978-1-163555-187-7)

On the Fly by PJ Trebelhorn. Hockey player Courtney Abbott is content with her solitary life until visiting concert violinist Lana Caruso makes her second-guess everything she always thought she wanted. (978-1-163555-255-3)

Passionate Rivals by Radclyffe. Professional rivalry and long-simmering passions create a combustible combination when Emmett McCabe and Sydney Stevens are forced to work together, especially when past attractions won't stay buried. (978-1-163555-231-7)

Proxima Five by Missouri Vaun. When geologist Leah Warren crash-lands on a preindustrial planet and is claimed by its tyrant, Tiago, will clan warrior Keegan's love for Leah give her the strength to defeat him? (978-1-163555-122-8)

Racing Hearts by Dena Blake. When you cross a hot-tempered race car mechanic with a reckless cop, the result can only be spontaneous combustion. (978-1-163555-251-5)

Shadowboxer by Jessica L. Webb. Jordan McAddie is prepared to keep her street kids safe from a dangerous underground protest group, but she isn't prepared for her first love to walk back into her life. (978-1-163555-267-6)

The Tattered Lands by Barbara Ann Wright. As Vandra and Lilani strive to make peace, they slowly fall in love. With mistrust and murder surrounding them, only their faith in each other can keep their plan to save the world from falling apart. (978-1-163555-108-2)

Captive by Donna K. Ford. To escape a human trafficking ring, Greyson Cooper and Olivia Danner become players in a game of deceit and violence. Will their love stand a chance? (978-1-63555-215-7)

Crossing the Line by CF Frizzell. The Mob discovers a nemesis within its ranks, and in the ultimate retaliation, draws Stick McLaughlin from anonymity by threatening everything she holds dear. (978-1-63555-161-7)

Love's Verdict by Carsen Taite. Attorneys Landon Holt and Carly Pachett want the exact same thing: the only open partnership spot at their prestigious criminal defense firm. But will they compromise their careers for love? (978-1-63555-042-9)

Precipice of Doubt by Mardi Alexander & Laurie Eichler. Can Cole Jameson resist her attraction to her boss, veterinarian Jodi Bowman, or will she risk a workplace romance and her heart? (978-1-63555-128-0)

Savage Horizons by CJ Birch. Captain Jordan Kellow's feelings for Lt. Ali Ash have her past and future colliding, setting in motion a series of events that strands her crew in an unknown galaxy thousands of light years from home. (978-1-63555-250-8)

Secrets of the Last Castle by A. Rose Mathieu. When Elizabeth Campbell represents a young man accused of murdering an elderly woman, her investigation leads to an abandoned plantation that reveals many dark Southern secrets. (978-1-63555-240-9)

Take Your Time by VK Powell. A neurotic parrot brings police officer Grace Booker and temporary veterinarian Dr. Dani Wingate together in the tiny town of Pine Cone, but their unexpected attraction keeps the sparks flying. (978-1-63555-130-3)

The Last Seduction by Ronica Black. When you allow true love to elude you once and you desperately regret it, are you brave enough to grab it when it comes around again? (978-1-63555-211-9)

The Shape of You by Georgia Beers. Rebecca McCall doesn't play it safe, but when sexy Spencer Thompson joins her workout class, their non-stop sparring forces her to face her ultimate challenge—a chance at love. (978-1-63555-217-1)

Exposed by MJ Williamz. The closet is no place to live if you want to find true love. (978-1-62639-989-1)

Force of Fire: Toujours a Vous by Ali Vali. Immortals Kendal and Piper welcome their new child and celebrate the defeat of an old enemy, but another ancient evil is about to awaken deep in the jungles of Costa Rica. (978-1-63555-047-4)

Holding Their Place by Kelly A. Wacker. Together Dr. Helen Connery and ambulance driver Julia March, discover that goodness, love, and passion can be found in the most unlikely and even dangerous places during WWI. (978-1-63555-338-3)

Landing Zone by Erin Dutton. Can a career veteran finally discover a love stronger than even her pride? (978-1-63555-199-0)

Love at Last Call by M. Ullrich. Is balancing business, friendship, and love more than any willing woman can handle? (978-1-63555-197-6)

Pleasure Cruise by Yolanda Wallace. Spencer Collins and Amy Donovan have few things in common, but a Caribbean cruise offers both women an unexpected chance to face one of their greatest fears: falling in love. (978-1-63555-219-5)

Running Off Radar by MB Austin. Maji's plans to win Rose back are interrupted when work intrudes and duty calls her to help a SEAL team stop a Russian mobster from harvesting gold from the bottom of Sitka Sound. (978-1-63555-152-5)

Shadow of the Phoenix by Rebecca Harwell. In the final battle for the fate of Storm's Quarry, even Nadya's and Shay's powers may not be enough. (978-1-63555-181-5)

Take a Chance by D. Jackson Leigh. There's hardly a woman within fifty miles of Pine Cone that veterinarian Trip Beaumont can't charm, except for the irritating new cop, Jamie Grant, who keeps leaving parking tickets on her truck. (978-1-63555-118-1)

The Outcasts by Alexa Black. Spacebus driver Sue Jones is running from her past. When she crash-lands on a faraway world, the Outcast Kara might be her chance for redemption. (978-1-63555-242-3)

Alias by Cari Hunter. A car crash leaves a woman with no memory and no identity. Together with Detective Bronwen Pryce, she fights to uncover a truth that might just kill them both. (978-1-63555-221-8)

Death in Time by Robyn Nyx. Working in the past is hell on your future. (978-1-63555-053-5)

Hers to Protect by Nicole Disney. High school sweethearts Kaia and Adrienne will have to see past their differences and survive the vengeance of a brutal gang if they want to be together. (978-1-63555-229-4)

Of Echoes Born by 'Nathan Burgoine. A collection of queer fantasy short stories set in Canada from Lambda Literary Award finalist 'Nathan Burgoine. (978-1-63555-096-2)

Perfect Little Worlds by Clifford Mae Henderson. Lucy can't hold the secret any longer. Twenty-six years ago, her sister did the unthinkable. (978-1-63555-164-8)

Room Service by Fiona Riley. Interior designer Olivia likes stability, but when work brings footloose Savannah into her world and into a new city every month, Olivia must decide if what makes her comfortable is what makes her happy. (978-1-63555-120-4)

Sparks Like Ours by Melissa Brayden. Professional surfers Gia Malone and Elle Britton can't deny their chemistry on and off the beach. But only one can win… (978-1-63555-016-0)

Take My Hand by Missouri Vaun. River Hemsworth arrives in Georgia intent on escaping quickly, but when she crashes her Mercedes into the Clip 'n Curl, sexy Clay Cahill ends up rescuing more than her car. (978-1-63555-104-4)

The Last Time I Saw Her by Kathleen Knowles. Lane Hudson only has twelve days to win back Alison's heart. That is if she can gather the courage to try. (978-1-63555-067-2)

Wayworn Lovers by Gun Brooke. Will agoraphobic composer Giselle Bonnaire and Tierney Edwards, a wandering soul who can't remain in one place for long, trust in the passionate love destiny hands them? (978-1-62639-995-2)